BETRAYED

BETRAYED

The Nicole Jones series

Karen E Olson

This first world edition published 2016
in Great Britain and 2017 in the USA by
SEVERN HOUSE PUBLISHERS LTD of
19 Cedar Road, Sutton, Surrey, England, SM2 5DA.
Trade paperback edition first published
in Great Britain and the USA 2017 by
SEVERN HOUSE PUBLISHERS LTD

British Library Cataloguing in Publication Data
A CIP catalogue record for this title is available from the British Library.

ISBN-13: 978-0-7278-8681-1 (cased)
ISBN-13: 978-1-84751-784-5 (trade paper)
ISBN-13: 978-1-78010-853-7 (e-book)

All Severn House titles are printed on acid-free paper.

Severn House Publishers support the Forest Stewardship Council™ [FSC™],
the leading international forest certification organisation.
All our titles that are printed on FSC certified paper carry the FSC logo.

Typeset by Palimpsest Book Production Ltd.,
Falkirk, Stirlingshire, Scotland.
Printed and bound in Great Britain by
TJ International, Padstow, Cornwall.

ONE

My name is Tina Adler, and I am an addict.

My addiction is not defined as such by the experts, although I could write an entire chapter on it and then some. There is no twelve-step program, no church basements with pots of coffee and fellow addicts with whom to share stories. No coins to mark sobriety, no common prayer.

The only thing I have is time. One day, one hour, one minute that I count without using.

I'm not naïve enough to think that I won't relapse. I did once before, and I will again.

Maybe even today.

I am escorted into a cold, concrete room, a metal table and two chairs in the middle. A big mirror adorns one wall, but I'm not stupid. They're watching me. The door slams shut behind me. I circle the table, running my fingers along its edges, sidestepping the chairs.

The laptop sits in the center of the table. It's open, the screen dark. I wiggle my fingers before making two fists. *I will not touch it.*

It's been thirty-four days since I handed over my laptop. Since I've been online. Thirty-four days, ten hours, and thirteen minutes, according to my watch. Yes, I've been keeping track. It keeps my mind occupied. I count seconds, minutes, my head spinning with the distraction.

I continue to walk in circles around the table, my eyes glued to the laptop, as though it's a mirage in the desert and if I look away, it will disappear. I want to feel the keys underneath my fingers, the power surging through me.

The door swings open, startling me, and my heart beats faster.

He comes in, closing the door behind him.

'I'm Agent Tilman. Please sit.' He holds a folder with papers in it. How old-fashioned – just like my old-fashioned wrist-watch. He indicates the chair next to me and, without waiting, he plops down in the other one across from me. His rumpled suit makes me wonder if he's slept in it, if he's been here all night.

He waves his hand again, silently telling me that I should sit, but I keep standing. If I sit, it means I'm here for the long haul. If they're going to put me away, they might as well just do it. It's not as though I haven't been preparing mentally for this for a long time.

I don't ask if I need a lawyer. Maybe I do, but I don't have one, and I don't know where I would find one. If I tell them this, they'll probably send me a young, overworked, underpaid public defender.

'I'm sorry for the inconvenience,' he says, as though he does not hear my heart pounding inside my chest. 'We felt it would be better to do this here, rather than at your place of business. Less public.'

They were waiting at the bike shop when I rode up this morning, anxious to make a pot of coffee and start my day. It's slow this time of year – there aren't as many tourists – but we do repairs, and I have three bikes that need tune-ups. They showed me their badges and said that the shop owners – Beth and Roger Connors – were already at the station. 'Just routine,' they said casually, as though having FBI show up at the door was an everyday thing. 'Just a few questions.'

Agent Tilman frowns. 'Please sit, Ms White. This shouldn't take long.'

For a second, I forget my alias, forget that he believes I'm Helen White, and then I mentally shake myself. I am so tense that I'm afraid I'll break in half if I sit, but I don't want to disobey, so I do as I'm told. The chair squeaks against the floor as I slide it out, and I settle into it, my arms folded across my chest.

'Do you recognize this laptop?' he asks, and again my eyes are drawn to it.

There's nothing special about it. 'Not really. Should I?'

'It was in the office at the bike shop where you work.'

I'm not sure where he's going with this. 'And?'

'Do you use this laptop?'

My heart quickens even more. 'No.' I've been clean for thirty-four days. I should get a coin for that.

'You've never used this laptop?' His voice is a low timbre, and his eyes meet mine.

We stare at each other like this for a few moments, and finally I give in. 'No. I don't know what you're looking for here.' I will myself to stay calm, to keep my voice steady. Agent Tilman clearly thinks I'm connected somehow to this laptop.

I begin to wonder if I *should* find myself a lawyer.

'Do you know who *does* use this laptop?'

I shrug, trying to appear nonchalant. 'Beth and Roger. It's their shop. Their laptop.'

'You've seen them use it?'

I am trying not to stare at the laptop, wondering what is going on.

'Sure. It's usually in the back office, but I am normally in the shop. I don't have anything to do with running the business. I do tours sometimes, but mostly I fix the bikes.' I realize I'm talking too fast, protesting too much, giving him answers to questions he hasn't asked.

'So you *have* seen them use it, Ms White?'

Without thinking, I ask, 'Did someone use this laptop for something illegal?'

Immediately, I regret my question, but he doesn't seem fazed by it.

'That's what we're trying to determine.'

I can't help myself. I start picking apart the possibilities that would lead the FBI to it: child pornography, illegal drugs or weapons, human trafficking. I wonder about Beth and Roger. I can't see them involved in anything like that. They seem too normal. But then again, I seem normal, too.

If the FBI were investigating something, they must have traced the IP address. If I were the culprit, I'd make sure that no one would be able to trace me, so I would reroute the IP address through a VPN. I wonder if this is what's happened. If someone has done just that, and Beth and Roger are innocent in whatever crime is connected to this laptop. I open my mouth to tell Agent Tilman this, but then shut it again. I don't want to show my cards. He can't know what I know. He can't know that I know anything about rerouting IP addresses. That I have skills that go beyond repairing bicycles.

'Besides Beth and Roger Connors, have you seen anyone else using this laptop?' he asks, pulling me out of my thoughts.

'I really can't say for sure who has used it and who hasn't. I know I haven't.'

'Do you have your own laptop, Ms White?'

'No.' I say it quickly, definitively, because it's true.

One of his eyebrows rises above the other. 'No? You don't own a laptop? What about a desktop computer? A tablet?' Agent Tilman's tone has gotten frosty. He doesn't believe me.

'I don't even have a smartphone, Agent Tilman.'

'That's unusual in this day and age.'

Maybe I should have lied. Because it *is* unusual. I quickly say, 'I don't want the distraction in my life. I lead a very simple life.' I pause. 'What exactly did you find on that laptop?'

He narrows his eyes and purses his lips, and for a second I don't think he's going to tell me. But when he finally does, a chill runs through me because I may not be able to escape this time.

TWO

'Do you know who Tony DeMarco is?' Agent Tilman is asking.

I shake myself out of my thoughts and try to concentrate. I can't possibly admit it. That I do know him. That Tony DeMarco was my father's business associate, that his testimony is what sealed my father's fate and his death in prison. That I stole from him and he tried to have me killed almost two years ago. That he offered me a job hacking for him.

'I've heard of him,' I say vaguely. 'Someone tried to kill him?'

Agent Tilman nods, all the while watching me. I resist the urge to cringe under his stare. 'He's going to live,' he tells me, as though I am concerned about Tony DeMarco's well-being. 'But whoever put out the hit on him may go after him again.'

There is probably no shortage of people who want to kill Tony DeMarco, but the more pressing question is: 'You think that this laptop is somehow involved?'

'We know it is. Whoever put the hit out definitely had access to it.'

I can't help but be curious about this. I consider again how easy it would be to reroute the IP address, although now something else strikes me, something that should have occurred to me as soon as he told me about Tony DeMarco.

It's as though my brain is on a time delay.

Why would someone conveniently either use this particular laptop or reroute the IP address here, where *I* live? When he is putting out a hit on Tony DeMarco, who is so connected to *me* in so many ways?

There is no coincidence. Someone knows that I'm here; he wants me to be revealed. He wants me to pay for his crime.

My fingers itch to pull that laptop toward me, to begin a search, to delve deep into it to find out who is doing this. Instead, I fold my hands tightly in my lap and try to concentrate on Agent Tilman, although I keep the laptop in my peripheral vision.

'Why don't you have a laptop, Ms White?'

We are back to this. I can't tell him about my addiction, although one of his colleagues knows it all too well.

FBI Agent Zeke Chapman. He knows I'm here. He knows where I live, where I work.

'No. I told you, I don't have a computer.' I look him straight in the eye when I say it.

Agent Tilman finally seems satisfied with my answer. 'Do you know whether Beth or Roger Connors knows Tony DeMarco?'

I give a short laugh before I can stop myself. 'No,' I say. 'I doubt it, anyway.' I have to backtrack. 'They are very honest people.'

'*Honest* is an interesting word to use.'

'That's what they are.' I hear belligerence in my tone, and I regret it immediately when his eyebrow rises.

'That's exactly what they say about you,' he says.

I am pleased to hear it. But it's not going to get me out of here.

'What do you know about Jerry McNamara?'

The question throws me for a second, but I see where he's going with it, and it's definitely to my advantage. It's as though a beam of light has penetrated the darkness. 'Jerry set up the new wireless network at the bike shop. I don't really know him.' Could Jerry have done this? I don't see any sort of motive; Jerry is a local guy and any possible connection to Tony DeMarco would be slim at best. But I'm willing to play along, throw suspicion around so it doesn't come back at me.

'He knows computers,' Agent Tilman states simply.

I shrug nonchalantly. 'He does.' My eyes stray back to the laptop. With a few keystrokes I could find out who'd been inside.

Agent Tilman stands. 'Thank you, Ms White.' He picks up the laptop, and his expression tells me that he expects me to get up and follow him out. 'If we have more questions, how can we reach you?'

I give him the phone number at the house, since I don't have a cell phone.

I don't see Beth or Roger or Jerry as I am led through the corridor and out through the front. I pass two police officers who stop talking as they watch me leave. I wonder how they feel about lending their interrogation rooms to the FBI, whether they are involved at all in the investigation, or if the FBI commandeered the whole case. I tend to think the latter.

I turn down the offer of a ride and walk back to the shop, my head spinning. I can't help but think that I've dodged a bullet. My identity, for now, is still under wraps; the FBI thinks I am Helen White, bike shop employee and computer Luddite. I can only hope that they don't go digging. If they do, they will find that Helen White doesn't really exist, that she has no history before the last few months here in Falmouth.

All it will take is a photograph. *Do you know this woman?*

Lines will be drawn; they will come after me.

What I need to do is disappear. It will make them look at me more closely and they will make the connection sooner, but I can't take a chance and stay. I am not safe.

No one is at the shop when I arrive. I don't bother to go inside. I unlock my bike from the rack out front and head for home.

THREE

I push open the back door and step inside the mudroom. I hang my bike helmet on the hook on the back of the door and slip off my sneakers, heading into the kitchen. The house is still, yet I am not at all startled to see Agent Zeke Chapman sitting on the couch, leafing through a magazine, waiting for me.

'How'd it go?' he asks lightly, as though his being here is completely natural.

The last time I saw him, I gave him my laptop and told him to leave. I never wanted to see him again.

'Maybe you should just tell them to arrest me,' I say. 'I don't know why you haven't.'

Zeke sighs. He closes the magazine, leans over, and puts it on the table. 'No one's going to arrest you, Tina.' He has still not looked at me.

I roll my eyes. 'Why not?'

'You're innocent, aren't you?' I hear a tinge of doubt in his voice, doubt that I actually am innocent. And now he does look at me; his eyes meet mine and he knows.

I am capable of it. And maybe in another time, another place, I would have done it. Or at least thought about it. Conceived a way to do it. But would I have gone through with it? There is no way of knowing.

'Tony DeMarco has more reason to put a hit on *me* than the other way around.' Sixteen years ago, I stole ten million dollars from bank accounts online, two million of which was

Tony DeMarco's money. Because of that crime, I have been living off the grid all these years. 'Anyway, I gave you my laptop. I haven't had one since.' I am not lying about this, and somehow he senses it. But . . .

'This was put in motion before I saw you. Before you gave me your laptop.'

I try not to let him see that his words startle me. This is why he doubts me. Why there is a question in his eyes.

'So, then, why *don't* you arrest me?' Something changes in his expression, and it dawns on me. 'You don't have any way to prove it was me, do you?'

He shakes his head. 'It's more complicated than you think.'

I glare at him, and it comes out before I can stop myself: 'Then why don't you find *Tracker* and have him help you? Why don't you arrest *Tracker*? Bring *him* in for questioning? Maybe *he* is the one who did it. He is just as capable as I am.'

I do not know for sure that no one knows his true identity. That Agent Zeke Chapman is a hacker called Tracker, and he has been hiding online behind that screen name for over twenty years. Tracker was my best friend and he helped me steal that money, but I only found out a month ago who he really is.

'Tina, is there any way you would consider helping us find out who put the hit out on DeMarco?'

I spent two months trying to get inside Tony DeMarco's deep web site to find proof of illegal activity so that the FBI could arrest him. I remind Zeke of this and add, 'You don't give a rat's ass about Tony DeMarco, and if he dies, you would not lose sleep over it.'

He grins and holds up his hands. 'Guilty as charged.'

'So, then, why do you want to find out who put out the hit?'

He looks visibly uncomfortable, then says something completely unexpected. 'That laptop at the bike shop? It's yours.'

I don't understand.

He sees my confusion. 'It's not *physically* your laptop. But someone hacked into it and uploaded your data into it.'

I still don't understand. I don't have any *data*. I say as much.

'It's data from that laptop you had last summer.'

My heart quickens. A shadow had infiltrated my laptop with a remote access Trojan and demanded two million bitcoins in ransom, threatening my friends' lives if I didn't pay up. I transferred the bitcoins, but we were unable to trace them – or trace the ransom demand back to DeMarco, even though we were convinced he was behind it.

Zeke continues. 'The messages about the ransom are on the laptop we found in the bike shop. There were other files on it, too. Software that would allow you to get into the deep web. Software that someone like you would know about.'

Someone like me – or like him. It must be Tor – The Onion Router. The federal government set it up for its own purposes; however, anyone who wants to be anonymous uses it, not just for selling drugs and guns or human trafficking or hiring hits, but journalists protecting sources, whistleblowers. It's easy to download.

'But the laptop can't have anything that directly leads to *me*,' I say. 'Otherwise that Agent Tilman would have arrested me instead of just asking me questions. Right?'

Zeke nods. 'The moment I saw what was on the laptop, I knew it was targeting you. Whoever is doing it also knows your screen names, the ones you use in the chat rooms. I couldn't get to you before the FBI did, but they don't know who you are, so I figured you'd be fine.'

I almost laugh. I'm not *fine*. 'Why didn't you tell them? About me, I mean?'

I am afraid of what he's going to say, and my fears are confirmed.

'I want you to help me find out who's doing this.'

Although I know it's for my own benefit, I am still uncertain about teaming up with him. It's not so much about the FBI, but it's *him*. Zeke Chapman is Tracker, my long-time online partner. I'd harbored fantasies about Tracker, who he was, what his life was like. I'd idolized him; he was my mentor. But this man sitting across from me – he is not even remotely part of that fantasy.

Ever since Zeke told me he was Tracker, thirty-four days ago, I have been grieving for the one person in the whole world I felt I could trust, my best friend, the person on the other side of the screen who looked out for me and helped me in so many ways.

I will never look at Zeke Chapman and see Tracker.

What makes me so angry is that he knows this. He understands. Like Tracker would.

He sees my hesitation. 'Whoever did this knows you work in the bike shop, Tina. Knows who you are, because of those things on the laptop. The FBI hasn't connected the dots because I never told them about the shadow or you specifically; I only told them that I was working with an informant, a hacker.

'I'd like you to reconsider. Work for me. Work with my team. Under the circumstances, it's in your best interest to find out who tried to kill Tony before he finds out that you might be involved.'

A shiver runs through me. 'I'm not a team player.'

'You're being framed, Tina, and we need to find out who's framing you. As soon as possible.'

I see nothing but sincerity in his eyes. But I also see something else, something I can't pinpoint.

'Why?' I ask. 'What's really going on?'

He hesitates a second, then says, 'The trail doesn't only lead to you. It leads to me – to Tracker – too.'

FOUR

My first thought is that someone has managed to set up both me and Tracker, a feat that at one point I would have believed was impossible.

But then something dawns on me. It sounds as though he has not told the FBI about his alter ego. 'Why don't you tell them that you're Tracker? They'll believe you that there's someone setting us up.'

He narrows his eyes at me. 'You don't get it, do you? They already think that whoever uses those screen names is behind the hit on DeMarco, and they'll see the connection between us. They'll think that *you're* setting *me* up. Unless we find out who it actually is and can hand him over on a silver platter.'

'But you could tell them, couldn't you? That I can't be behind it.'

Zeke takes a deep breath and runs his hand through his hair. 'There is enough said in those ransom notes to lead back to the bank job.'

'You're afraid they'll find out about your role in that, aren't you?' He helped get me inside the source code to find the account numbers I needed to transfer the money.

'It's complicated, Tina. You don't know the whole story,' he says softly.

I put my hands on my hips. 'OK, so why don't you tell me? The *whole* story.'

He stands, coming so close to me that I can physically feel him without touching him. 'We don't have time.'

'Short version.' I struggle to keep my voice steady; I can't let him know that he is unnerving me.

He backs away, circles around the coffee table a couple of times. 'OK, OK, long story short.' He runs a hand through his hair again and begins to pace in front of the fireplace. 'I was like you when I was a kid, Tina. I was online; I was hacking. But unlike you, I got nailed. I hacked into a place I shouldn't have and got caught.' Even though I'm curious, he doesn't elaborate, merely continues. 'They were lenient with me, said if I helped them online, I could wipe my record clean. So I did. That's when I met you.' He stops pacing. 'I was fifteen.'

I was seventeen when I met Tracker online; we had eight years together.

'You were so good,' Zeke says. 'I couldn't believe it. We didn't do anything really illegal for a long time. Not until . . .'

His voice trails off and I finish his sentence in my head. *Not until I asked him to help me get into the bank accounts.* 'Why did you do it?'

He gives me a small smile. 'You need to ask?' He is close again, closer than before, and I remember how he looked when he first showed up at my father's house all those years ago. I thought he was there about my father – the FBI had been watching him for years – but it had been about me. When I realized that he suspected me – without knowing who he really was – I fled to Paris with Ian Cartwright, the man I'd done the job for.

Zeke followed us and asked me to run away with him. He said he'd even left his wife for me. But Ian had a gun, and I ended up accidentally shooting Zeke. I thought I'd killed him. I left Ian to clean up my mess and disappeared to Block Island, off the coast of Rhode Island, where I lived for fifteen years before Ian found me, demanding that I steal for him again, since he never got any of the money the first time.

It clicks then, what happened. 'The accounts were frozen,' I say slowly. 'That was you, wasn't it?'

He doesn't say anything, and I know I'm right. 'There were news stories about it, about the bank job. Someone told the papers that the FBI suspected me.'

'Ian said it was you. But there wasn't any real evidence. And you disappeared. We didn't have any real evidence against Ian, either, and then he went to work for DeMarco, so we kept an eye on him and used him for information.' He hesitates.

'What?' I ask.

He doesn't continue his story. Instead, he says, 'I've been living and breathing this. The sooner we get Tony DeMarco, the better.'

'I thought this was about finding out who ordered the hit on him,' I say softly.

'That's right,' he says, startled by my words. He realizes he screwed up.

It strikes me then, a possibility I never considered. What if *he* is guilty of this? What if, since he couldn't catch him online, *he* ordered the hit instead?

He's studying my face, and I shift uncomfortably. It's as though he knows what I'm thinking.

Tracker and I were always in sync.

He *had* the proof, the evidence, against me. He held my fate in his hands, and instead of turning me in, he came to Paris and offered to run away with me.

He is still protecting me, and I owe him for that.

He has not moved away from me, and in that moment, I

see him for the first time as Tracker. I put my hand up to his cheek before I can stop myself, and he leans in and I feel his lips against mine.

It would be so easy not to stop. But in a second of clarity, I see the truth. This man is Zeke Chapman, FBI special agent. He wants my help. Someone set *me* up, too. I was guilty once, but I'm certainly not guilty now, and I do have the skills to help.

I pull away and take a step back. Now it's my turn to circle the coffee table, keeping it between us.

'Tina,' he says, his voice husky with a passion I remember.

I hold my hand up. 'No, Zeke, we can't. There's too much baggage here.'

'OK. I get it. It's a lot to process.' He tries a small smile on for size.

I vowed to hate him forever for his betrayal. I gave him my laptop and I said never again.

Yet here I am, considering this.

'I gave it up.' He knows what I'm telling him.

'Consider this a relapse.'

'A one-time thing?' Living without a computer is so much simpler. I feel freer, as though a weight has been lifted. Yet the idea of navigating the deep web, crawling around the codes and catching the person who framed me is like a magnet, drawing me into Zeke's plan. I don't know if I start up again that I will be able to walk away again.

He shifts uncomfortably, his eyes moving around the room. There is something else going on.

I am almost afraid to ask when he finally takes a deep breath and looks me in the eye. 'Tina, I need to be honest with you.' He pauses, and I stop breathing as I wait. 'I don't know any other way to say it but straight out. The statute of limitations on the bank job ran out after ten years. We never charged you, never arrested you.'

I'm not quite sure what he's talking about, but then I focus on the words 'statute of limitations' and the pieces begin to fall into place. Before I can say anything, he continues.

'You're not a fugitive. You're as free as I am.'

FIVE

can't speak. My brain is on that time delay again. It's as if I've had a stroke and I have to learn how to think all over again.

The statute of limitations ran out. I was not arrested, charged. I'm not a fugitive.

I'm not a fugitive.

I think about all the years I've been hiding. All my years on Block Island, the year in Canada, my months here on Cape Cod. All the aliases I've used, the identities I've taken.

Rage surges through me, and I feel my face flush with the anger. 'You didn't think to tell me before now?' I ask, my voice low, deep, strangely calm despite my emotions.

'I'm sorry about that. I was going to tell you in New York, but you took off on us. And then when I found you here, I decided that I would tell you first about me, and you were so angry, you threw me out before I could say anything.

'I have to tell you now, because this thing with DeMarco could change everything for you. He knows what you did with the bank job. If you're tied to the hit, if you're linked to another crime, the FBI can come after you for everything, even the bank job, since you *were* a person of interest. Statute of limitations would mean nothing. And then there's DeMarco. If he thinks you're trying to have him killed, he will kill you first. Or at least try.'

My head is reeling. For five seconds, I was safe. I was free.

Zeke is still talking. 'You have amazing survival skills, Tina. Use them now. Help me find out who's setting us up. You can put all of it behind you if we can catch him. You can start all over again; you can come out of hiding.'

I blink a few times, trying to bring it all into focus, but the anger still simmers. I take a step backward and bump into the bookshelf. Zeke instinctively reaches out, but I hold up my arm, wave him off, and stumble up the stairs. I hear him follow, but I don't stop. I go into the bathroom down the hall and shut the door behind me. With only a moment to spare, I lean over the toilet bowl and retch.

I haven't had any breakfast, no coffee, so there is little to come up. When I feel as though I'm done, I sit back and lean against the wall, still on the floor, my head in my hands.

I barely register the soft knock at the door, and it opens a crack.

'You OK?' Zeke peers around the door, a worried expression on his face.

I shake my head, and he comes in, drops down on the floor in front of me. There isn't much room, and he has to keep his knees up. His hands cover mine, and they are warm, slightly calloused. I don't want to feel comforted; I want to stay angry, but the emotion dissipates the longer we sit like this.

'The FBI came after me in Block Island,' I whisper.

'No. They followed Ian there. It was all about Ian, not you.'

The memory of my panic is still so vivid.

'I should have told you.'

'In New York.' It had been a shock to find out he was still alive. I finally look up at him, forcing myself to get back to the matter at hand. 'You should have told me then.'

He nods. 'Yes. But I thought—'

'That I would help you get Tony if I was still running, if I still wanted to protect myself.' I pull my hands out from under his and tuck myself further into the corner, away from him.

'I'm sorry, Tina.'

I peer at him out of the corner of my eye. He does look sorry, and I hate him for that. For being sincere.

'But now I'm stuck again, aren't I? I have to help, or I really will be running.' I am so tired of it; the idea of being able to be *me* again is overwhelming. But then it strikes me. Who am I, really? I feel as though I left Tina Adler behind so long ago that the idea of being her again is foreign to me. Amelie Renaud was a brief moment in Paris; Susan McQueen was desperation in Quebec. Hélène LeBlanc and Helen White are one and the same, and the person I am pretending to be now.

Nicole Jones was who I was on Block Island and the only

identity I've ever had that I was completely comfortable with. When I was Nicole, I was happy.

But can I get her back again? Can I ever be Nicole again?

The bigger question is: Can Nicole Jones be a hacker and still be happy? Because underneath it all, despite the different names, the different lives I've lived, I am still a hacker at heart. I can't change that part of me.

I may have quit, but the addiction is there. And I am suddenly struck by the truth: I don't want to give it up. I never did, or I never would have gone back. It is who I am.

Zeke is watching me sort this all out, waiting for me.

'You pretended to be dead,' I say, remembering that he'd told me the FBI planted the story in the newspapers so they could smoke me out. 'They must have known about me.'

'They just wanted to question you.'

'But why did you have to be dead?'

He shifts uncomfortably and doesn't meet my eyes. 'I went undercover for a while.'

'How long?' I ask.

'Two years.' He doesn't elaborate, and I can tell by the way his jaw is set that I'm not going to get any answers if I push.

'You going to be OK?' he asks softly.

I hate it that he can see through me, that he can see into my head so easily. I want to separate Zeke and Tracker, but it's futile. They are one and the same, and I have to try to get used to it. I swallow hard and nod. 'Guess so. Don't have much of a choice, do I?' I make an attempt at a chuckle, but it comes out garbled and I sound as though I'm choking.

'So you're on board?'

Maybe if I do this, I can walk away, set up a life somewhere. I can leave Helen White behind. Start afresh. No one coming after me – not the FBI, not Tony DeMarco.

Not Zeke.

'Yeah,' I whisper. 'I'm in.'

'So, about the team,' he says, all business now, even though we are still sitting on the bathroom floor. 'You'll like them.'

I doubt that. I like the anonymity of being online, shrouded by a screen name, no one knowing who I am. But then I think about my screen names. How someone has managed to discover my identity despite my best efforts. 'So I would actually meet this team?'

'Yes.'

I open my mouth to object, but he puts his hand up. 'We've got a place. Everyone needs to be on the same page.' He pauses. 'I know hackers aren't team players. I know you're not. Team building is not something we do, but my hands are tied. I've got funding, and I need to submit reports.'

He wants me to believe that he is being forced to play along with the bureaucracy, but he doesn't seem too upset about it. If he were, he'd go undercover as Tracker and leave it all behind. I can only surmise that he likes being FBI, and he likes running this team.

'When?' I ask. There has to be a deadline. They will want closure soon – and if not the FBI, then Tony DeMarco.

He confirms this. 'Soon as possible.'

'How involved are you?' I ask.

He knows what I'm getting at. Can he be Tracker and Zeke Chapman at the same time? Can he show his cards as a hacker?

'I told you, they know about me, but not about Tracker.'

My thoughts are pinballing. 'How do I know I'm going to be safe?' My voice trails off as I try not to think about the repercussions, how Tony DeMarco has his own form of justice.

'No one knows where my team is, and it's going to stay that way.'

Zeke's eyes meet mine, and in them I see him again: Tracker.

'We're all like you, Tina,' he says. His tone is so soft that I barely hear him, but I do hear what's behind the words. What he's trying to tell me about his team.

It's not that we're all hackers.

We all have something that we want to hide.

SIX

'So tell me how you got into that laptop. What led you there?' I ask.

Relief floods his expression. He knows now for sure that I'm going to help. 'There are conversations.'

'Conversations about what?'

'A hit. On DeMarco.'

'You're kidding, right? There are actual messages discussing this?'

'Yeah.' Zeke helps me up off the floor. 'Come on. Let's go downstairs,' he says.

On the way, I ask, 'How are we going to find out anything if we don't have the laptop? We really need to get in there. I want to see what's inside. Maybe whoever planted that stuff in there left some sort of calling card that we can use to trace him.' Just as he was able to throw down footprints that led into the laptop.

'Don't worry about that. Come on.' Zeke grins. When we get back to the living room, I see what I didn't notice before: the messenger bag on the floor next to the sofa. He pulls a laptop out of it and waves it in front of me. He opens it, boots it up, and sets it on the coffee table as he sits. He pats the cushion next to him, and I squeeze between him and the sofa's arm. He doesn't move over, but I am unaware of being uncomfortable as I stare at the laptop. It's worse than when I was in the interrogation room – the *need* that rushes through me. Before I can stop myself, I reach out toward it, my fingers grazing the edge. I want nothing more at this moment than to touch the keys, feel them under my fingertips. The desire overwhelms me, and I feel myself taking a short intake of breath.

Zeke turns the laptop toward me, pushing it closer. I yank my hand back as though I've touched fire.

'Is this *the* laptop?' I ask, aware that my voice cracks.

I clear my throat as I wait for him to answer, but he doesn't; he merely touches a key and the screen pops to life. I see the messages I got last summer in Quebec, the ones telling me my laptop had been hijacked and the hijacker wanted a million bitcoins. I read the exchange we had about the bank account that the FBI never found – I had set it up for Tracker – and I realize something.

'Isn't it evidence?' I ask, referring to the laptop

'I can't do my job without it,' he says, but he doesn't explain how he is able to take evidence and just walk off with it.

I decide I'm not going to nag him about it. He's the one who will get in trouble if they find out. Instead, I study the messages on the screen.

'He never actually says what bank account or anything that implicates me,' I say softly, thinking out loud.

'No, he doesn't, but this did raise some flags – wondering exactly who the messages were aimed at. They know that whoever it is, is allegedly responsible for the hit. The IP address was like a gift.'

'Isn't it a little too obvious?' I ask. 'I mean, wouldn't your people figure that someone wouldn't be that stupid?'

'Criminals are really stupid, Tina,' Zeke says with a short chuckle. 'You have no idea.'

'But I'm not that stupid.' As I say it, though, I know that I'm wrong. It was a stupid move on my part that led Ian – and Tony's people – to find me on Block Island. Zeke, who knows this, doesn't bother to contradict me.

I want to change the subject, so I go back to the laptop's contents. 'What about the pictures? Of Steve and Jeanine.' My friends in Block Island who were threatened.

'Go ahead,' he tempts me, the laptop even closer now.

I can't help myself. I pull it on to my knees. Zeke watches me, but I barely notice. A few keystrokes and there they are – it's too easy to find the pictures. I know now that this is definitely a set-up. It wouldn't be *that* easy.

But as I'm thinking that, it also strikes me that the shadow never used Steve or Jeanine's names – just called them my friends – and from the photographs, it might be difficult to identify them or where the photos were taken.

For a moment, I forget about what I'm doing – my willpower gone and my relapse all too real – as I gaze at the pictures, even though I don't need them to remember them. All I have to do is close my eyes, and they're in front of me. In that second, I realize something. If I'm free, maybe I can go back. Back to Block Island.

Zeke is closing the laptop cover. 'We don't have time for this now, Tina. We've got to get going. Whoever put these things on this laptop knows you're here, probably knows that you've been questioned, and may even be watching the house right now.'

I catch my breath. 'But why?'

'That's what we have to figure out.' He won't meet my eyes. He knows more than he's saying. He's had some time with that laptop, and I know what he can do.

'I want to see the conversations about the hit.'

'We have time for that later. I'm curious, though, how much you know about anyone in the chat room. Besides me, anyway.' He looks at me now. His face is so close, and again I am aware that his leg is pressed against mine and I can feel the heat coming off his body. I squirm a little, but I don't have any room to move.

I force myself to consider his question, which is curious. 'I don't know much about anyone there – not personally, anyway. We're all anonymous. Supposedly,' I say. 'Do you think the shadow is someone in the chat room?' That would be a huge betrayal. Everyone on the chat site is there anonymously, but it is a place where that anonymity is respected.

At least that's what I always believed.

Zeke shrugs. 'I think we need to find out more about the people on that site. It might narrow things down a little. Process of elimination.' He stands. I am relieved that he is no longer so close physically. It makes me uneasy, reminding me of what we had a long time ago and how I do not want to repeat it. Yet there is still an attraction.

'I tried to find out about Tracker,' I say slowly, wondering if I should even admit it.

He gives a short chuckle. 'And you couldn't find out anything? I'm surprised. I found out about you pretty easily.'

I stand and face him, trying to force my competitiveness down but not being too successful. 'I was a kid.'

'You were twenty-five.'

'You didn't know who I was before then? Before the job?'

He smiles. 'No. Even though I tried to find out.'

I can see something in his expression, and it dawns on me. 'Something gave me away. *I* gave me away somehow, didn't I?' I try to remember what I might have said, what I might have done back then, but it's too long ago, too much time has passed.

He's not going to tell me, either. He's too busy putting the laptop back in the messenger bag. He goes over to the front window and stares outside.

'They wouldn't be so bold that we'd see them, would they?' I ask.

'No.'

'If someone's watching the house, then he knows you're here. With me.'

'We have to make it look like this is normal.'

'You and me?'

He smiles. 'It might not be so difficult. For either of us.'

I choose not to address what he's really saying. 'So, what, he sees us leave together?'

'We have to make it look like you're not leaving for good. That it's just another day for you.'

'It's not, though. I would be at the shop now, at work.'

'Maybe that's what you have to make him believe. That you're going back to work. That it's business as usual.'

I'm dubious, but I don't have a choice. He's right: I can't stay. I already knew that, but the difference now is that I'm not leaving alone.

SEVEN

I am packing again. The backpack that made it through Quebec and all the way to Cape Cod is again going to hold all of my necessary belongings. Everything else gets left behind.

I desperately want to think that this is the last time. The last time I ever have to pack like this, the last time I ever have to leave a place like a fugitive.

I remind myself I'm not a fugitive anymore. Never was. But I can't seem to wrap my head around that. Being a fugitive is habit. It's been my way of life for so long.

I pause in front of the bedroom window, and I can see the water from here. Its color changes with the seasons; instead of a bright, deep blue, it's more silver today, reflecting the clouds that hang lower in the sky. Sometimes I walk along the beach and find a place to sit, my fingers tracing the cool sand, digging up white, shiny shells. If I had my own house like I did on Block Island or Isle-aux-Coudres in Quebec, I might collect those shells in jars. I used to have jars filled with the smooth rocks I found on the beaches on Block Island. But here, I don't have my own house. I have been housesitting for an elderly couple who go south once the air begins to get frosty.

My eyes snap open when I realize I have to contact them, let them know that I won't be coming back, that they need to find someone else to live in their house and water the plants.

'You can't do that,' Zeke tells me when I mention it.

'But I can't leave the house unattended. Let me call someone.'

'I'll take care of it.'

I narrow my eyes at him. 'How?'

'I'll take care of it,' he says impatiently, grabbing the pile of clothes that I've laid out on the bed and shoving them into the backpack.

I take the pack from him and pull everything out. He watches me sort through the T-shirts and jeans, neatly rolling them up so more will fit. I've got this part down.

I am on my bike, my pack on my back. I feel the burn in my thighs as I pedal hard; I am not used to the weight anymore. I am wistful as I pass through the familiar neighborhoods, nodding at other bikers, joggers, women pushing strollers. I hate it that I have to leave yet another bicycle behind. I wonder if I will be able to get another one wherever we are headed.

The plan is for Zeke to meet me in the alleyway behind the bike shop. He'd parked his car around the corner, in front of someone else's house, as though that would fool anyone. If he is right that someone has been watching me, he is as exposed as I am.

The scent of the ocean hangs in the air – salty, briny. I think about my watercolors hanging in the gallery in Woods Hole. Through my art, I have tried to capture the magic of this place, of the places where I've found refuge these past years. I never knew I had any artistic talent; I spent all my time in front of a computer screen before I went on the run. But once I discovered this about myself, I embraced it, just as I embraced my new identities. I was reborn in so many ways, and again I wonder about my new destination – I still don't know where I'm going; I'm almost afraid to find out.

I reach the bike shop much too soon. I want to take the whole day, make my way down Cape, maybe even go as far as Provincetown, where I can't go any further and the ocean spreads out in front of me as far as I can see.

The shop is locked up; Beth and Roger must still be tied up at the police station. Either that or they've decided to stay closed today. Maybe they're at the Coffee Obsession, huddled over a couple of lattes and pastries, trying to figure out how their laptop got all tied up with a hit on a mobster.

I open the side door and walk my bike past the front desk and into the workshop. I breathe in the rubber smell, close my eyes, and commit it to my memory. I have a feeling that I may not be part of this sort of life again for a while.

I lean my bike against the wall and scurry out, not wanting to linger or I may never leave. I lock up the door I came through and go around to the office and slip outside.

Zeke is waiting in an SUV. I toss my pack into the backseat before climbing into the front.

It seems so clandestine.

I am not sure I want to go with him to be squirreled away with some unknown hackers whom I don't know. I have been on my own – alone – for so long that the idea of cohabitating is not appealing. I touch the jade necklace in the shape of a dragon that sits against my chest. It has given me strength before, and I'm afraid I will have to call on it again.

'I don't understand something,' I begin when we are a few miles away, heading toward Boston. 'Why have you continued to use the screen name Tracker after all these years? Why didn't you give it up?'

The SUV slows, stops at a light, and he turns to look at me. 'Would you have trusted me if I wasn't Tracker? If I was someone else?'

'So this is about me? Finding me?' It's too simple.

He reaches over and touches my cheek. 'Yes.'

The light turns green, and the SUV shoots forward. I can still feel his fingers on my skin, and I wonder if he is telling the truth.

'I'm not only Tracker, though,' he says suddenly, interrupting my thoughts. 'Like you, I've got a few screen names. They do know about those; they know what I can do. That's how I was able to assemble the team. Cybercrime is on the rise.' He says this last bit as though it's news to me, as though he's reading a script. He is smiling now, too, to show me that he is spouting the company line.

'Who are they, this team you've got? And why do I have to meet them? Hackers don't meet each other, Zeke.' I pause. 'It will be the biggest regret of their lives.'

He tenses up and bites his lip. I am throwing Tracker's words back at him, the ones he wrote to me so many times when I suggested we meet and he refused.

'You met me anyway,' I accuse before he can say anything,

aware that my voice is getting louder as my anger rises, but I can't help myself. 'You came to my father's house under the pretense of watching him, and you met me. You knew who I was; we already had a relationship. But you took it a step further, didn't you? You seduced me.'

He chuckles then, despite himself. '*You* seduced *me*, Tina. Remember?'

I shrink back in my seat. Yes, I did. It was all part of my plan to make Ian Cartwright jealous. But looking at it now, Zeke set it all up. He showed up; he put everything that happened afterward in motion.

'I didn't know what was going to happen between us, Tina,' he says softly, reading my mind, which makes me even angrier. He isn't Tracker. Not now. Tracker lives online. He is not flesh and blood. He is not this man who lied to me. Betrayed me. Tracker would never do that.

And yet he did.

I slump down in my seat and watch the world pass by outside the car window. I want to ask where we're going, but at the same time I don't want any more conversation. I watch the highway signs and see that we are nearing Boston. I turn the radio on, the music swirling around in my head.

Zeke reaches around behind me and pulls out a large white envelope, which he drops in my lap. I frown, opening it. I take out the driver's license and the passport, both in the name of Susan McQueen, the name I used when I lived in Quebec. I raise my eyebrows at him.

'I'm Susan again?'

'Figured you'd answer to it if someone used it.'

He's right about that. I was Susan for over a year, and I got used to her. 'But why not use my real name? I mean, if I'm not a fugitive?'

He pauses, as though thinking about how best to answer this. Finally, 'There are news stories online.'

He's right. Stories about my father. About how he bilked his rich and famous clients out of millions and ended up in prison. How he died there. I wonder if taking back my real name is not a good idea after all. Even if I am not a fugitive, even if the bank job never comes back to haunt me, my father sealed my fate. I can never come completely clean if I want to build a new life.

I shake the thoughts aside and study the documents. I don't recognize the street address on the license, but the city is Miami. The photograph is one I took of myself when I was in Quebec with the idea that I could use it for this purpose, but I never followed through. How did he get it?

'It was in the laptop,' he says.

The one that I gave him over a month ago when he told me he was Tracker and I vowed never to go online ever again. Even though I wiped it clean, he was able to find this photograph; he was able to pull it out from deep inside.

For a moment, despite myself, I do think of him as Tracker, as the person on the other side of the chat room who could do anything, whose skills surpassed anyone else's I've ever known. The hacker I wanted to emulate, the one I learned from, trusted.

And when I realize what I'm doing, I push the thoughts aside and allow myself to become angry again. He infiltrated my laptop. What else did he find?

'You needed documents,' he said.

'And you just so happened to have my laptop and just so happened to have those documents made up. Were you so sure of me? That I would say yes?' The fury rises as `I think about it, how I have played into his hands so easily. I reach for the door handle, forgetting that we're going seventy miles an hour. 'I want out. Now. I'm done.'

The car swerves to the side of the road and I hear the screech of tires as the cars behind us brake and veer around us. I'm thrown against the door as we jolt to a stop, despite the seat belt, and he throws his arm across me as he unclasps his own seat belt with his other hand. Even if I want to escape now, I cannot open the door for the weight of him.

'You can't,' he hisses in my ear, his breath hot against my skin.

I try to yank back, but the seat belt keeps me from it, and I am more a prisoner than I was in that interrogation room.

'I thought this was a free country,' I mutter.

'You are on tenuous ground, Miss Adler.' He is reminding me that a new crime could unearth my old one.

I glare at him. I hold his secret; I am not the only one who is at risk here. But he doesn't seem concerned.

'I'm going to sit back,' he says softly, as though I am a danger to him and to myself. 'You have to stay in the car.'

I am more than aware that he could overpower me again, so I mutely nod. He settles back into his seat, and although I do not try to get out again, I try my best to disappear into the crack between the seat and the door, as far away from him as I can get.

'You and I are a part of this,' he says. 'Someone made it his business to set us both up. It's in our best interest to find out who, so maybe we can both move on with our lives.'

His voice does not rise as he speaks; his tone is as though he has merely invited me out to lunch. But the threat is present. I need to help him or I will never be free. As it is, he has been searching for me for years and has finally gotten me where he wanted me all along.

'How much of this is saving our own asses and how much is it about finding Tony DeMarco's site and making sure that he's locked up forever?' I ask.

'It's about both.'

I think about this for a few minutes. Both are intertwined; one will lead to the other, but I'm uncertain which will come first. Or if it even matters. Sort of like the proverbial chicken-and-egg question.

'Tell me where we're going.'

'To the airport.'

He lets that settle between us for a few seconds before he starts the car up again and we head back into the traffic.

'I can't believe you're going to let me use fake documents to fly. What if I get caught?' I ask.

'You won't.'

He sounds so sure.

'Listen, Tina, we make fake documents for people all the time.'

He probably means people in witness protection. Maybe that's what I am now. Perhaps not a witness, but I definitely need protecting. At least until Tony DeMarco is taken care of.

'Where are we flying to?' I ask.

He is not stupid enough to think that I have let this go, but after a moment he speaks.

'We're going back to where it all started.'

EIGHT

I have not been back to Miami since I left more than sixteen years ago, yet when I step outside and breathe in the warm, tropical air, the first thought I have is 'I'm home.' Immediately, I feel as though I have betrayed my adopted home of Block Island, where I lived for fifteen years under the radar: no Internet, only my bike tours and paintings and Friday nights at Club Soda with Steve.

I push the memories aside and consider the reason we are here.

Tony DeMarco lives here.

We are in a nondescript rental car heading south on the South Dixie Highway. The road runs parallel with the monorail; the concrete landscape is flat and stretches as far as I can see. Pale pink-and-white stucco strip shopping malls, gas stations, and palm trees tell me that I'm not on Cape Cod anymore, but I could be anywhere in Florida. We are nowhere near the bustling, vibrant, neon South Beach. Outside the car's air-conditioned cocoon, the air is familiarly damp; it's still hurricane season, although it's late enough in the season that the risk is low.

I watch Zeke's profile as he drives, staring straight ahead. He's wearing sunglasses; he pulled them out from his duffel bag when we got to the car. He notices me staring at him, and he glances over, a broad grin breaking across his face. It is so familiar, just like the air, and brings me back to the days more than sixteen years ago, when he would come to my father's house and take me to the beach on the back of his motorcycle.

For a moment, I allow myself to remember how that smile wrapped itself around me and made me feel safe. I went into the relationship with Zeke for all the wrong reasons, and I was never head over heels for him as I was with Ian, but from the first moment Zeke stepped across the threshold into my father's house, there had been an attraction, a sense that when I was with him I didn't have to be anyone but myself.

Just like with Tracker.

I take a deep breath and look away, folding my hands over each other and tightening my grip. Did I somehow subconsciously know who he was back then? Is that why I allowed myself to get caught up with him, convince myself that to find out for sure whether Ian loved me, I needed to have an affair with an FBI agent – three weeks after we'd stolen ten million dollars?

'You knew who I was,' I say flatly as I stare out the front windshield.

'Yes.'

'And you were married.'

'Yes.' Out of the corner of my eye, I see his jaw tense.

'Do you still keep in touch with her?'

'No.' His monosyllabic answers indicate he doesn't want to take that trip down memory lane, but my curiosity is piqued. Who was she? Why was he so willing to throw it away for me?

I remember something. 'You told me she was a teacher. You were trying for kids.'

'*She* was.' His tone is terse, and I need to give it up, but I'm not ready yet. He's taken me for this ride, and I have an uncanny urge to pick at this like a new scab. 'We were very young. Too young. I was trying to be someone I wasn't.'

'Why?'

He grips the steering wheel so tightly his knuckles turn white. 'You really want to do this now?'

I don't, not really. But there have been so many lies. I lean my head back on the headrest and close my eyes. Before I can stop myself, I say, 'I loved you.'

'No. You never did,' he says roughly.

He's right about that, and I am instantly sorry, because I wasn't talking about Zeke.

'Tracker,' I whisper, just to say it, to hear the way it sounds in my throat.

He is quiet for a second, then says, 'I was a fantasy to you, Tina. I wanted to be real. I *was* real. For a while.' There is a catch in his voice, and I don't want to open my eyes because I don't want to see it in his face.

'After this, will you let me go?' is all I ask.

'You can do whatever you want.'

We don't speak again until we pull in behind a bright pink stucco apartment building which, at a distance, looks fresh and new, but the closer we get, appears to be more worn around the edges. I have made a pact with myself that I will lay off Zeke. Right now it's all about finding out who put the hit out on Tony DeMarco and who set us up. Granted, Zeke has a broader goal, but I'll deal with that when I have to. With any luck, both birds can be killed with one stone.

Zeke looks tentatively at me as he parks. 'Are we good?' he asks. It's as though he, too, has decided to call a truce with the past and let me off the hook.

I nod, and we get out of the car. He goes around the back and takes my backpack and his duffel out of the trunk. I hold out my hand to take the pack, but he shrugs me off. 'This way.'

He leads me through an archway and into a courtyard. What used to be a fountain sits in the middle. It is round, covered in multicolored small mosaic tiles, and a stone dolphin looks to be leaping out of it. It is quite likely the ugliest fountain I have ever seen, although perhaps with water it might be a little bit better. I peer over and see about two inches of mucky water and a couple of dead goldfish.

'Does anyone ever clean this out?' I ask, but Zeke is already heading toward a staircase on the opposite side of the courtyard. Palm trees adorn all four corners. They are old and tall, and their fronds reach out toward each other, keeping the sunshine out.

I follow him up the stairs, noticing orange stains in the pink stucco. A small lizard scurries across the floor when we reach the hallway, its tail flipping up behind it. I begin to wonder how long I'm going to have to stay here. I hope it's not too long.

Zeke stops at a door, taps twice, then turns the knob.

'Welcome home,' he says, pushing the door open, letting me go in first.

NINE

I t's nothing like what I expected.

It is a normal living room with a couch, a couple of chairs, a coffee table. A small galley kitchen is to the left. A sliding glass door leads out to a small balcony overlooking the parking lot. At least it's not the sad fountain in the courtyard. There are no pictures on the walls, no decorations.

Music emanates from somewhere down the hall. I raise my eyebrows at Zeke, who nods and moves ahead of me again, carrying our bags. He tosses his duffel in one bedroom to the right, across from the bathroom, and takes my backpack into a larger bedroom at the end of the hall. This is where the music is coming from.

I reach the doorway and stop. The girl – or, rather, young woman – is dancing in the middle of the room. She wears a short pink sundress that only grazes the tops of her thighs; her feet are bare. Her hair falls in a long, thick blonde braid down her back. When she turns around, I am struck by her bright green eyes and rosy cheeks. She looks like someone's little sister.

She does something with her phone and the music halts. 'You must be Susan,' she says, but the innocence falls away for a moment and I see her gaze flit from me to Zeke. She's not happy I'm here.

I give her a stiff smile, uncertain how to navigate this situation. Zeke flashes me a look that says I need to get over whatever I'm feeling, because it's pretty obvious that she and

I are going to be roommates. And then I remember Zeke's bag in the other bedroom. Great. Three is most definitely a crowd.

'This is Heather,' Zeke says to me as he puts my backpack on the twin bed across the room. A twin bed. I only slept in a twin bed once in my life: that one semester in college. I am not enjoying this.

But it seems as though Zeke is, and I resent him for it. He's talking to Heather about the music, which I don't recognize, distracting her from the fact that I have still not said a word.

I go over to 'my' bed and survey the rest of the room. There is only one dresser, one closet. Again, no decorations, no artwork on the walls. It's going to be like living in a monastery.

'It's not so bad.' Zeke is suddenly next to me. 'Anyway, you won't be here too much. Heather, why don't you head over, and we'll meet you there in a few?'

'It's nice to meet you,' I say. Even though I try to sound friendly, I don't think it's convincing.

Heather merely gives me a nod, confirming that I'm right, and turns to Zeke. 'I'll see you later,' she says, flashing a bright smile at him before she disappears down the hall. I see enough in that smile to know that three truly may be a crowd – at least as far as Heather's concerned.

'She's got a crush on you,' I say, my tone light as I tease him.

'She's a kid.' He pauses. 'Maybe you're jealous?' He gives me a sly look.

I give a short chuckle. 'You're right. She's a child. Nothing to be jealous of.' However, I am oddly aware of an irrational competitiveness. I shake it off and change the subject. 'What happens if you slip up and call me Tina in front of everyone?'

He narrows his eyes at me, giving me the impression that he is not fooled. But he leaves it alone. 'You're right. Maybe you should have just stayed Tina Adler.'

Again I wonder if I could ever go back to her. I push the thought aside. 'So Heather doesn't know who you really are?'

He gives me a quizzical look, one of the first times he hasn't known exactly what I'm asking, but then the light bulb goes on. 'Oh, you mean about Tracker?'

I'm a little uncomfortable with him talking about himself in the third person, but it does sometimes feel as though another person is standing here with us. 'Yes.'

'No. She doesn't know. No one else knows.' He says it as though I'm special because I'm privy to his alter ego. I don't feel special. I feel trapped.

I try to ignore the claustrophobia. 'How many of us are there?'

'Counting me, there are six.'

'Only two women?' I almost say 'girls,' and I mentally slap myself. I'm hardly a girl, although I'm not sure just how old Heather is. She may not even be twenty yet, but I'm not great at guessing ages.

'You know the odds.'

That hackers are mostly boys or young men. 'Yeah. But Heather looks like she should still be in school or at the mall with her girlfriends. She's really a hacker?'

'She's good.'

I let that hang between us a few seconds. We'll see.

'So what's the deal here?' I look reproachfully at the bed again.

Zeke chuckles. 'It's not that long, Tina. You won't be here that much anyway,' he says again.

'Where is the hub of all the activity, then?'

'Corner apartment. It's a lot bigger.'

'Servers?'

'Off site.'

'Safe?'

'Of course.'

'We're going to be inside a lot of code that we're not supposed to be inside,' I point out.

'No kidding.'

'So why didn't you just get your own apartment? Why are you staying here?'

He stops smiling now. 'I have to keep an eye on you.'

'So I don't take off.'

'So you don't take off,' he repeats. 'You're pretty good at
that.'

I can't help but smile. 'Yeah, I am, aren't I?'

'Do you want to shower or anything before we go?'

'No, I'm fine.'

'Then let's get to work.'

He's right about the corner apartment. It is much larger, and
even though it doesn't have any artwork on the walls either,
it doesn't matter here. The moment I walk in, I can concentrate
only on the tables of computers and the wires that snake around
between them. In a way, I'm a little disappointed because it's
just so clichéd, but it does work.

Heather is hunched over a keyboard across the room, and
I study the other three who haven't even looked up. They all
wear headphones, music filling their heads while their eyes
are glued to the screens filled with code. My fingers begin to
itch.

Zeke brings me over. 'This is Susan,' he says loudly, and
only two pull off their headphones and look at me. Heather
gives me a sidelong glance before turning back to her
screen.

One of the hackers is scruffy, with a day-old beard and
greasy hair, wearing a bright orange T-shirt. Zeke tells me his
name is Jake. The other, called Charles, is Asian, his black
hair sticking up straight, although it looks clean. He has a
wide face and broad nose, with glasses perched on its end.
Both of them look to be in their late teens, maybe early
twenties. I assume they have to be eighteen and legally adults,
but then again, Zeke had documents made up for me, and I'm
probably not the only one.

Despite my age and gender, they don't seem very curious
about me, simply stick their headphones back on and return
to their screens.

Zeke goes over to the third hacker, who still hasn't glanced
up, and taps his shoulder, startling him. I know that feeling,
and I suppress the urge to chuckle. He isn't like the other two,
even though he looks younger – maybe not even old enough
yet to shave. He is dressed as if he's older, however; as if he's

got a real day job somewhere other than in a corner apartment in a worn-out apartment building: white button-down shirt, chinos. His hair is short, slicked back, and he's got a rich-boy air of arrogance around him. I am struck by a sense that I know him, but I chalk it up to growing up with privilege myself. Hacking doesn't discriminate.

'Meet Daniel,' Zeke instructs.

'Hello, Daniel,' I say.

Daniel doesn't respond; he merely turns back to his screen. I'm not offended; it's what he does. I was hardly socially competent when I was his age and had no use for real human beings, either.

Zeke is clearing a place for me in front of an extra desktop I hadn't noticed next to Heather. She flashes a bright smile at him, but barely registers that I'm in the room.

There is suddenly too much togetherness. It's almost as though the walls have begun to close in on me. I grip my hands tightly in front of me as Zeke boots up the desktop, and my gaze wanders to the sliding glass door that leads out to a small balcony, similar to the one in the other apartment. It's turned dark outside; this morning at the police station feels like a million years ago, and exhaustion overwhelms me.

Without a word, I cross the room, open the door, and step outside.

I can't stay.

TEN

I am at the door to the other apartment by the time Zeke catches up with me. My heart is pounding within my chest. My head tells me I'm having an old-fashioned panic attack, while at the same time it's as though I'm going to die right here, right this very moment.

'What's wrong?'

I take a couple of huge gulps of air into my lungs, willing myself to calm down.

'Are you OK?' Worry laces Zeke's tone, and he takes another step toward me.

I hold up my hand to keep him at bay and shake my head. 'I can't work in there. I can't work like that.'

I expect him to scold me, tell me that I'm being unreasonable. Instead, he unlocks the apartment door and leads me inside. He doesn't say anything, just goes to his room, leaving me in the living room, wishing I'd stood up to him, told him I wouldn't come with him.

'Maybe this is better.'

I twirl around at the sound of his voice and see him standing behind me, holding the laptop. I shake my head. 'I don't know.'

He holds it out closer to me now. Reluctantly, I take it from him. Its weight feels comfortable in my hands, and I pull it to my chest, clutching it.

'I don't care where you work,' he says, 'as long as we get the job done.'

I don't believe him. He brought me here, to Miami, for a reason. To be on that *team*.

'It's fine,' he assures me, and I can see he understands what's happening to me.

Still clutching the laptop, I sink down on to the couch and put my head between my legs.

'You'll be OK,' he says. 'Do you want me to stay?'

Without looking up, I shake my head. I feel his hand on the back of my neck. I wonder if he's making sure I'm not really dying, and as if to prove that I'm not, he says, 'I'll be down the hall.' And just like that, Zeke is gone. He has left me alone here.

I slowly pull myself up and lean back on the couch, taking a few more deep breaths. After a few moments, I begin to feel a lot better. Enough so that Zeke's sudden disappearance strikes me as a little odd. So much for keeping an eye on me. Instinct makes me glance around for some sort of device – a camera maybe – that is spying on me, that will tell him whether I'm staying or leaving. I do a quick search of the room, the kitchen area, but nothing. That doesn't mean it's not here, though.

And then I see it. The lamp in the corner is on, and a small wire is visible in shadow behind the shade. On further inspection, it has come a little loose, which is why it's no longer completely hidden.

If he is watching, then he will see my face peering into the camera. I don't really care. He brought me here because I'm smart, maybe sometimes smarter than he is.

Which is why I do a search in the bedroom, too, and find another camera in the ceiling fan.

I don't like being spied on. I know I'm a flight risk, but there has to be some sort of trust. I told him I'd help; that should be good enough for him to know that I won't go back on it. The bubble of irritation successfully erases the lingering remnants of the panic attack as I consider the situation. The sooner I can get this job done, the sooner I can leave Zeke's watchful eyes behind. Still holding the laptop, I go back into the living room and take one last deep breath before sitting on the couch and opening it, booting it up.

The screen is still dark when I get back up, pacing. What am I doing? I could walk away now. The cameras be damned. I could leave this apartment with my backpack, catch a bus or even hitch a ride. I've managed to escape before; I have no reason to think I can't do it again. I could go to Miami city hall and find my birth certificate, apply for a driver's license, get a passport, all with my own name. I could get a bank account. Legitimately. *I* would be legitimate.

I don't have to hide anymore.

I'd told Zeke that I didn't need to freshen up, but suddenly I want a shower. I leave the laptop on the coffee table and find a towel in the hall closet. I make sure not to get undressed in the bedroom under the camera's watchful eye. I wonder if Heather knows about the camera.

Within a few minutes, I am standing under a hot stream of water, my eyes closed, thinking about freedom.

Until I have an idea.

My eyes snap open, and I shut off the water, wrapping the towel around me as I pad into the living room. I sit in front of the laptop and hit a few keys. I don't even think about what I'm doing. I just do it.

*   *   *

He finds me here, like this, my hair air-dried, still wrapped in the towel, the code scrolling in front of me. The apartment is dark except for the light from the screen and the moonlight that splashes through the sliding glass doors across the dingy carpet.

'Tina?'

His voice startles me; I didn't even hear the door open. The light comes on, bright, and I blink against its harshness.

I realize I'm wearing a towel and nothing else. My hair springs around my head in ringlets. I have no idea how long I've been like this.

I give him a wan smile. 'Sorry,' I say, although I'm not sure what I am apologizing for. Maybe it's because I abandoned the team, abandoned him. Or maybe it's not. Maybe it's because I need something to say, and I don't want to tell him that I looked for him in the chat room, forgetting that he was a few doors down and no longer Tracker. I'd caught myself before I wrote a message, staring at the screen.

'You OK?' Zeke asks, still standing, still staring, a worried expression on his face. Maybe he's reconsidering his decision to leave me here in the midst of a panic attack.

I give a little snort. 'Sure.' I force myself to stop looking at the screen, to get up, pull the towel tighter so it doesn't fall off. I brush past him toward the bedroom, where I shut the door and rummage around in my backpack until I find the oversized T-shirt I sleep in and pull it over my head. Since he is here and not on the other side of the cameras, I feel a little confident that I can change without anyone watching. Still, I make an effort to cover myself. I come back out with the towel and hang it on the rod in the bathroom before heading back into the living room.

I expect to see him still standing, but instead now he is at the laptop, checking out what I've found.

The first thing I discovered was the remote access Trojan, one that Beth or Roger – or maybe Jimmy, who set up the new wireless access – had inadvertently installed through an email link. This is the portal that allowed the shadow to upload all of the messages that we exchanged several months ago. I also found a back door, so the shadow could get in even if access was denied, and the port where the shadow managed to reroute the IP address. I see it jumped to three other locations before ending up in Falmouth, Massachusetts, but where it originated is still a mystery, although I could deduce from this that the shadow is likely using Tor, which randomly causes the original IP address to bounce around and makes it less traceable.

'I didn't really find anything,' I say. 'I mean, nothing you haven't already seen.' The galley kitchen is across the room, and I head for the refrigerator. Milk, eggs, bread, a six-pack of beer. It's not what I'm looking for. 'Do you have any cognac?' I ask. I need a short one.

'Upper right cabinet,' he says, not even looking up. It's as though he turned into me – or Tracker – the moment he sat down.

I find the bottle and pour two glasses, bringing one out to him. He sips it, his eyes still trained on the screen. The liquid is hot and warm against my throat, and I welcome the small diversion. I'm curious, though, and I lean over to see what he's doing.

The code is splashed across the screen, and I see where the photographs were inserted, the ones of Steve and Jeanine. I stick my hand out and point at it. 'The pictures,' I say. An uncomfortable feeling washes over me. I don't like that someone had been spying on them, taking their pictures without them knowing, and then using them in the ransom demand.

'Yeah, but that's not all. What else do you see?'

My breath catches in my throat. *What else do you see?* I can close my eyes and see the question on the screen, the question Tracker always asked when we were working on something together. He was constantly quizzing me, forcing me to push myself, to see the whole picture myself and not rely on him.

Zeke is watching me, waiting for my answer, waiting to see if I can see what he's already found.

Does he know what he's done? I can't tell from his expression.

I shake off the memory as I try to concentrate on the screen. There. There it is. 'That's not all he inserted,' I say, always the dutiful student. This isn't a mystery to Zeke, who's had this laptop in his possession since the FBI found it in the bike shop. He's been poking around inside it, as I wanted to when Agent Tilman had it on the table in front of me. He knows how to try to unearth its secrets. Zeke is a few steps ahead of me, just like Tracker always was.

I don't have time to ruminate on that, however, because a picture of Adriana DeMarco fills the screen and makes me forget all about Tracker.

'Why would the hacker put in a picture of Adriana?' I ask softly, the sound of my voice startling me, since I wasn't even really aware I'd spoken out loud.

As far as I know, the circle of people who know that Adriana is my half-sister and not Tony DeMarco's biological daughter is quite small. I don't even know if she knows. So there's only one explanation.

Whoever is setting me up may not have necessarily only wanted the police to arrest me for Tony's hit.

He wants me to know that he knows about me. Everything about me. And he is taunting me.

'This has to be the same person who shadowed me,' I say. 'He knew things; he knew about the bank job. He knew about *you.*' The shadow had gotten into my laptop through a URL he embedded in a link Tracker had sent me for a private chat room.

Zeke settles back on the couch. We've both taken our eyes off the laptop screen.

'He doesn't know who Tracker is,' he says slowly, as though he's thinking about what he's going to say at the moment that he says it. 'I mean, he doesn't know it's *me*. But he does know about Tracker. He's created conversations in the chat room archives, but conversations I never had. Stuff having to do with the deep web. Instructions to a few hackers about how to navigate Tor.' He pauses. 'I wouldn't do that. Most of the people on the chat know about Tor, are using it, and they don't need any help with it.'

'Who did you supposedly have these conversations with?'

'A few people.' He hesitates, then says, 'You.'

ELEVEN

I am not quite sure how to react, what to say. Finally, 'Me?'
'Well, your screen names, anyway. Tiny and BikerGirl and p4r4d0x, mostly.'
'I haven't been using anything for the last month,' I protest. 'Like I said, this started before you gave me your laptop.'
'It's not me.'
'I know. It's not me, either. But someone wants everyone to think it is us.'
I think for a second. 'Who even knows who "us" is?' I ask, making quote marks with my fingers. 'We haven't had public conversations in the chat room for a long time.'
Zeke stares at me thoughtfully. 'You're right,' he says after a few seconds. 'But it's someone who knows about the French phrases.' We'd devised a way to identify each other, to prove that we were who we said we were.
'The shadow knows about them,' I point out. He used them to get me to click on the link that let him inside my laptop. 'So we are back to him. An unknown person who clearly knows who I am, and possibly knows who Tracker really is.' I begin to feel a little paranoid. 'No one here knows who I am?'
'No more than they know I'm Tracker.'
'The conversations don't seem like anything that should be particularly suspicious, though.' I pause when something strikes me. 'They lead directly to the hit on Tony DeMarco, don't they?'
He shifts a little. I've struck a nerve.
'My team found an anonymous instant messaging service. They traced the chat log, where there's a conversation about how to take DeMarco out.'
I sit next to him, put my glass on the table. 'Show me.'
It only takes him a few minutes. I would be impressed if I didn't know he'd already been here; he already knew how to

find it. I scan the messages, which don't seem too incriminating. Tracker and p4r4d0x, a screen name I set up when I lived in Quebec last year, are merely having a conversation about how they haven't been in touch for a while. If my shadow is the culprit behind this, then I'm not surprised he found p4r4d0x, since I was using that screen name when he first showed up in my laptop. I hadn't realized, however, how deeply he'd infiltrated it, since I had been very careful about clearing everything. But it shows how, even when you think you're being careful, it's extremely difficult to wipe a computer completely clean.

I scan a few screens and am about to say that this is nothing, when the conversation turns.

> *p4r4d0x: He sent someone to kill me.*
> *Tracker: Are you sure?*
> *p4r4d0x: Yes.*
> *Tracker: What do you want to do about it?*
> *p4r4d0x: What we did before.*
> *Tracker: I don't know if we can. There are more firewalls now.*
> *p4r4d0x: That wouldn't stop us. But that's not what I mean. You know.*
> *Tracker: I have a few connections.*
> *p4r4d0x: I can pay. It's left over. Saved for a rainy day. This is the rainy day.*

I stop reading. Zeke is watching me.

'Someone went to a lot of trouble,' I whisper.

'Yeah. It gets worse.'

'I don't want to know. If I keep reading, the words will be stuck in my head, and what if they come out? What if someone's questioning me and I accidentally repeat something from here?' I close the laptop cover. 'No, I can't read anymore. Just tell me the gist of it.'

'OK. p4r4d0x talks Tracker into getting in touch with his connections, and then the conversation ends. But in another conversation, a couple of days later, Tracker tells p4r4d0x that it's all set up and it'll happen over the weekend. He tells her to transfer bitcoins. We found the transaction, but it went into the wind. We're still trying to figure out where it originated and where the bitcoins ended up. DeMarco got hit on Sunday, in front of his daughter's apartment building.'

'And all that's in there?'

He nods.

'But is DeMarco ever mentioned by name? How would this be connected to him?'

'His daughter's address in New York. It gives the time and place, where he's going to be.'

I think for a few seconds. 'So your team finds these messages and they trace them—'

'To the bike shop. That's right. They followed p4r4d0x.'

'But I haven't been online as p4r4d0x since Quebec.' When the shadow infiltrated my laptop. Whoever is setting me up has to be connected to the shadow, if not the shadow himself.

There is no other way to know my screen name.

But then I realize something. 'They haven't found Tracker,' I say slowly.

Zeke shakes his head. 'No, and I haven't been online as Tracker. Not since you left New York.'

When I went to Cape Cod.

'The team isn't after *me*, they're after *him*.' He pokes at the screen, where 'Tracker' lives.

So if we can trace this Tracker, we may be able to find out who's behind the hit on Tony DeMarco.

'If they're as good as you say, they might figure out every-thing.' I think about those four kids in that room down the hall. It's a ticking time bomb. If they find out who I am, who Zeke is, and if the evidence points at us, we will both be on the run.

'That's why I brought you here.'

I make a face at him. 'You're kidding, right? You're setting me up, more than even the shadow is.'

'No, that's not right. I brought you in because I know you and I can stop it. We have to be here, keep an eye on them.'

'I could've done this from anywhere, and so could you. We don't have to be in Miami.'

'You don't get it.'

'Enlighten me.'

'What happens is that you're on the team. You have to be here because I have to be here. We have to keep an eye on them, watch what they're doing, set it up so they don't find out anything. In the meantime, you and I can actually try to find out who's doing this.'

I grab my glass, go into the kitchen, and pour myself another drink. When I've drained the glass, I finally speak again. 'I think you've completely lost your mind.'

'You and I can do this, Tina.'

'Do you think whoever is doing this knows who *you* are, too?'

I see from his expression that the thought has crossed his mind. 'Perhaps. If he does, he's pretty damn smart, but I'm not sure he's smarter than we are.'

I'm not as confident as he is. 'You and I,' I start, hesitating because I don't quite know how to put it.

But he does. 'You don't think we can do it. Like before.'

I shake my head. 'It's not like before. You and I are definitely not like before. So, no, I'm not sure that we can do this.'

'But what if we could?'

'We can't go back. You should never have told me who you are. It might actually be your greatest regret, like you always used to tell me.'

Zeke gets up and comes over to me. I take a step back, but I am standing too close to the wall and I'm trapped. The light from the moon spills across his face. His hand slips around my waist, and I hold my breath as he leans in, his lips brushing mine, but he doesn't kiss me. Instead, he whispers, 'I will never regret this.' And then he does kiss me.

For a moment, I melt into him, his mouth warm, his desire infectious. I feel his hand under my shirt, against my skin, and I press myself further into him, wanting him right now as much as he wants me.

I don't know why it's at that very moment that I realize something. I had always suspected that Tony DeMarco was behind the shadow, but all of this mixes it up a little bit. Why would Tony have me set up for the hit on him? He could merely find me and kill me himself.

So if the shadow isn't the one framing me—

I jerk away from Zeke, moving around him quickly, as though the laptop is going to disappear before I reach it. I am sitting in front of it, scanning the code, my fingers on the keypad, scrolling through it.

'There,' I say, turning the screen around so he can see it.

Zeke is watching me, and I am more than aware of what I've done, that I've interrupted an intimate moment, but he seems rather nonplussed. I don't know if I should be upset or relieved. Either way, it proves one thing: he is like me. This addiction – this need that we have – supersedes any desire we have for each other. Realizing this makes me unbearably sad.

He stoops down and studies what I'm showing him. 'Holy shit,' he says softly.

'You do see what I see, don't you?' What I see is a string of beautifully written code, code that I'd be proud to write. But it's like a masterpiece that's been spray-painted with graffiti. Right in the middle of it is a small string that's so sloppy that the same person couldn't have written it.

'Someone added to the code,' Zeke says. 'It's not just one person doing this. It's at least two.'

TWELVE

I tell Zeke my suspicion that someone has piggybacked on to the shadow in order to set us up.

'But that would mean that person—'

'Is also setting up Tony DeMarco,' I finish for him.

He runs a hand through his hair and sighs. 'OK, let's play devil's advocate for a moment. Let's say it's still just the shadow, but what if it's open source? *Anyone* can modify it.'

'So one person wrote the code and then opened it for anyone to see or modify? What's the motive in that? If the shadow wants to get at us, why let anyone else in? Why make it open source? That doesn't make any sense.'

'Can we get in there? Maybe there's a back door.'

I am already one step ahead of him.

I can't find any sign, however, that it's open source, which leads us back to two people – at least – behind this. I lean back on the couch and close my eyes. None of this makes any sense.

'This is almost too personal,' Zeke says. 'Who would be after you or me – *us* – like that?'

I sit up straight and shake my head. 'Tony has been after me ever since the bank job, and I'm pretty sure he was the one behind the shadow. But he didn't know about you, doesn't know who you are online. I didn't even know about Adriana until you told me, so no one I've ever had contact with – except you – knows she's my sister. Tony knows, though. It all leads back to Tony DeMarco.'

'But why would Tony DeMarco put a hit out on himself and then make it look like you and I are responsible for it? He got shot, Tina. He's in the hospital.'

Exactly what I was thinking before we went on the open source wild goose chase. I don't want to say I told him so. 'So say it's someone who wants to get all *three* of us. This goes back to the bank job. It has to.'

I don't have to see the look on his face to know what he's thinking. There is only one person who has any motive to go after all three of us: Ian Cartwright. Ian still thinks I owe him because he never got the money we stole; Tony DeMarco forced him to work for him to pay back the money we stole; Zeke and I were lovers. And it's more than possible that Ian knows about Adriana. She resembles the younger version of me – we both look like our father; he couldn't possibly not see it. Yet . . .

'I don't want to think it,' I say. 'Ian and I, well, we were pretty complicated back on Block Island, but he went back to his wife, his family.'

'He also went back to DeMarco.'

'I transferred money to Tony's account to help him.'

'It wasn't enough.'

'I didn't know that we stole from Tony. I only had account numbers, no names.'

'I knew.'

My head snaps back so I can look at him. 'When?'

'Back then. I knew who the victims were.' His voice is barely audible. Of course he knew. He was FBI; he probably had a list of names from the get-go.

'But didn't you say that the money didn't really go anywhere? So we really didn't steal from him, did we?'

He chews on his lip for a second. 'I told you it was complicated.'

I don't like the sound of this. 'So we *did* steal from him? What happened?'

He sighs. 'The money transferred; you saw it yourself. I had to make it look good for you. But I couldn't get it all back.'

'What do you mean, you couldn't get it all back? You knew where it was going.'

Zeke narrows his eyes at me. 'You had another account set up.'

'The one I gave you access to – to pay you and anyone else who helped.'

'No one else helped. It was just me. And it didn't work.'

I don't understand what he's saying. What didn't work? I don't have to ask, though, because he knows what I'm thinking.

'You transferred two million dollars into that account,' he reminds me. 'That was Tony DeMarco's money. And it's like it went into a black hole. The account never existed.'

'Of course it did.' I am really confused now.

'No, Tina. When I tried to get to the money, I got a dead link. And then you were gone. Just like Tony DeMarco's two million dollars.'

I don't know how to wrap my head around this. The account was real. I did some of my best work setting it up.

'The shadow knew about the account,' I say, thinking out loud. 'He said the FBI couldn't find it. Who did you tell?'

'No one, Tina. I didn't tell anyone. I figured you had the money somewhere. That you had transferred it out before I could get to it, that you were living on it all those years.'

And if I had really done that, then I betrayed him by running.

I study his face to see if he believes this, if he thinks I've been lying to him, but I can't tell. I can't read him. I find myself wishing desperately again that he is merely Tracker, the person on the other side of the screen. Tracker and I trust each other. Zeke – well, I'm not so sure about where his trust lies.

'Did Ian—'

I hold my hand up to silence him. 'Ian doesn't know anything about computers,' I say. 'You know that. Ian didn't do it. He came looking for me last year. He wanted me to steal for him again. He wouldn't have bothered if he'd gotten even two million back then, and if he'd somehow gained computer skills in fifteen years, he wouldn't have needed me to help.' Something changes in his expression, but I don't have the energy to interpret it. I am suddenly so tired that I can barely think, much less put it all together. 'I think I have to go to bed.' I say it before realizing the effect my statement might have, and I worry that he's going to make another move, but he just nods.

He closes the laptop cover. 'Go in and get some sleep. We can get a fresh start in the morning. It's been a long day.'

I stand up. 'What about—'

'Don't worry about them.'

But I do worry. I worry that one of his team will be lurking around online tonight and find out who Tiny or BikerGirl or p4r4d0x really is while I'm sleeping.

Zeke stands and steers me toward the bedroom, gives me a chaste kiss on my forehead. 'Get some sleep.'

I stumble through the dark room and collapse on the bed, vaguely aware that the front door has opened and closed, and I have been left alone.

Heather is sleeping in the bed across the room from me when I awake. Her blonde hair is tousled and her arm is hanging over the edge, but she doesn't stir even though I accidentally bump my backpack against the dresser, making more noise than I expect. I pull the pack with me into the bathroom, noticing on the way that Zeke's door is closed.

I turn on the water at the sink and splash some on to my face. I'm having a hard time believing that I'm actually here, back in Miami after all these years. Zeke Chapman made it happen, just like Tracker made it happen sixteen years ago when he arranged the travel documents for Amelie Renaud and I ended up in Paris with Ian. It was Ian's idea that I take that name, the name of the woman who would become his wife.

I look at my reflection in the mirror. I still have the reddish hair from my makeover in Montreal, but it's longer now; I haven't kept it as short and styled. It's growing out a little funny, and it makes me look sloppy. I wet my hands and try to smooth it out around my ears but the curls keep popping up. I am wearing my glasses for the first time in a few months. When I suggested taking along the contacts and their solution, Zeke overruled me, explaining that I wouldn't be able to bring it through airport security. It was easier to leave them behind, easier to wear the glasses, as I'd done since Paris.

A knock on the door startles me.

'You coming out?'

Zeke.

I open the door, realizing that I have been thinking about everything and anything except what I found out last night.

And I know what I have to do to find out the truth and who's behind it all.

I nod at Zeke. 'OK, let's get to work.'

THIRTEEN

Only Jake and Charles are hunkered down in front of their desktops, their eyes trained on the screens, their headphones keeping out any outside sounds. Heather is still sleeping back in the apartment, and I assume Daniel is also getting some much-needed rest wherever his bed may be.

How can Zeke keep an eye on any and all of them? Does he trust them that much that they won't take off on him?

Of course, I am the only one who is being held hostage by the threat of Tony DeMarco, so I am probably the only one who thinks constantly about escape. The rest of them seem content to do their work. It's not a bad gig for a young hacker. They get to hack legally and get paid for it.

For a second, I consider that option. The one that's been offered. And then I dismiss it again. My life is better without this.

Zeke has come with me, and we are carrying the coffees he'd picked up before I got up.

'What about them?' I ask, cocking my head toward Jake and Charles.

'They like something a little stronger.' He chuckles and indicates the empty cans of Red Bull that clutter the desk area.

I am about to sit when he puts his hand on my arm and looks into my eyes. 'I'm sorry about last night.'

The kiss. He's apologizing for the kiss.

'It's OK,' I say, uncertain if it really is, or if I am just saying it to put it to rest.

'Maybe when this is all over—'

I shake my head. 'I don't know.'

'Of course you don't,' he says lightly, but I can hear a disappointment behind the words. I choose to ignore it; we don't have time for a conversation about it. I honestly don't know where we're going to stand when all this is over, and I can't even begin to speculate.

The computers are lined up, three to each side, on a very long table that stretches across the room. Jake and Charles are on this side of it. I go down to the end, nearer the glass sliding door. I pull the chair out and sit down, hitting a couple of keys to get the computer out of sleep mode. I haven't used a desktop in a long time. The mouse feels odd underneath my hand, and although the keyboard is only slightly larger than my laptop's, it feels obscenely big. Not to mention the screen.

I feel as if I've entered another dimension.

'You might want to check out the Waste Land.' Zeke is across from me, hovering.

I frown.

'The Waste Land. Like the T.S. Eliot poem.'

I have no idea what he's talking about.

'"April is the cruellest month."' He's quoting it, but it doesn't jar my memory. I never paid attention to anything except my computer when I was in school. I don't want to admit that I'm impressed. There are more layers to Zeke Chapman than I realize.

He looks disappointed that we can't connect on this.

'OK,' he finally concedes. 'You're not a poetry reader. But the Waste Land is a good place to start.'

'What is it?' It bothers me that there's a site I don't know about, but there are so many sites that are constantly popping up and coming down that I shouldn't feel inadequate. At least that's what I tell myself.

'It's on the deep web.' He cocks his head toward Jake and Charles. I am uncertain whether they are even aware we're in the room. 'We found *Tracker* there.' The way he says it, I can tell that the Tracker he's talking about is the imposter.

He is giving me a directive. He wants me to see if I can't find him. Find *Tracker*.

I turn away from him and back to the computer, my hand over the mouse. I get into Tor, which is easily accessible with its Firefox add-on. Before going to the Waste Land, though, I head to the Hidden Wiki, which lists search engines and links to sites and chat rooms. I haven't been here in over a month; things change quickly, sites are pulled down or blocked, new sites pop up. The link to the chat room is still here, and I can't help myself, so I click through. Instead of signing on with any of my usual screen names, I create a new one and begin lurking. The conversations are fairly benign, and this is not what I'm online for, but it's merely habit. I am about to sign off when I see him.

Tracker. He's here.

I feel a little jolt in my gut, then think: *Is this Zeke or is it the Tracker imposter?* Zeke said he hasn't been online as Tracker, but what if this is a test? What if he *is* here and wants to see what I'll do?

I poke my head over my computer. Zeke is across from me. His head is down; he's concentrating on his own screen. Without another thought, I send Tracker a message, asking to meet him in a private chat. I use one of our French phrases: 'Le soleil brille aujourd'hui.' *The sun is shining today.*

I wait to see if he looks up over his desktop, but he doesn't.

I am playing a stupid game, so I look back at my screen, ready to sign off for real this time. But this very well might be the imposter Tracker. Maybe I should wait around, see if he responds.

A message from Tracker pops up, saying that he's in the chat room. When I click through, I see the message: 'Non, le ciel est nuageux.' *No, it's cloudy.* Again I peer over the top of the computer, but Zeke is still immersed in his own world. Since the shadow knew about the French phrases, it could be the imposter. But what if it really is Zeke?

No one here knows he's Tracker, so he can't give himself away. If it *is* Zeke, he can't exactly leap up and give me a high-five over the computers between us.

'Did you find anything yet?' he is asking. The question makes me think that this is Zeke, not the imposter. Zeke would be careful, too, to make sure that he couldn't be traced. We also have to be as discreet as possible in our conversation.

'No. I came here first.'

'Old habits die hard.'

'Yes. Have you found anything?'

'Just lurking for now. Maybe you could see what you can find out.'

It's casually said, but I know what he wants me to do. I've gotten into the private chat rooms before.

But my search is futile. I don't recognize anyone here; there's nothing suspicious going on. I don't even see Angel, who'd been a regular in the chat room and was well acquainted with Tracker and a couple of my own screen names. I'd had the idea that I could reach out to him – or her – discreetly, but Angel's absence seems to be just another sign that I am most likely on a wild goose chase. Until I wonder whether Angel could somehow be connected to what's going on.

I don't like that I'm questioning anyone in the chat room, much less Angel. But when faced with a faceless enemy, anyone can be guilty.

There is another message in the private room from Tracker. He's sent me a link to the Waste Land. 'Be careful,' he writes. 'You don't know who's watching.'

I would be willing to bet that *he* is watching, which means I can have no missteps.

I glance over at Jake and Charles, who are still concentrating on their own work. Since neither of them seemed to react when Tracker showed up in the chat room, I can only surmise that they're not watching the site at the moment – which bothers me a little. If this team is supposed to track down Tracker and p4r4d0x, they're not exactly doing a great job, even though Zeke said they're the ones who found the conversations in the first place.

I navigate to the Waste Land, and I have to set up a sign-on. Since I'm using Tor and I've also got VPN – and I assume everyone else on the site is taking the same precautions – the sign-on seems a little ridiculous, but I do it anyway. Again, I choose a username and password that have nothing to do with any others I've ever used, which also underscores the redundancy of the process.

When I finally get in, the site is remarkably like any other that has items for sale, but there are categories for drugs and weapons and sex. I click on 'miscellaneous.'

If Zeke hadn't already gotten me documents, this would be the go-to place for them. Passports, driver's licenses, credit cards – I could create yet another identity for myself if I wanted to. For a moment, I consider it. Susan McQueen is a known entity. But I could pick another name at random and disappear completely.

And then I remind myself that I don't have to.

The idea of being free, not having to hide, is still so foreign to me. I feel almost silly for not knowing about this myself. Granted, I spent fifteen years without a computer. But when I did get one, I could have gotten the answers I needed with just a few keystrokes. I never even considered that this was a possibility, though, so why would I do a search?

I can't dwell on it now. I have a job to do, and then I can ruminate and figure out what exactly my next step will be.

I could turn to the deep web for that next step. Spirits of aborted babies and ghosts that will tell me my future are for sale here. 'Miscellaneous' is right.

Everything for sale must be purchased with bitcoin, the

virtual currency. To get it, you have to link an actual bank account to a bitcoin wallet. I have no bank account. But I do have the FBI, and I'm sure that Zeke's got a wallet just for this purpose.

I skim through the occult listings that would allow me to buy spells to put on people, and I wonder how many of those are sold. Probably a lot more than most people would think.

There must be a chat room here somewhere. But pride prevents me from asking. I want to find it myself, or at least give it a little more time before I concede defeat.

And I'm glad I do, because when I turn back to the screen, it's staring me in the face.

FOURTEEN

It's a link for a chat room. This must be the one where our alter egos had the conversation about putting the hit out on Tony DeMarco. I peer over the computer at the top of Zeke's head.

All of my instincts tell me that whoever is setting us up is playing games. Although Zeke's team found the conversations here that led them to the laptop, it is too pat, too easy. This seems like the logical place for something so criminal, but maybe it's a little *too* logical.

My first impulse had been to look at the laptop, but I abandoned the idea when I second-guessed it. Maybe I wasn't wrong. Maybe we need to go back to the laptop and go backward, not start here and go forward.

I stand, and Zeke looks up.

'Where are you going?' He's not admonishing me; he is merely curious.

'I need to get the laptop.'

He nods. 'OK.' He stands, too, and it's clear I'm not going alone.

'I'm only going back to the apartment. I'll be right back.' I don't want him to follow me everywhere, but it seems as though he really is concerned that I'm going to take off because he shrugs me off.

'I need to get something anyway.'

Jake and Charles still don't seem to notice us as we head out.

'What's going on?' Zeke stops me when we get outside.

'It's not in the deep web.'

'What's not?'

'Where this started.'

He frowns. 'What do you mean?'

'Someone wants us to think that they're messing around on the deep web.'

'You don't think so?'

'I think whoever did this is sending us in circles. He knows me. He knows you. He knows what we can do. It seems simple. Too simple. But still we can't trace it. You've got IP addresses, right?'

He nods.

'They go from that site to the laptop?'

'And back again,' he says, getting it now. 'It does go in a circle.' He pauses. 'So what's the plan?'

'Start with the laptop. The IP addresses are key. He had to have left a trace, but it's not going to be easy to find, because he's smart.'

'Not smarter than us.'

I give him a wan smile. 'Maybe. Maybe not.'

'Speak for yourself. I've got a reputation to uphold.'

'I don't have a reputation. I don't even exist.' As I say it, a wave of sadness overwhelms me, and I turn away, leaning against the railing that overlooks the courtyard.

His hand tucks itself around my waist. 'I'm not sure I can do this.'

'Do what?'

'I told you I was Tracker for a reason. And not for the reason you think.'

I twist around to look at him; his hand remains on my waist. 'So it's not because you want my help?'

'No. It was purely selfish. I could have done it alone.' He leans closer, his breath hot against my neck. 'I don't know how to do this,' he whispers. 'I thought I had it under control, that we could work together like we've done before, but it's not the same. I'm not Tracker. I mean, I am, but he's not me. He's not *really* me.'

He doesn't think I understand, but I do. 'What we do online isn't who we are, I know that. And I know you aren't really Tracker, but Tracker is who I know. He's the one I've trusted all these years. I don't know how to meld you into one person.' A flashback assaults my memory. Zeke, in my bedroom, looking at my laptop. He didn't realize I'd seen him, and I didn't let on. Again I wonder: *Did I know then?* No. I couldn't possibly. I never knew.

He steps away, and I shiver even though the air is damp and warm. I study his face as he watches me. Tracker and I are always so in sync – even only a little while ago when we were online – but Zeke and I are struggling. I have no idea how to have a relationship with him.

'We have to find a way to do this. Together,' I say slowly. 'Because whoever did this seems to be after both of us for some reason.'

He clears his throat and nods, shoving his hands in his pockets. 'Yeah, you're right. I'm sorry. I'm being unprofessional. It won't happen again.'

'OK,' I say, but I don't know if it really is.

Zeke starts walking in the opposite direction of the apartment.

'Where are you going?' I ask his back.

'You go on. You can get started. I need to clear my head a little. I'll be back in a few.'

I watch him disappear around the corner. We're going to need to get answers soon, because I'm not sure either of us is going to survive this if we don't.

Heather is coming out of the shower when I let myself into the apartment.

'Oh! You startled me,' she scolds, standing in the hallway, wearing only a towel.

'Sorry.' I wonder again if she knows about the cameras, if I should tell her.

As I'm debating this with myself, though, she comes out into the living room instead of going into the bedroom to change. 'So what's your story? Zeke thinks you're the second coming or something.' She frowns, studying my face as though looking for my lies.

I don't owe her anything. 'Don't worry about me,' I tell her. 'I'm no threat.'

'Oh, I didn't think you were a threat.' It is the way she says it that convinces me that's exactly what I am to her. Which concerns me. Even though I am no longer – or ever was, apparently – a fugitive, I am still very protective of my identity. 'I was just wondering what's between you and Zeke. It's pretty clear that it's *something*.'

I consider how to respond. 'I'm an old friend of his.' For the first time in a long time, I am not lying about something. 'That's about it. Nothing more.'

'Doesn't seem like it's nothing,' she says, her eyes narrowing as she studies my expression, which I struggle to keep neutral.

'We knew each other a long time ago.' I don't want to say any more than this, but I can tell she's not going to stop.

'Were you *involved*?'

I debate how to answer her and finally decide on the truth. 'Yes. But it was a long time ago.' I feel compelled to emphasize this for some reason. 'He thinks I can help.'

'Why?' The hard look in her eyes tells me she's not going to let this go.

'Why what?'

'Why would he want *you* to help find out about Tony DeMarco?'

I consider what to say and finally settle on the truth. 'Tony DeMarco and my family have a history. It's personal.'

Heather's eyes narrow as she decides whether to believe me. Finally, she nods. 'OK.' She turns and heads back into the bathroom, leaving me alone.

I can tell that she's a bit of a pit bull, and it is not going to be as easy as that, but I am happy to have the reprieve. I am also feeling claustrophobic. She is no longer in the room, but she is still in the apartment. She and I are sharing a room. Zeke is always going to be just a few steps away.

After being alone for so long, this is too much togetherness.

I hear the blow-dryer in the bathroom. It's time to move. I move quickly into the bedroom, grab my backpack, which is still mostly packed, and go back into the living room.

I scoop the laptop up off the coffee table where I'd left it earlier and let myself out of the apartment.

FIFTEEN

I start toward the other apartment, then stop. The idea of going back there, of working in a room with five other people on top of each other, makes my heart beat faster. I told Zeke I'm not a team player. He's the only one I've ever worked with, and we were not in the same room. I like being alone; I like my own space. I couldn't stay there before, and I doubt I'll be able to last more than ten minutes there now. Zeke – Tracker – will understand.

I've made my decision, so I turn around and swiftly go down the stairs. I pass the fountain, and instead of going out the way we came in yesterday, I end up on a sidewalk in the front of the building. Another stucco apartment building is across the street, although this one is lime green. I'd forgotten that about Miami, about Florida, how everything is in pastels. Maybe that's why I was so drawn to Block Island, where the houses are white or gray clapboard, classic, not looking as though they've jumped out of a child's chalk drawing on the pavement.

I hesitate, glancing behind me for a second in the direction of the parking lot. I wish I'd paid attention to where Zeke had left the car keys, but it's probably better that I don't have the car. It would be too easy to track, even though it's just a rental.

But it leaves me with a dilemma. Even though I'm in a city, it's not the kind of city, like New York, where you can hail a cab on every corner. Miami is spread out, and even though I haven't been here in a long time, that hasn't changed. I do have some cash in the backpack, but I don't have a cell phone. I wonder if pay phones still exist.

I also anticipate another problem.

I am still holding the laptop, so I open it, booting it up. I don't need Internet to find the GPS tracker that Zeke has installed. He knows better than this. It's easy enough to disconnect, and I do that before I continue on my way.

As I walk along Sunset, the backpack heavy against my back, I begin to feel a little overheated. I'm wearing jeans and a T-shirt – it's too much clothing. On the Cape, I was wearing fleece and even gloves while I rode my bike; it's hot here in South Florida. The brightness of the stucco and concrete blinds me, and I wish I had sunglasses, but I'll need a prescription, or at least another pair of contacts. I didn't remember to bring my prescription with me; Zeke pushed me out too fast.

I spot a small coffee shop up ahead. I duck inside and order an iced coffee. I know where I want to go, but I can't possibly walk the whole way. I consider public transportation, but I don't want to navigate. I sidle up to the counter and ask about how I could go about calling a taxi.

'Don't you have a cell? You could Uber.' The young barista is trying to be helpful, but she doesn't know who she's talking to.

'I just want to call a cab.'

'Uber will be here faster, but you need the app.'

'I don't have a phone that has an app.'

She eyes me curiously, then says, 'Hold on.' She goes over to another barista, whispers something, and then slips around the counter and comes out next to me. 'Come on.'

I follow her outside, where she pulls a phone out of her pocket. 'I'm not supposed to do this, but it's my good deed of the day.'

While she orders the ride, I glance around at the patrons sitting at the tables outside: two moms with kids in strollers, a young man on a laptop, and a girl texting.

The barista is talking. 'It's all set, but you have to pay me. It's going on my account.'

'No problem.' I take some cash out of the backpack pocket

and make sure that she gets a very nice bonus for helping me out. She frowns when she sees how much I've given her.

'That's too much,' she tries, but I put my hand up.

'No, it's not. I really appreciate this.' I pause. 'You might want to be a little careful, though, with using the Internet here.'

She frowns.

'Can I see your phone for a second?'

She looks dubious, but hands it to me. I check the wireless settings. Just as I suspected. 'You're not on the store's Wifi,' I tell her, cocking my head toward the young man using the laptop. 'You're on *his* Wifi.' I switch networks on the phone after showing her.

She doesn't understand.

'He's got a device under that newspaper next to him. It creates a wireless hotspot and it's probably stronger than the store's Wifi – that's why you're hooked up to it automatically, and so is everyone else, most likely. He can get all your information.' He hasn't done a very good job hiding the device, but it's small and most people won't know what it is.

She finally understands. 'You mean, he's stealing my passwords and shit?'

'Yeah. Listen, you did me a favor, so I'll do you one.' I go over to the young man. He's maybe in his early twenties, with bedhead and a spray of acne across his forehead. He's wearing cutoff jeans and a white T-shirt that's a little too large. He could be one of Zeke's team.

'Hi,' I say, sliding into the chair across from him. 'You know, I could have you arrested right now for what you're doing.'

'What are you talking about?' He's trying to act nonchalant, but I can see the worry in his eyes.

I reach over and take the router out from underneath the newspaper. 'I'm with the FBI. Cybercrime unit.' I never thought I'd rely on Zeke's team like this, but it's worth the look on his face. 'I'm going to take this now, if that's OK with you. Or, if you'd rather, I'll make a call and you won't see the light of day for a few years.'

'Um, your ride is here.' The barista is standing next to me, staring at the small square device that fits neatly in the palm of my hand. She indicates a blue Toyota waiting at the curb.

I give her a smile as I slip the router into my backpack. 'Thanks.' I give the young man a quick glare. 'I know you'll get another one, but I'd be careful if I were you. We're everywhere.' As I get up and turn to walk away, I say to the barista, 'Make sure he doesn't pull that again. And keep an eye out. Those things are legal, even though what they do with them isn't.'

'Thanks so much, Miss . . .'

I hesitate only a second before I say, 'Jones.'

'I'm Sadie. If you need anything else, let me know.'

'You've done more than enough. Thanks a lot.' I go over to the Toyota. I'm not sure about protocol, so I open the front passenger door and climb in.

The driver is older than me, maybe around Steve's age – sixty-five or so. That's where the resemblance ends, though. This man is bald, and he's clearly spent a lot of time in the sun. He wears a bright blue Hawaiian shirt with palm trees all over it that barely covers his potbelly, a tuft of white chest hair visible above the top button. He gives me a smile. 'Where to, Miss?'

Without thinking about it, I tell him.

I don't know if what I'm doing is the right thing, but I have to go. It's as though I'm being drawn there.

'From out of town?' the driver asks.

'Pretty obvious, is it?'

'Up north?'

'Yes.'

He chuckles. 'You might want to get a pair of shorts. It's a scorcher today.'

'I'm OK,' I say, and I am – for the moment. The car is comfortably air-conditioned, and I settle back in the seat. The passing landscape is as familiar to me as the stonewalls and bluffs on Block Island, yet at the same time it's been so long since I've been here that I feel more like a tourist.

We pass the entrance to Vizcaya, and I close my eyes for a moment and picture the Italian villa and gardens that spread as far as the eye can see. But then the memory of Ian's hand in mine as we watched the flamingos shakes me out of my reverie.

Soon the water spreads out in front of us, on either side, as we enter the Rickenbacker Causeway. I am thankful that the driver hasn't continued conversation. I worried that he might feel obligated to befriend me, and I'm not in the mood.

I twist around and look behind us. The Brickell Avenue skyline stirs up even more memories. After I got kicked out of university my father got me a job at an advertising agency as a receptionist. I lasted three weeks. Nothing could hold my interest except my computers.

I twist back and watch as we cross on to Key Biscayne. I remember how it felt the first time I set foot on Block Island: as though all my troubles had disappeared. But now my shoulders are tense, and I'm afraid I'm going to be sick.

I'm really home.

SIXTEEN

The driver drops me off at the Palm Court Resort. I give him a generous tip before waving him off.

He is right about the heat – and about the fact that I am going to need a change of clothes soon. I can already feel the sweat drip between my breasts and down the back of my neck. I'd forgotten how oppressive the heat can be here.

First, though, I have to get a room.

The Palm Court Resort is little more than a motel, but its sign advertises 'Cottages with an Ocean View.' The lobby is cool, with a white tile floor and bright white walls accented by two orange-and-red-striped plush sofas across from the desk, where a woman about my age stands and smiles at me.

'Can I help you?'

'I'd like a room.' I pause. 'I should tell you that I don't have a credit card, only cash.'

'That's fine.' She says it so quickly that I wonder about the other guests here. Are they all escaping their lives in some way?

We exchange the cash for a key, and she directs me outside and down a path to a small cottage that does overlook the water. It's not as pricey as I thought it might be, and for that reason I am surprised that it actually offers what it claims it does. But I'm not going to complain. Just having the ocean in sight is therapeutic.

The room is also a surprise. It's larger than I expected, with a small kitchenette. Sliding glass doors lead out to a wooden deck with a couple of plastic chairs and small table. I drop the backpack on the bed and pull open the door and step outside. A small path leads toward the water. I forget about everything as I walk. I pull off my sneakers and my toes sink into the soft sand. The beaches on Block Island were rocky, with pebbled sand – not like this.

I finally reach the water and put my feet in. I almost expect the frigid chill of the northern Atlantic, but instead it's warm, like a bath. I want to shed my clothes and immerse myself, but although I don't see anyone nearby, someone could come around the corner at any moment. I make a mental list in my head: shorts, another T-shirt, a bathing suit, flip-flops. The uniform I wore for years here.

I sit just beyond the water's edge and draw a palm tree in the sand next to me. The turquoise and cobalt colors of the sea meet and mix, and I wish I had my paints to capture the essence of it. When I lived here, I had no idea what I could do with a paintbrush and an easel. If I'd known, would I have ever left? Maybe I would have studied art, become an artist, had a gallery of my own. My mother would still have died, my father would still have gone to prison, but I would have been OK. I would have had a life I didn't have to run away from.

I take a few deep breaths, drawing in the scent of the salt water. The ocean has healing powers for me, and when I finally begin to head back to my room, I am much more relaxed.

I close the glass door to keep the cool air inside and take the laptop out of the backpack. I open it and reach to turn it on, then stop myself. I'm not ready yet. I'm not in that much of a hurry. Before I begin, I have to do what I came here to do.

There is a small safe in the room, and it's large enough to fit the laptop and most of my cash. I put it all inside and set the code. I unpack the backpack so it's nearly empty and swing it over my shoulder as I head back out.

I feel as though I haven't been on a bike in months, even though it's only been two days. I push the pedals harder than I need to; I'm not in a race, but I like the way it makes my legs, my calves, feel. It's a pretty good bike for a rental. The guy at the shop gave me a map of the island and told me to check out Crandon Park. He mistook me for a tourist.

I bought some bike shorts and a tank top, as well as a helmet, so I'm a little less overheated. A bottle of water fits in a holder. I'm feeling a lot more like myself – at least the person I've been in the last sixteen years. It keeps me a bit disconnected from the person I was when I lived here.

Harbor Point is on the other side of the island from where I'm staying. As I ride, my senses are assaulted by the scents and sights of my past. Palm trees line the roads; flowers reach toward the sun, which is high in the bright blue sky. Colors are more vivid here than anywhere I've ever been.

I pass a couple of houses that weren't here when I was growing up, but their ostentatiousness matches the lifestyle I was accustomed to – a lifestyle I am now ashamed of. There was too much money, too many possessions. No wonder I turned out the way I did: a girl who hid behind a computer screen name in order to make friends. A girl who was talked into committing a crime by a man I would have done anything for just because he said he loved me.

I was so desperate for him.

My father saw that, which is how he was able to manipulate him into manipulating me. Did my father know how good I was? Did he know that I'd be able to actually do it? Was he surprised when I did?

I left so soon afterward that I never had the chance to ask him about it. I never had the chance to confront him.

He died before I could talk to him again.

A pang of regret hits me, and my foot slips off the pedal a little, the bike tips to the left, and I struggle to right myself.

It's then that I see it. Straight ahead. The house looms large beyond the gates that are securely shut, keeping strangers like me at a safe distance. The lush greenery is a contradiction, feeling welcoming despite the property's standoffishness.

A 'For Sale' sign hangs from the gate; the realtor's name and phone number prominent. I don't need her, though, to know what lies beyond.

I stand with the bike between my legs and close my eyes. Instead of a sad fountain with dead fish as at Zeke's apartment building, the fountain here, in front of the mansion's entrance, is made of sleek Italian stone, its water clear and cold as it rises and splashes against the sides.

Inside, the chandelier studded with real diamonds hovers over the foyer, a spectacular welcome. An ornate gold mirror hangs over the marble table that was always adorned with a huge spray of orchids, my mother's favorite. Walk down the hallway and it opens up into a gigantic great room with floor-to-ceiling windows overlooking the infinity pool and, just beyond it, the ocean. The Oriental rugs, plush sofas and chairs, teak coffee tables, and Tiffany lamps lend a homier feel than expected.

A sudden rush of emotion overwhelms me. I should never have come here. It serves no purpose except to bring back all the pain I've fought so hard to forget. This house that is so beautiful on the outside hid the ugliness inside. My mother's mental illness. My father's criminal activity. A lonely girl who became a criminal herself.

I turn my bike around and brush the back of my hand against my cheek, wiping away the tears. I take a few deep breaths and adjust the helmet, tightening the strap under my chin. I glance up the street and decide in a split second what is best for me mentally right now. I map out the island in my head just as I used to map out Block Island for my bike tours: Crandon Park on one end, Bill Baggs Cape State Park on the other. I can go down Harbor Drive and around to the light-house. From there, I'll figure out what I want to do.

I climb on to the bike, but as I begin to take off, a sleek

black BMW screams past me, nearly knocking me down. I stare at it as it moves further away from me. I know who lives up ahead. It's part of the reason I'm here, although not the entire reason. I was going to save the visit for later, after I'd confronted the demons of my past and made more peace with them. But the black car has piqued my curiosity. So I follow it.

I pedal fast, fast enough so that when I arrive in front of this house, I am just in time to see him getting out of the car.

Ian Cartwright.

SEVENTEEN

I duck behind the fronds of a small palm tree, pulling my bike back with me. I peer around and am relieved that he has not noticed me. He flips his keys around in his hand as he saunters toward the front door, leaving the car out front. As he approaches, the door opens, but I cannot see who opened it for him.

I watch until he is inside the house, and I let out my breath. I didn't even realize I was holding it.

I never expected Ian Cartwright to show up at Tony DeMarco's house. Although, the more I think about it, I wonder why I wouldn't. He works for Tony; he's indebted to him. Miami was his home as much as it was mine, way back when.

Tony's house isn't at all like my old house in that it's far more modern, looking somehow like an office building, all glass and concrete. It is on a long, narrow lot and fills it completely. There is no high gate here, just a semi-circle driveway, although I am sure that one step in the wrong place will alert a sophisticated security system and staff that an intruder is on the property.

I can't stay here, watching the house. Someone might see me lurking and call the police. I don't want Ian to know I'm here. It's bad enough he drove right past me a few minutes ago. I touch the edge of my bike helmet, as though it has protected me from something worse than a fall. Ian knows that I bike, but I'm out of context here. He doesn't expect to see me, so he doesn't. I'm invisible. At least for the time being.

I start to leave when movement catches my eye. The door opens, and Ian comes back out, but this time he's with a woman. I go deeper behind the palms. The woman is tall, blonde, wearing a white sundress that accentuates her perfect tan. She is beautiful. I recognize her as Amelie. Amelie Renaud, Ian's wife.

Ian opens the passenger door for her. Before she climbs in, he brushes her cheek with his lips, and she lifts her face and smiles at him, running her fingers along his jaw. Then she disappears into the car. As he walks around the front of the car to the driver's side, I study him. He is a little leaner since I saw him last on Block Island; he's lost some weight and his hair is grayer. He is nattily dressed in a pair of khaki slacks and a short-sleeved linen shirt that's untucked.

He is no longer the man I fell in love with, but I can see the shadow of that man in his face. The way he smiles at his wife is the way he used to smile at me, but I know now that it can be a lie. He used her as much as he used me, but she didn't leave him.

They have two children. I saw them online. Two little boys. A family portrait. Could that family have been mine?

An unexpected pang of jealousy ripples through me. He was involved with Amelie before he met me; he went back to her and she gave him the account numbers that allowed me to steal for him. When I left him in Paris, he married her. My only consolation is that he never got the money.

The black car begins to move. I have to get out of here.

He is going to see me – a woman on a bike – but my back is to him; he won't see my face. I pump the pedals as hard as I can so I can feel it in my calves; I am hunched over the handlebars. I look to my left, toward the ocean.

I am like this as the car passes me, its exhaust fumes mixing with the heat and filling my lungs. I cough a little, but I dare not look up. He might see me in the rear-view.

I have rented the bike for the whole day, but instead of the ride I anticipated, I merely head back to the motel. I leave the bike outside the room, leaning against the side of the building, under the window. Once inside, I pull off the helmet and toss it on the small counter in the kitchenette on my way to the safe, where I retrieve the laptop. I leave the cash inside.

I resist the urge to do a search on Ian – or, rather, Roger Parker, the name he is using now. I push thoughts about him aside and concentrate on the reason I'm here: Tony DeMarco. My focus has been on myself and how I can clear my name, but it might help if I look into what exactly happened in New York outside his daughter's apartment. I don't want to rely only on the information Zeke gave me.

The New York newspapers have the story, which relates how the gunman had taken the shot when Tony emerged from his car just outside his daughter's apartment building. No one saw anyone with a gun; no one saw anything at all – not even someone fleeing. They just heard the shot, saw Tony fall. I picture the outside of the building, the long awning, the doorman, just as it was last summer when I was there.

The doorman.

I frown to myself. There is no mention of a doorman in the story, and my imagination takes over. Perhaps the doorman was in on it. Perhaps he alerted the gunman when Tony's car arrived.

No one else was injured, the story reports, and the gunman fled quickly; he is in the wind. Tony DeMarco is in the hospital in stable condition. His daughter will not comment.

I think that the story must be finished, but no. It goes on to say that this was a hit ordered through a dark web Internet site and traced to a small town on Cape Cod. It talks of persons of interest being questioned, but no one has been arrested.

A person of interest? That must be me. Or maybe it's Jerry, the guy who set up the laptop's wireless connection. Either way, the story ends in Falmouth, and it's quite possible that the media is camped out at the bike shop. I got out of town just in time.

I lean back on the bed and rest my head against the head-board, looking up toward the ceiling. I don't know how long it will be before Zeke shows up here. I may have disconnected the GPS, but he is tenacious. He found me in Paris, and he found me in Quebec; he will find me here.

He's been here before, too.

I take a quick trip to a small sandwich shop, buy a salad for lunch, and bring it back to the room. I absently pick out the red onions. Although it makes sense to go back online and try to find out who is setting me up, there might be another way. Granted, Zeke had the laptop before I did and probably already has done what I'm about to do, but on the off chance that he missed something, it's worth another try.

If a remote access Trojan was used to install the messages that incriminate me, then it's possible the shadow's IP address is still floating around somewhere inside the laptop.

I got rid of my laptop over a month ago, but there is one thing I did not get rid of. I push aside the salad, grab my backpack, and rummage around in the front pocket until my fingers find it: a flash drive. Zeke doesn't need to know I have a program on it that might possibly track the IP addresses that have connected to the laptop.

I stick the USB into the port and run the program when it's done downloading. As the display pops up on the screen, there are several established connections. I want to see which ones have connected to this laptop from another computer.

I am disappointed that I find nothing. It doesn't prove anything, though, one way or another. What I check now is where the computer that wants to install something sends the data through other devices.

Again, I find nothing.

My head is spinning with ideas, but I am sure that Tracker has tried all of them. Is there anything he wouldn't think of?

I eat some more salad and wish I had gotten something a little more substantial. I don't want to go out again, though, because I don't want to risk running into Ian. It's possible that he and Amelie are far away from here, but I have no idea where they might have been going. They were dressed casually but elegantly; in Miami, that could mean lunch or a party or an afternoon on a yacht.

I wonder where their children are, but imagine them with

their own friends. They might even be teenagers now; the website with the family portrait was ages old.

Out of habit, I find myself navigating to the chat room. I am a little surprised to see Tracker. Although he'd been in the chat room with me earlier, he'd made it pretty clear that he wasn't making a habit of that, that he hadn't been online as Tracker for a while. At least not since his team had been looking for him.

I can't help but want to know what he's up to.

I have come here via Tor and my VPN, so I feel fairly confident that he won't be able to trace me even if he discovers I am lurking. The last thing I want is for him to find me before I'm ready to be found.

I am so busy making sure I'm shrouded that I almost miss it.

Tracker and p4r4d0x disappearing into a private chat room.

EIGHTEEN

It's disconcerting, seeing my own screen name and knowing that it isn't me. I wonder if this is the way Zeke felt about discovering the other Tracker online.

I have the strongest urge to snoop, as though I'm in a stranger's house and want to peer inside cupboards and peek into drawers. I've gotten into the private chat rooms before, and Zeke knows about that. I do have the thought that this might be his imposter, who might not be aware of this. If it really *is* Zeke, I'm sure that he's got a handle on it and is dealing with p4r4d0x the way he wants to, but my curiosity is too strong. Within minutes, I am eavesdropping – so to speak – on Tracker and p4r4d0x.

Tracker: She's back in town.

p4r4d0x: What are you going to do?

Tracker: Once I get the money, she won't even know what hit her.

p4r4d0x: So she does have it.

Tracker: She says she doesn't, but I found the account. I just can't get into it.

p4r4d0x: What makes you think she'll get you in?

Tracker: She trusts me.

p4r4d0x: You fucked with her. She doesn't trust anyone, much less you.

Tracker: It's different now.

p4r4d0x: Keep your eye on the prize and don't let your feelings for her get in the way.

Tracker: She fucked with me, too. She's going to get what's coming to her.

p4r4d0x: Look what happened in New York. You didn't finish the job.

Tracker: I'll finish this one. I'll finish them both.

Suddenly, they are gone. They have both left the chat room at the same time, and I am here, all alone. I stare at the screen, their words jumping out at me, taunting me.

I reach over and close the laptop, not turning it off, just putting it to sleep. Their conversation replays itself in my head; it doesn't matter that I'm not reading it anymore. It's as though I have suddenly gained a photographic memory and I can't shake it off.

I get up and go to the glass doors, sliding them open and stepping outside. The warm breeze slips through the palms overhead and gently touches my skin. I shiver, despite the heat.

Suddenly, I am shaking, and I drop down on my knees, unable to hold myself up any longer. The fear rushes through me. My head is telling me that this must be Zeke's imposter, whoever it is who set us up, because p4r4d0x is definitely not me. But the rest of me wonders if it's not real, if it's really Tracker – no, Zeke – and he's lured me to Miami for a reason, to keep me close, to get his hands on the money in that account, and then he'll do to me what he's already tried to do to Tony DeMarco. Tracker's part of the conversation could easily be Zeke.

Zeke hates DeMarco. He is desperate to catch him at something illegal. But would he really try to kill him?

He also has reason to hate *me*. I rejected him after using

him; I shot him and left him for dead. And then I disappeared for sixteen years before he finally found me.

Tony DeMarco is not personal. I am.

I consider p4r4d0x. There are two people involved in this conspiracy, and I suddenly remember the sloppy lines of code. Zeke had seemed surprised about that, so maybe this *is* his imposter, but then again, I don't know Zeke well enough to know how good a liar he is.

I sit cross-legged on the deck, staring out at the ocean, willing it to work its magic, to calm me down. I take some deep breaths and try to empty my head, but it's spinning and I can't focus on anything. I rock back and forth, my heart pounding.

Why can't I give Zeke the benefit of the doubt? If it *was* Zeke and not his imposter, then the conversation could have been his way of luring p4r4d0x to reveal his identity. It's possible he was trying to trace p4r4d0x's IP address.

I try to convince myself that Zeke is setting up his imposter and p4r4d0x and does not actually want to kill me himself, although the conversation feels all too real.

Maybe there's a way to trace both Tracker and p4r4d0x, find out at least where they are. I get the laptop, pulling it into my lap again, and go back inside the chat room. But neither Tracker nor p4r4d0x are anywhere to be seen.

I'm kicking myself now that I let my emotions get the better of me and I didn't try to track both of them when I had the chance. They were right here on the screen, within my reach. And I blew it.

I go inside and start pacing, circling the room. I do my best thinking on my bike, and the bicycle is just outside on the deck. I still can't chance it, though, that Ian and Amelie will drive by and I go unrecognized a second time. So I sit again and pull the laptop closer, peering at the screen for a few seconds.

The French phrase pops up in the chat. But it's not Tracker. It's Angel. Looking for me.

My fingers freeze on the keys. How would Angel know the French phrase? Do I answer? Do I reveal myself? What if he is my shadow?

I yank my hands back, away from the keyboard. I am filled with dread. If he traces me back here, if he can somehow get through the firewall I've created, the VPN, Tor, I may not be able to escape again.

But then I come to my senses. I am well protected. So before I can stop myself again, I respond with my own French phrase and a link to a private chat room.

'Where the hell are you, Tina?' he asks when we are both there.

It's Zeke. It takes me a second to digest that. He's hiding behind Angel's screen name. Maybe his team saw the previous conversation we had and are on high alert.

'Tina?'

I've used a different screen name, but the French phrase clearly told him who I really am. So much for anonymity. 'No names, remember?' I shouldn't have to tell him that. I wonder for a second how he'd react if I used his real name here.

'You were here one minute and gone the next. Heather said you just took off.'

Again with the real names, but I have no doubt that this is really Zeke. 'I couldn't stay. It's not my thing.'

'It's for your own safety.'

'So you say.'

'What's that supposed to mean?'

I take too long thinking about how to respond when he continues.

'I can find you, you know.'

I don't doubt it for a second. He could have already found my IP address, regardless of my safeguards. He's found me when no one else could.

I still don't respond.

'Tina, you're in a lot of danger. Please come back. I found the imposter, and he's here. In Miami. He's got a hit out on you. He wants you dead.'

NINETEEN

I leave the chat room without saying goodbye. He'll know the exact second I've left. I am shaking again; the fear is palpable.

I'm not afraid of p4r4d0x. He is still an anonymous, faceless screen name. No, I'm afraid of Tracker. Of Zeke.

There is no way he could have known about the hit on me unless he was the Tracker of the conversation I saw. There was no imposter. Has there ever been?

And if he is the Tracker in that chat room with p4r4d0x, he is the one who is going to kill me.

Again, I play devil's advocate with myself. What if he is undercover? What if he is online as Tracker only to trick p4r4d0x into revealing himself? No, I cannot be certain; the conversation points to Tracker as the one who shot Tony, who tried to kill him.

I can understand why Zeke is so hell-bent on arresting Tony. Tony's got his hands in a lot of criminal pots, and arresting him would be a coup for any FBI agent. But killing him? I wonder what really happened when Zeke was undercover. He didn't say anything about what he did, exactly. Was he immersed in Tony DeMarco's organization? If so, what did he see? What was he asked to do? What *did* he do?

From the conversation I've just witnessed, Tracker means to kill Tony and kill me, too. Why didn't he kill me when he found me in Falmouth? Why put all that stuff on that laptop to incriminate *me*; why get me involved? Or is it some sort of backup plan? If he can't kill me, maybe he thinks he can frame me so I'll finally pay for my crime.

It's these questions that make me think twice again about whether the Tracker I saw with p4r4d0x is really Zeke. He's had so many opportunities, if he was so inclined, to kill me in the last couple of days, not to mention ever since he found me in Quebec. I am a non-person; I don't exist. No one would ever know what happened. It could be the perfect crime.

Am I merely trying to talk myself out of believing this could be Zeke?

And then it hits me. He can't kill me until he gets the money.

I pull the laptop toward me. Discovering someone's identity in Tor, behind a VPN, is difficult at best, but nothing is impossible. There are always traces of us left behind. Zeke is no stranger to this either, since the FBI has developed malware to deliver users' IP addresses to servers outside the Tor network, de-anonymizing those users.

Since Tor runs on the Firefox application, there have been security holes, holes that the FBI has created itself. But software patches have been developed to counteract that effort. I wonder if Zeke has been trying to compromise Tor by infecting those patches. If so, however, he can't have been successful, since he would already have found Tony DeMarco's site – and whoever has been setting us up.

If it's not Zeke himself.

Without thinking about it, I type 'Zeke Chapman' into a search engine.

The first things that pop up are the news stories from sixteen years ago, the ones that reported Zeke's death on the houseboat in Paris. I've read them before; they don't tell me anything new. There are Zeke Chapmans on social media, but as I click on each one, I don't see his familiar face. There are white pages that list Zeke Chapman in various cities and towns across the country; none of them seem to be him. I call up the images, and none of those men even remotely resemble him.

It is unusual these days for someone not to have some sort of Internet footprint. But maybe not for someone like Zeke, who wants to hide behind screen names online. Maybe in the world of the Internet, Zeke Chapman truly is dead.

There isn't even a mention of him *before* Paris. It is as though he existed for only that one moment.

I scroll back to one of the stories about his death and scan it. Yes, there it is. 'He is survived by his wife, Lauren.'

I type 'Lauren Chapman' and 'teacher' into the search engine.

There are a lot of Lauren Chapmans. I click on all the social media links, but none of them are teachers. I find one history professor at a small college in Idaho, but she is considerably older, a professor emeritus. No, she can't be the one.

I could search for 'Lauren' and 'teacher,' but I don't even want to think how many I'd find. I don't even know where they lived; Zeke was here in Miami, but that's not to say that he lived here with her.

I lean back and close my eyes. I wish I'd found out more about her, more about him, but he always seemed so simple. FBI agent. Married. Unhappily. Easy to seduce. What more did I need to know back then? I wasn't thinking long-term. And then when I saw him again in New York, when I found out he wasn't dead, I was in shock. And even more shock when he told me he was Tracker.

My eyes snap open. I know nothing about him. Nothing at all.

Nothing except what he's told me. Which is what, exactly?

I shut the laptop and scramble to my feet.

An idea skitters through my head, and I need a phone. It means going back out, but I can't stay hidden in my room forever. Zeke doesn't know where I am; Ian didn't recognize me. I convince myself that this is a good idea, that it's the only idea.

My trip to the 7-Eleven is uneventful. I chide myself for being paranoid. Zeke might guess that I've come home, so to speak, but he doesn't know where I'm staying. I've disabled the GPS in the laptop, and there are plenty of hotels and motels to choose from. It could take a little while for him to discover this one. I'm not going to be here too much longer anyway.

I am not one of those hackers who regularly use social engineering. I hope I don't sound boastful when I say that I am more gifted with coding than tricking someone with words into giving me information. My father was the one who used his words, his personality, to get everything he wanted from people. His smile and seemingly easygoing personality drew in his clients, made them trust him while all the time he was conning them behind their backs. I never wanted to go that route, be like him. But right now, I am going to try.

I find the phone number for the local FBI field office online, and I punch the number into my new disposable phone. I almost hang up before someone answers, but when I hear the voice and it's not a machine, I clear my throat and begin.

'I'd like to talk to your human resources department, please.'

'I'm sorry, but you need to call our main headquarters in Washington, D.C.'

I was afraid of that, but I'm ready for it. 'I'm with Sun Bank, and I just need to verify that someone works there.' I sigh deeply, so she can hear. 'I screwed up, and I was supposed to get this information two days ago, but I forgot. Can you just tell me if Zeke Chapman works there and what his official title is? I would really appreciate it.'

'Um, well, I'm not supposed to—'

'I'll get fired,' I say. 'Seriously. He applied for a mortgage, and we're doing a background check. You must know about that, right?' I'm laying it on a little thick, but hopefully she won't notice.

'OK, hold on a sec.'

I am on hold only a few minutes when she comes back.

'Zeke Chapman?'

'Yes.'

'A mortgage?'

I am beginning to feel a little queasy. 'That's right.'

'You're sure he works here, at the FBI?' Her voice is hushed now, furtive.

'Yes. That's what he put on his application.'

'I'm sorry, but I don't know where you got that information. There is no Zeke Chapman here. He's not an agent here, and he doesn't work in any other department. I even checked the database to see if he's with another field office in another state, but he's not. I'm sorry. I don't know what else to tell you.'

TWENTY

I hang up the phone without saying goodbye or thank you. My hands are shaking, and I make two fists and take a deep breath. Does Zeke even work for the FBI? Did he ever?

Last summer, Zeke wanted me to go undercover with Tony DeMarco, who'd offered me a job hacking for him. I am not a fan of bureaucracy, but Zeke had been so quick to make that plan, to push me to do it without any obvious sign that he'd cleared it with his superiors. I'd suspected he was going rogue, but maybe it was worse than that.

I get up and begin to pace. I am not safe here. Why did I get on that plane with Zeke? Why did I allow him to talk me into this, coming with him, agreeing to help him? He fed my fear of Tony DeMarco, my fear that I could still end up in prison for what I've done.

I stop pacing and sit back down in front of the laptop. I do a quick search and through my research discover one thing: Zeke's reveal about the statute of limitations, my status as a fugitive, is correct. So at least I know he didn't lie about that.

My head is spinning. What about Tracker? Has he lied about being Tracker, too? I don't have any real proof that Zeke is Tracker, except that he repeated the French phrases to me. If he'd been privy to our conversations online, he would know this. The shadow in my laptop did.

For a while, I'd suspected that Tracker was the shadow. The shadow knew everything about the bank job, about Steve and Jeanine, about the account I'd set up that the FBI hadn't found. Only someone close to me would know those things.

Zeke wants to get close to me, or at least that's what he's said. He said that finding me wasn't about the bank job. It was about me. I close my eyes and can still feel his lips on mine. For a second, I wanted him as much as he wanted me. But what if that's a lie, too? What if it really is about the money, just like 'Tracker' told p4r4d0x? What if he's trying to seduce me into helping him get both the money and Tony DeMarco? I seduced him the last time, as he reminded me. Now, maybe he thinks it's his turn.

I wrap my arms around my torso, wishing I could disappear into myself. I am alone in a city I barely know anymore. I have limited funds. I can trust no one.

I find myself on the beach again, my little room in the distance. I am taking a risk, coming out here, but I need to see the water, feel it around my feet. I walk along the edge of the sea and spot a bright orange kite in the sky, hear children laughing.

My heartbeat has slowed, and I begin to think more clearly. I consider the reason I am here, the reason I had to leave Cape Cod, and not just because Zeke told me to. I *was* interrogated by the FBI, and I don't believe that was a lie. A crime was committed; Tony DeMarco got shot.

I don't know that much about it, just what I've read online in the news reports. Tony DeMarco is in stable condition. Ian is staying in his house. I'm not sure what his role is in Tony's operation, and I'm not sure that he's still feeding information to the FBI. He might be. He also might be responsible for the hit.

However, Ian – or at least the Ian I used to know – is not prone to biting off the hand that feeds him, so to speak. Even if he'd somehow gained a multitude of computer skills, I am not convinced that he is behind this.

I am calmer when I am not thinking about Zeke, so I decide I have to turn my attention away from him. See if I can't find out what's going on with Tony. Find out who p4r4d0x is. I don't need Tracker to do this. I've used him as a crutch for far too long. I am perfectly capable of doing it myself.

I head back to the room and do a little sleuthing online, but I still cannot find any updated information about Tony DeMarco's condition. All of the news sources say that he is hospitalized, but there is no more information than that.

The more I think about this, about how someone was hired to kill him, the clearer it is that whoever did it, failed. Which means either that the hitman was not truly a professional or that Tony DeMarco wasn't really supposed to die.

It is not difficult to find Adriana DeMarco's cell phone number. Of course, it's not listed, but it's remarkably easy to get inside the carrier's code. There are only three or four wireless carriers that anyone uses, and I choose the one that has the widest service areas. It is a no-brainer. Anyone could have guessed right.

As I punch in Adriana's number on the disposable phone, I realize that she may be in the hospital and she won't pick up. But she answers on the second ring.

'Hello?' Her tone is tentative; I am coming up on her phone as 'unknown caller.'

I am nervous, and I hope that my voice doesn't waver. 'Miss DeMarco?'

'Yes?' I can hear her tone become even more guarded; she is wary, and I don't have much time to win her over.

For a second I consider telling her the truth: that I am her sister. She most likely doesn't know she has a sister, any more than I knew all these years. Would she embrace it? Would she call me a liar? Would she confront her father once he recovers? Would he tell her?

For the first time, I wonder if he would want me dead only if to keep the secret that she is not truly his daughter. My father is dead, as is my mother. There is no one, then, to tell.

Except Zeke. How, exactly, does he know?

The thought throws me off for a second, and I struggle to regain my composure. 'Miss DeMarco, my name is Agent Nancy Lyon and I am with the FBI in Miami. I just want to confirm with you that you are aware that Roger and Amelie Parker are staying at your father's home here.' Impersonating an FBI agent is probably one of those criminal acts that can dredge up my past, but if it's a way in, I need to take it.

'Hold on a moment, please.'

I am not sure what's going on, and I am ready to hang up and abandon the whole thing when she comes back on the line.

'I'm sorry, Agent Lyon, but I was with someone. What can I do for you?'

I want to find out who she's with, but that would raise red flags, so instead I say, 'I'm verifying that you're aware that Mr and Mrs Parker are staying at your father's residence on Key Biscayne.'

'Yes. Is there a problem?'

'No. Just a precaution.' I pause. 'I'm sorry about what happened with your father.'

Silence. I've made a mistake. Again, I'm ready to end the call when she finally speaks.

'Well, you are the first one to say that, and I appreciate it. It's almost as though all of you think he should have died.' Her voice has an edge to it. 'What are you doing about finding the man who tried to kill him, anyway?'

'We're doing all we can,' I say, hoping that since I'm telling the truth she'll hear it in my voice. 'How is he doing?'

'He's stable. They think he can go home soon.'

'That's good news. Will he come back here, to Miami?'

'Yes.'

'Will you come home with him?'

'Of course.'

'Who will run your businesses?' She owns two spas in New York – her father is suspected of laundering money through them, but she most likely doesn't know that, either. 'I'm sorry, I don't mean to pry,' I add. I may be pushing it, but she hasn't hung up on me yet, and I admit that the longer I talk to her, the more I wonder about her. Her tone has gotten less defensive now; it's soft, gentle, almost trusting. Everything that I'm not. I saw her once, last summer, and she is young – the same age I was when I did the bank job. She looks like me at that age. Her hair is darker, but her face is mine – our father's. I wonder what Tony DeMarco thinks when he looks at her. Does he see my father, a reminder of his wife's infidelity, his best friend's betrayal? It doesn't seem as though he has taken it out on her, which speaks well of him – possibly the only thing good in him.

'That's all right,' she is saying. 'I have people who can take over while I take care of Daddy.'

Her use of the word 'Daddy' to describe DeMarco tells me more about their relationship than anything else.

'Will you be there when we arrive?' she asks.

'No. I'm being assigned to another case in a day or so.'

'You've been very kind. I wish you all were like that.'

So do I. 'Thank you, Miss DeMarco. I'm glad to hear that your father is doing well.'

'He was very lucky.'

'Were you there?' I ask it before I think. If I were real FBI, I would know this.

But it doesn't faze her. 'No. I was in my apartment. I heard the shots.'

'And you have no idea who would do this?'

She laughs, and I shouldn't be, but I'm surprised. She laughs like me. Not for the first time, I think about how my father had very strong genes. I wonder how much she's like me in other ways.

'Daddy has a lot of enemies, but you already know that.'

'Yes.'

'It was ordered online. The hit. But you know that, too.'

'We're working on that.' Another truth. But I have to get back to what I'm looking for, and I have to take a risk. 'Is it possible for you to give me Roger Parker's cell number? We'd like to set up a time to go over and make sure the house is safe for your return.'

She hesitates, but only for a second. 'I'm not sure I can give that out.' She's smart; I wouldn't give it to me, either.

'I promise not to abuse it,' I say, forcing my tone to be much lighter. 'It's a precaution. We wouldn't want you to be compromised on your return, and we have to make sure that Mr and Mrs Parker are safe as well.' The idea that they might be in danger, too, lingers.

'I never thought of that,' she says softly. 'If it would be helpful . . .'

'Yes, it would be incredibly helpful.'

She rattles it off the top of her head, which makes me wonder about Ian and how well he knows this girl.

I repeat the phone number back to her, and she murmurs that I've got it right.

'Thank you,' I say.

'I have to get back.'

'Yes.' I am not quite sure how to say goodbye. I have an urge to stay on the line, to ask her more about herself. 'I'll pass this along. Take care.' I hang up before she responds. I have what I set out to get.

TWENTY-ONE

Tony DeMarco is not dead; he is doing well enough to come home soon. I don't know exactly when, so I have to take advantage of this immediate window of opportunity. Getting Ian's phone number out of Adriana was easy, maybe too easy, and it's very possible that she's going to tell him about the nice FBI agent who called, concerned about him and his family. She might even tell him tonight – if they are friendly enough.

It's more than likely that Ian knows the truth about Adriana. He met me when I was in college; the resemblance between me and my half-sister is pronounced. He may not know the whole story, but he is not stupid and could piece it together.

I think about the phone call, hearing her voice. I have no family left except her, and she doesn't even know I exist. What would it be like to have a sister? Is it too late to have a relationship with her? Could we be friends? Would we find a deeper bond between us as time went on? When I was young, I used to fantasize about having siblings. An older brother, maybe, or a sister around my age with whom I could share secrets. Either way, it would have been someone who could share the burden of my parents.

The laptop needs to be powered up. I grab the backpack and rummage around in it, pulling out its cord. Something's tangled in it, and I am holding the small box, the wireless router device, that I confiscated from that teenager at the coffee shop.

I eye the cell phone number I've written down on the small pad on the table. I had the crazy idea that I could try to call Ian, maybe talk to him about Tony, find out what's going on. But a different idea begins to form.

Besides impersonating an FBI agent, I'm about to do something else that's probably not very legal. After plugging in the power cord, I turn to the laptop and find my way to Tor. I locate the link to the site I've read about. I've never done this before, but it's so straightforward. I download the program and it only takes a few minutes. Tracking cell phones has never been so easy, and from the software's description, Ian will never even know that the application has been installed remotely on his phone.

It doesn't take long. A small blinking dot appears on a map. I zoom in and see exactly where Ian Cartwright's – or, rather, Roger Parker's – cell phone is.

They are at a South Beach restaurant. I don't know how long they've been there, how long they'll stay, so I will have to move fast.

I am not completely familiar with the wireless router and how it works, but it's not difficult to figure out once I turn it on. The device activates a hotspot wireless network that I manage to program so that it will automatically override any other network in the vicinity. It's a pretty strong signal, which makes me pause for a second and wonder if I shouldn't buy some sort of stock in it.

I go online and do a search for the router. Although I am initially surprised that the teenager I took it from hasn't deactivated it, I discover that the data doesn't expire once it's purchased. There is no name attached to the device. Maybe the teen stole it from someone who doesn't know it's gone. I find my way into the source code of the program's software and create a new account that only I can see and administer. Whoever this belongs to is out of luck right now.

The website informs me that the router can go about eight hours before having to be recharged. It looks as though there are about seven hours left. I'm uncertain if it's enough time, but I don't have much choice, since I don't have a charger.

While I've been sitting here, I can see four other users have come into the network. It's easy to monitor through the site. With just a few keystrokes, I could be inside their computers. People need to be more careful about noticing which network they're connected to online.

Since I don't have the time or the inclination to peek into these other computers, I turn off the router to save the battery and tuck it inside the front pocket of my backpack. It's a long shot, but the only one I've got.

For the second time in just a few hours, I am pedaling the palm-tree-lined street toward Tony DeMarco's house. I don't even look when I pass my old home; I'm not here to reminisce.

I don't see anyone around, not even any cars. It's as though this whole neighborhood has been abandoned. The houses are quiet, a few lights in windows. I cast a shadow in the pools of light from the street lamps as I pedal down to the end of the road, which circles back around and up again. I strain to hear something, anything, but the only sound comes from the crash of the surf in the distance.

I take care in front of Tony's house, certain about that elusive security system that probably has a motion detector to make my presence known. I lean the bike against a palm tree and walk around out front, holding up the phone as though I'm taking pictures, all the while glancing around, seeing if I can spot anyone anywhere. But still I see no one.

I reach around behind me and take the wireless router out of my bag and flip the switch. I stoop down and tuck it next to the driveway, under some bushes so it's concealed.

And then I move away, back down the path to the street, around the house, and to my bike.

When I get back to the motel, I bring the bicycle inside this time. Zeke is probably out looking for me, and if he sees a bike, he will automatically think of me. I don't want to make it too easy for him.

The laptop is where I left it, powering up. I peel off the bike helmet and drop it on the nightstand. I sit cross-legged on the bed and pull the laptop toward me, its cord snaking across the bedspread. I'm not sure this is going to work, but I flip open the cover, waking it up from its sleep mode.

I had been afraid that I would need to be within range of the router in order to see the information within it, but it's a powerful little device. I make a mental note to get one for myself as I manage the information that's popped up on the screen. Five devices have connected to the network I've created.

The username for one of them is Amelie. It's not a common name, at least in the States, so when I see it, a little jolt rushes through me. There is nothing more rewarding than a hit on the first try when hacking.

It doesn't take me too long to get into her system. She's not online, but the computer is still connecting to the network. It's possible that she isn't aware she left the computer on. I'm not even going to speculate why she wouldn't either turn it off or put it in sleep mode.

It's not her work computer, but she has work-related files: memos, job evaluations, copies of payslips. She's no longer working for the bank in Paris, but she's working at a bank here, on Brickell Avenue, as a vice president. I wonder what the bank would say if they found out she's the one who supplied Ian with the numbers for the accounts we stole from.

I quickly move on, because there is limited time with the router.

She's got a file with passwords – why people insist on keeping those on their laptops is a mystery. I make a copy of the file, for future reference. There is a folder with memos pertaining to her kids' schools and downloads of their report cards. I have no interest in any of these things. A quick look through Amelie's Internet search history tells me that she's concerned about wrinkles, she's shopped online at Neiman Marcus, and she's spent a lot of time looking at friends' pages on Facebook. A little further searching turns up nothing in the deep web, no Tor software.

There's nothing here linking her to Tony DeMarco, despite the fact that she's living in his house at the moment.

I can't help myself, though. I open the program that contains all her photographs. The first is dated today – she must have her phone linked – and it's a picture of Ian holding up a glass of beer and grinning. It takes me aback, because it's so familiar. Again I see the young man I fell in love with in his face. How many times had he looked at me like that? And not so long ago, either. I would be surprised if Amelie knows how well Ian and I reconnected last year on Block Island – if she knows anything at all.

I scroll through a few more pictures that have a more artsy feel to them: wine glasses on a glass table, a sunrise over the ocean, the shadow of a palm tree against a full moon. I wouldn't be surprised to find this batch posted on Amelie's Instagram account.

The screen is full of thumbnail shots, and I click on one of two boys – or, rather, two teenagers, standing side by side, their arms slung around each other's shoulders.

And now I know why Daniel – Zeke's Daniel – looked so familiar. It wasn't that he's a hacker.

It's because he's Ian's son.

TWENTY-TWO

It's as though the wind has been knocked out of me. I stare at the photograph, at Daniel, trying to make sense of this. I have no idea what game Zeke is playing, but I don't like it. He has to know who Daniel is. He must have been waiting for me to see the resemblance, make the connection. I feel stupid that I didn't see it right away for myself, even though I had a feeling that I knew him from somewhere. Zeke had to know that I'd pick up on it at some point. Maybe he's laughing because I hadn't.

My hands are shaking, and I sit back and close my eyes, trying to calm down. It's one thing after another with Zeke, it seems. Why? Did he bring me here to humiliate me and then have me killed or kill me himself?

Am I overreacting?

My eyes snap open with the thought. Am I? Am I seeing things that are merely figments of my imagination? Zeke has made no secret of how he feels about me, but – as I discovered – I really know nothing about him.

No, I can't assume that I'm imagining all of this. In fact,

I have to assume that my worst fears have been realized, so I'm on alert and ready for anything until I can find out the truth.

The truth that may be right here in front of me.

I take a deep breath and stretch my fingers before continuing.

I get out of Amelie's computer and check out one of the others that joined my network. Whoever owns it is streaming a movie, a crime drama set in England. I'm pleasantly surprised that the network switch was seamless enough so the viewer didn't notice, or if he or she did, it didn't register. I poke around a little bit behind the scenes. I don't see anything familiar, just a lot of music and videos. Nothing raises any red flags with me. It could be anyone, but I'm pretty certain that it's not Tony DeMarco or anyone who's living in his house at the moment.

I move on to the next computer in the network. At first it looks benign, but it's *too* clean. Most people's desktops are littered with files, photographs, but this one is completely clear of any clutter. I look for any documents or images, and there are no files here either, raising even more suspicion. When I see the Internet history, I realize this computer is definitely not benign.

There is no Internet history. Nothing. Whoever owns this computer has been clearing everything.

The Tor software is not hard to find. First, I think this must be Daniel's computer; who else, besides a hacker, would install a program that would provide such anonymity? But then I wonder if it's not someone else. Daniel has access to everything he could ever want with even more anonymity through Zeke's computers in that apartment in South Miami. Unless he's sneaking home and doing some extracurricular work that Zeke might not know about.

I didn't have to check the IP address on Amelie's computer, because it was clearly hers, but this one is a different story. However, when I get the IP address, it doesn't pinpoint a specific street address, only Harbor Point. So it could be any computer within range of the router.

As I'm pondering my next move, I see it. Someone is using

this computer, either in person or remotely. I watch as he – or she – opens the Tor program. I should feel ashamed; I felt so violated last summer when the shadow was watching me, and here I am, doing the very same thing. I justify it by telling myself that I am not like the shadow; I am not going to hold this computer for ransom, demanding money for its release. Instead, I silently watch the user navigate the Hidden Wiki, not unlike the way I did just a few hours ago.

Every muscle is tense; I feel as though I'm going to snap in half.

And then it's gone.

The entire screen goes black. Suddenly, the pop-up screen with the router information opens, and I see what the problem is: there was a lot less time on the battery than I thought. It's run out of juice.

I still have the IP address, but access might be beyond reach. Whoever owns this computer clearly knows about security and firewalls. I have to try anyway. I use my advance port scanner program and input the IP address to see if there are any open ports. But there aren't any; there's no way in. He probably has it set up to reject any incoming traffic and to prevent ports from opening.

I fall back against the pillow and close my eyes. I've at least found out who Daniel is, so it's not a complete waste. But I'd spent too much time on that, and not enough time looking for a possible link to Tony DeMarco. In retrospect, I also forgot to get Amelie's IP address. Her computer seemed benign, but there might have been something in her email or other documents that could have told me something more.

Although I've come a long way after a long absence, I am still rusty; my instincts are still too slow.

I spring up off the bed and walk across the room and go out on the deck, the warm ocean breeze wrapping itself around me. I have another sudden urge for a paintbrush, an easel. I want to paint the sky, the water, capture the moment. Maybe it would ease the nervous knot in my belly. I want to try to bypass Zeke and catch Tony DeMarco myself, but I have to concentrate on the end game and keep from getting distracted. Maybe then I can finally put the man in prison. Justice would be served – for my father, who died behind bars because his former friend and business associate threw him under the bus.

I conveniently push aside the fact that my father stole from Tony, just as he stole from every other person he came in contact with.

What he stole from me was worth far more than money.

I often have wondered if my mother had not been mentally ill, would my father have been different? Was he a criminal before she became ill? Was he stealing from his clients from the beginning or did he discover that he could do it somewhere along the way? I don't know. But as I well know, no one really changes; our personalities are set from the start. I am a criminal as much as my father was one. Nature *and* nurture both, in my case.

Would my father have had an affair with Tony's wife if my mother hadn't been ill? Could he have stayed faithful to her? He must have known about Adriana – or maybe he didn't. It's possible Tony's wife kept it from him. Adriana was still a child when he went to prison; she was only five when I left and she didn't look like me, not really, not yet. My father may have died not knowing he had *two* daughters.

I'm envious of Adriana. She has had a father in her life. Granted, Tony is not someone I'd be proud of, but she still calls him 'Daddy.' There is a closeness in that word, and she is at his side in the hospital.

I find myself back on the beach, my toes digging into the soft sand as the water rushes over the tops of my feet, tickling them with its warmth. The water on Block Island was always so cold, as though reminding me I should never get comfortable. I can get comfortable here; I *am* comfortable here. It's familiar: this water, this breeze, these palm trees. It's like a cup of hot tea and toast and a favorite television show on a cold night on a remote island in Canada. Or a hike through Rodman's Hollow on Block Island, where the shad blossom dances across its branches. But it's a little different. This place evokes my childhood, my teenage years.

I don't want to remember. I turn my back to the water and

go back inside, shutting the glass doors, the cool air conditioning causing goosebumps to rise on my arms.

The laptop sits on the table, its cover closed. The router might no longer work, but I still have skills without having to rely on an outside device. I should be trying to find out who p4r4d0x is, whether the Tracker I saw is really Zeke, what Zeke's real story is, but it's as though my brain has shut down, exhausted from the day's events.

So instead, I lie down on the bed and close my eyes, and soon I am asleep.

When I wake, it's dark outside. I glance at the clock by the bed and see that it's almost midnight. I've been asleep for four hours. I climb out of bed and go into the bathroom, splash some water on my face. I've done some of my best work in the middle of the night. Why should tonight be any different?

The laptop springs to life when I open the cover. I hadn't shut it down, and the site where I was tracking Ian's cell phone is still on an alternate screen. I hit the refresh button without thinking about what I'm doing.

The cell phone, not surprisingly, is no longer in South Beach.

What *is* surprising is that it's here.

At this address.

TWENTY-THREE

I sit up straighter and stop breathing for a second, as though whoever is carrying the cell phone is in the same room as me and, if I don't breathe, I will be invisible. But after a few seconds, I realize how stupid this is. I am alone; no one is knocking on my door.

Still, I stare at the blinking dot on the screen. It may not be right here, but it's somewhere very close. Panic begins to rise in my chest, and I struggle to stay calm. There is no way Ian could know that I'm here. Even if his son told him that there was a new hacker, he doesn't know Susan McQueen.

He's only known me as Tina Adler and then Nicole Jones. Susan is a stranger to him.

But the dot continues to blink at me.

It's dark outside, and the only light in the room is the glow from the laptop screen. It bounces off the glass doors. I didn't close the curtains, and shadows dance across the deck. I put my hand on the laptop cover and lower it until just a small stream of light slips through the crack, bathing the room in more darkness and allowing me to see the outlines of the palm trees outside. I don't see anything else.

I get up and move toward the doors, skirting around and gently closing the curtains until I'm shrouded inside. I stand as still as possible, straining to hear if anyone is lurking around outside.

I hear nothing. I go across the room and stand by the door that leads to the parking lot. A thick curtain covers the window next to the door. I strain to hear, but still nothing. That doesn't mean someone's not out there.

I know I'm being ridiculous. I tell myself the site must be wrong. It can't be accurate. Maybe Ian and Amelie weren't at South Beach. Maybe he's not here right now. But I haven't convinced myself.

Ian knows where I am. How, though?

What if it was the router? What if the person who was on Tor was Ian? Maybe Daniel has been showing his father around the Internet. What if he managed to trace my IP address through the router back here? If he did, it's possible he doesn't know it's me; it's just some hacker.

There are too many 'what ifs' and not enough viable explanations for anything.

I take a step away from the door and that's when I hear it: the crunch of gravel. I freeze. In my head, I picture Ian creeping around outside my room. I am not afraid of him, but I definitely do not want to be found. I glance over at the laptop. Did I disconnect the router program? I'm sure I did. I took care of the GPS feature, but what if there was more than one? Zeke could have easily installed something that I might not have discovered. He is still better than I am, as much as I hate to admit it. But if I was traced through a GPS in the laptop, rather than the router, then whoever is outside is somehow connected to Zeke. Maybe it *is* Daniel. He's the only link I know between Zeke and Ian. Except for me.

I think I'm so smart, but I'm standing in the dark, afraid to move or I'll be discovered when I am already exposed. I might as well go outside and confront him.

I reach for the doorknob, but snatch my hand back as the car engine roars on the other side of the door. Even though the car has started, it doesn't sound as though it's going anywhere; it's idling in place.

I move swiftly over to the table and lift the laptop cover enough so I can see the screen. I'm very aware of the light it casts, but I have to check.

The cell phone dot is still blinking in the same place.

If it's Ian, he should just knock on the door, let me know that he's on to me, that he knows where I am. Confront me. He had no problem doing that when he showed up on Block Island.

I'm being silly. Why am I cowering in the dark? He knows I'm here; I have to be on the offensive, not the defensive. I straighten up and walk over to the door. Before I open it, I pause at the window, my fingers pulling the fabric aside slightly as I peek outside.

A sleek black car that looks like the one I'd seen earlier at Tony DeMarco's, the one that Ian and Amelie got into, is in the parking lot. I can't make out who's inside; it's too dark. But it's got to be Ian if it's the same car.

The hell with this. I put my hand on the doorknob and turn, flinging the door open.

Just as I step outside, the car takes off, skidding across the lot and down toward the main entrance. I watch the red tail lights until it disappears into the night.

I'm not quite sure why he left. What was the point of sitting outside, watching my room, and leaving only when I finally came out?

Unless that's the point. He is only doing this to unnerve me.

I stand outside and consider my options. If he knows where I am, I should either go back to the apartment or find another place to hide. I'm uncomfortable with going back, especially since I've witnessed the conversation between Tracker and p4r4d0x. Until I can confirm that Zeke is or is not the Tracker I saw in that chat room, I don't think I can see him without letting on that I'm suspicious.

When I head back inside, I bump into the wheel of the bicycle that's leaning against the wall. I study it for a few seconds, weighing my options. I have to keep it. It's my only transportation. I don't want to borrow anyone else's Uber account or waste money on a taxi when I've got a decent way to get around.

It would be ironic, though, if I'm arrested for stealing a bicycle.

I eye the laptop, suspicious that I have not completely gotten rid of any GPS tracker. There could easily be a second one.

Now that I'm more focused, it doesn't take me long to find the tracker software that Zeke installed in the laptop. It's clever, how the software avoids detection by being in the firmware. I am momentarily impressed. I manage to disable it and tell myself that I have to stop thinking he's smarter than I am. By doing that, I'm allowing him more power over me than he deserves.

I check the cell phone GPS site again, and I watch the blinking dot as it maneuvers the island's streets, ending up back where I suspected it would: at Tony DeMarco's house.

I quickly stuff the laptop into the backpack and swing it over my shoulder. I grab the bike helmet on my way out and leave the key on the windowsill. I don't bother locking the door; there's nothing to steal.

It's the middle of the night. I'm not sure about my destination. It wouldn't be safe to go back to the mainland at this hour on a bike. I think about the beach at my old house, how I would lie on a chaise longue for hours soaking up the sun, listening to the soft crash of the waves against the sand. I was lazy then; if I wasn't on the beach, I was in my room on the computer in the chat rooms. I had no direction, no life. Ian and I would go to the clubs; he'd come back with me. My father never indicated that this was a problem for him, but now, in retrospect, I wonder about that. I wonder how he viewed my lifestyle. By then he was busy conning his clients out of their money, but he had built a business; he had created a life's work and his daughter was living the life of a party girl. No worthwhile employment, no direction.

I shake off the thought. It's water under the bridge.

I begin to doubt that it was a good idea to leave the motel. I am biking in the middle of the night, an easy target if Tracker and p4r4d0x have somehow discovered where I've been. If I'd stayed, at least I could have locked the door, hidden. I am not thinking straight. By bringing me here, Zeke has unleashed too many memories that have distracted me – not to mention stirring up an uneasiness about how I am still attracted to him while not being sure whether I can trust him. I crave more answers, and I am suddenly overcome by the need to have Internet, another reason to have stayed at the motel.

I navigate Crandon Boulevard, and as I begin to pass the Key Colony Plaza, I spot a familiar logo. Starbucks. It's long closed, but its Internet might not be.

There are a few steps, so I climb off the bike and bring it up with me. They've left tables outside, with the chairs sitting upside down on top of them, the umbrellas closed. I look at the street, and a few cars pass, but I think it's dark enough that no one will notice me if I stay to the back.

I pull a chair down off a table and take the laptop out of the backpack, happy that I'd powered it up so it's ready to go. The light from the screen startles me, and I glance around to make sure no one is around to notice.

I am right about the Internet; it's free, and all I have to do is agree to its terms. Whatever they may be. I know that public Wifi isn't usually private, but there's no one else here so the risk is worth it. I sign on to my VPN and find my way to the chat room. I create yet another screen name. I don't have to remember it; I'm only going to use it this once.

But before I can do anything else, he steps out of the shadow and I freeze.

TWENTY-FOUR

'What do you think you're doing, Tina?' I should have known he'd find me. 'Nothing,' I say. I sound like a belligerent child. I wish he didn't affect me this way, especially when he catches me off guard.

Zeke takes a few steps toward me, until he's standing right on the other side of the table. 'You're not going to ask how I found you?'

'Probably the GPS you put in the laptop.'

He grins. 'I had a feeling you'd find it.'

'Then why put them there at all?'

His expression grows dark, and he leans over, putting his hands on the table. 'Because I knew you'd run.'

I ran, but not for the reasons he thinks. I'm not inclined to explain it to him, though. I don't know that he'd understand *this*. It bothers me that he knew I'd take the laptop. That he'd rigged it with the GPS, taking for granted the fact that I wouldn't leave without it. I hate the idea that I'm so predictable, that he can guess my every move.

He's watching me closely, a frown etched in his forehead. 'What do you mean, *them*?'

I shrug.

'You said "them," not "it." Was there more than one GPS on the laptop?'

A chill shimmies down my spine. 'There were two,' I say softly. His reaction causes me to believe him, that he didn't know there was more than one. I tell him where I found both.

'The second one was in the firmware?' He's shaking his head, running his hand through his hair as he thinks about that. 'I used a standard GPS. I didn't do that.'

We stare at each other for a few seconds.

'Who had access to it besides us?' I ask.

'No one.'

But he's wrong. 'This is the laptop that was at the bike shop, right?'

He knows now what I'm thinking. That GPS code was installed before the FBI found it.

'Jesus, I can't believe I didn't see it. I was all over that thing,' he says, almost to himself.

'If it makes you feel better, it wasn't easy to find. Although I thought you were pretty clever to do it that way, and now I guess the clever one isn't you at all.'

'No, the clever one is the person who set us both up.' He stares me down. 'You need to come back with me.' He takes my silence as an invitation to keep talking. 'You'll get used to it.'

'Used to what?'

'Working in that room with them. Working with them. I had a hard time at first, too.'

I really hate it that he does understand. That he knows exactly how I feel at all times. He is what I'm running from more than anything. I like being alone. I'm used to my own company. I'm not lonely.

No. I'm lying to myself. I *am* lonely. I miss my friends. My real, flesh-and-blood friends. Steve, Jeanine, Veronica. Again I wonder if I can go back now. Now that I'm not really a fugitive. It's not that I was never myself with them; in a way, I was more myself with them than with anyone else. Even Tracker.

Zeke is waiting for some sort of response from me, but I'm too wary of him. I still don't know if he's the Tracker I saw online with p4r4d0x. I shiver involuntarily as I think about their conversation. He could take me out right now, kill me and walk away.

I take stock of my surroundings. The plaza is closed; no one is around. Only a few cars have passed on the street below the steps. I am in the shadows. I have no protection here; I am vulnerable.

He straightens up and holds out his hand. 'Come on.'

I don't move.

'Seriously, Tina, you have to get over this. You have to come with me, come back.'

'Why, exactly?' Every muscle is taut; I'm ready to run if he makes even one more move toward me.

'Because I found something online.' His tone is guarded, as though he isn't sure how much to say, until he says it. 'The person who's pretending to be me, pretending to be Tracker – he's after you.'

I don't say anything.

'You know, don't you?'

I shrug.

'You don't think it's me, do you? That I'm *that* Tracker?'

I wish it weren't so dark so that I could see his expression more clearly, his eyes. 'I don't know what to think.'

'It's not me.'

I scramble to my feet so we are face to face. 'Tell me, then, why the FBI doesn't know who you are.'

'What do you mean? What did you do?' He takes a step back and folds his arms across his chest.

'I called FBI headquarters. They said they didn't know who you are. She said she checked with other offices, and your name never came up.'

'So you think I'm lying?'

The words hang between us.

'I wish you hadn't done that.'

'Because it's true? You're not really FBI?'

He stops and faces me. 'I *am* FBI. But I told you, I've been undercover.'

'I didn't think you still were.'

He reaches around behind him, and instinctively I back up. He holds out his hand.

A shiny gold badge sits in his palm.

'Where'd you get that? Cracker Jack?'

'Very funny.'

I don't expect him to grab my other hand, turning it over. The weight of the shield sits heavy in my palm. I run my fingers across the raised letters. It feels real. I want to believe him. I want to believe that he has nothing to do with the Tracker I saw online with p4r4d0x.

Still, I hesitate.

'If this doesn't convince you, then how about this?' he says, pulling out his cell phone and punching in a number, handing it to me before he hits 'call.'

I take it, but I'm not sure what he's doing.

'Call,' he instructs. 'Ask for Agent Tilman.'

Tilman? That was the name of the FBI agent who questioned me in Falmouth. Zeke's nodding. 'Yeah, it's *that* Agent Tilman.' He grins. 'How do you think I managed to take a piece of evidence to Miami?' He means the laptop. The one that's sitting on the table in front of me. 'You don't trust me, I get that. I don't know if I'd trust me, either. But I'm asking you to. I need you.'

It could all be a set-up, but against my better judgment I begin to dissect the situation. If he were truly the Tracker I saw online with p4r4d0x, he's had plenty of time – and privacy – to kill me right here. No one would be the wiser.

'I need you to be honest with me, Zeke,' I say softy. 'I saw a conversation online. Between Tracker and p4r4d0x.'

His expression changes slightly, but he's standing in a shadow so I can't read it.

'I thought so. I wish you hadn't seen that,' he says.

I stop breathing and feel as though he's punched me in the gut. He *is* the Tracker I saw.

TWENTY-FIVE

'No, no, that came out wrong.' He takes a step toward me, and I take a step back, looking around to see what my best escape would be. He reaches his hand out, and I duck underneath it, circling around him, going toward the steps that lead back down to the street. I glance at my bike. Can I get to it?

He's too quick, though, and he grabs my arm. I drop both the phone and the shield as I try to wrench free, a small cry coming from somewhere deep in my throat. He's got me now, his arms around me, tight; I can't get free. 'Don't be afraid,' he whispers in my ear.

It's too late for that. I am more frightened than I ever have been. I struggle against him, but his hold on me is too strong.

'It's not what you think. It wasn't me.'

I don't say anything, just wait for him to finish me off. How will he do it? Will he strangle me? It seems easiest. I haven't noticed a weapon.

'*I'm* not going to kill you, Tina,' he says then, suddenly setting me free. I take the chance and run over to the bike, fumbling with the helmet which I had hung on the handlebars. I can't steer it like this, and the helmet falls to the pavement with a thud. I drag the bike around me until it's between us; he's cornered me. I shove the bike at him, and he catches it, forcing me back against the side of the building with it until I am completely trapped.

'I shouldn't have to prove myself to you. I got you out of Canada; I brought you here. No one knows where you are, and that's because I'm doing everything I can to keep you safe. I know someone's out to kill you. I know you were framed. I was, too – remember? There's someone online impersonating *me*. Impersonating *you*.' He's accentuating the last word of each sentence, making a point, trying to get through to me.

And then: 'Seeing you confuses me,' he says softly.

It is not something I have expected.

'I have loved you since I was fifteen.' His voice catches on the words as though it doesn't want to let them go.

I find my voice. 'You don't even know me.'

He gives a short chuckle. 'Tina, we know each other better than anyone else. We are the same person.'

'If you know me so well, then just let me go. Let me be. Let me disappear again. Tony DeMarco won't find me. I'm not afraid of him.' As I say it, I realize it's true. I'm more afraid of Zeke right now.

'I can't do that, Tina,' he says.

My entire body is shaking. I grip the bike to try to get control of myself.

'I'm not going to kill you,' he says slowly, louder now, as if I won't be able to hear him otherwise. 'I saw that conversation, too. We were probably both in there at the same time.'

'You're saying you're not the Tracker who said he tried to kill Tony DeMarco? That you haven't really found that bank account? That you aren't going to kill me, too?' The volume of my voice rises with each question, until I realize I'm shouting.

'No, no, and no,' he says. 'I don't know who put out that hit on DeMarco, and I have no idea where that bank account is, and I really don't want to kill you. I'm only trying to find out who my imposter is. While I was watching them in the chat room, I was doing everything I could to nail down the IP addresses, but I couldn't find them.'

'So why did they tell me at the FBI that you didn't exist?'

'Because I don't. Not to anyone calling the main number, anyway.' He chuckles. 'You've got to improve your social engineering skills if you want to get further than that.'

I already know that, so I don't respond.

'Do you believe me?' His tone is so tentative.

I don't know. My head is reeling, and I ask the first thing that comes to mind: 'You couldn't trace the IP address? What did you try?' I don't believe that with all my doubts about him, the fear that's overwhelmed me the last five minutes, I focus on this.

He notices. 'See, Tina? That's the way you and I are. My god, I was kissing you and you switched gears so fast, but I didn't even care because what we do online is what we do and nothing stops us.'

'What's wrong with me?' I ask, mostly to myself, but I say it out loud. I look him straight in the eye. 'You really could kill me right now.'

He smiles. 'But I'm not going to. It would be like killing myself.' He pauses. 'You're an extension of me. When you were gone so long, I felt like someone had amputated a part of me. Finding you again was like a miracle.'

I hear the words, but he hasn't tried to come closer. He hasn't tried anything. We are just standing here, the bike between us.

Call me crazy, but I believe him. Neither of us has been completely honest with the other from the start, but the part of him that's Tracker – the real Tracker – the part of him that

I know so well, he's the one who's talking to me now. I am more sure of that than I have been of anything in a while.

He reaches over and puts his hand over mine. 'Stay with me and you can be free,' he whispers. 'I'm offering you everything. Come back with me, Tina.'

I consider my options. I want desperately to be free, but if I leave now, I never will be. He senses that I'm wavering, but he does not push. He doesn't have to.

'If I go with you,' I say, ready to negotiate, 'I don't want to stay in that apartment. Not with you and Heather. I need my own place. My own space.'

'I'll see what I can do. Anything else?'

I haven't thought this through. I should have had a list of demands, because no doubt I'll come up with something and this might be my only chance to ask. But I can't think beyond my own privacy right now. I shake my head. 'I don't know.'

'OK.' Zeke leans down and picks up his phone and shield, putting them in his pockets before gently taking hold of the bike's handlebars and moving it out from between us. My hand is still on it, though. I don't want to release it. It's almost as if I do, he will be taking everything from me. Perhaps he is.

Finally, I let go. I watch him wheel the bike to his car, open the back hatch, and lift it up, placing it inside. I pick the laptop up off the table and stuff it into the backpack, shifting it over my shoulder, the weight of the pack my only comfort. He beckons me to the car, and I get in, a sinking feeling in my gut.

If I'm wrong about him, this could be the biggest mistake of my life.

TWENTY-SIX

He doesn't start the car up right away once we're inside and I wonder what he's waiting for. Finally he says, 'The reason we're here, in Miami, is because of DeMarco.'

I already knew that.

'But we're also here because Ian Cartwright is here.' He pauses. 'Ian and I are working together.'

Working together? I try to wrap my head around this, try to find the words that have escaped me. Finally, all I can ask is: 'Is that why his son is working on your team?'

He gives a short snort. 'I was wondering how long it would take you to see it. The resemblance, I mean.'

'Did you tell Ian I'm here?'

Zeke chuckles. 'God, no. Why would I do that?'

I consider this for a moment. How would Ian know where I am? The laptop? Zeke's GPS? Or the other one?

'Tell me how Daniel ended up on your team.'

'He got into trouble. He hacked into his school's system and changed grades.'

A boy after my own heart. I have no idea if Zeke knows my own history of doing just that at the University of Miami back in the day, a move that got me expelled, and I'm not about to tell him. I suddenly have some sympathy for the boy.

'That doesn't tell me how he ended up with you. And why isn't he in another school?'

'He graduated last year. Think of this as his gap year.'

'Working for the FBI?'

'Ian came to me—'

'He *came* to you?'

Zeke sighs. 'Tina, you've been away a long time. A lot has happened. Your old boyfriend is feeding us information from his boss, and he came to us because he was afraid if DeMarco found out what Daniel could do, he'd enlist him. So we got custody. Ian's strictly hands-off; he's got instructions to stay away. As far as DeMarco knows, Daniel's at boarding school. He doesn't really give a crap about Ian's kid, so it's not on his radar.'

'Ian's got another boy,' I say, remembering a search I'd done online.

'And *he* really is at boarding school.'

I feel a rush of sadness for Ian, for Amelie, for those two kids. I know what it's like to grow up in a house without attentive parents, but at least I had a home. My father would never have sent me away.

I shrug the thought away, though, and concentrate on something else. 'Ian's not strictly hands-off.'

'What do you mean?'

'I saw him. Earlier.'

'You saw him?'

'His car was outside my room. The room I had at a motel.' Before he can say anything else, I tell him. 'I tracked his cell phone.'

'How? How do you know it was him?'

I'm having doubts now about telling him, but it's too late. I tell him how I saw Ian and Amelie at Tony's house earlier. 'It was the same car.'

'You tracked his cell phone? How did you get the number?' I hear suspicion in his voice.

'You say I'm good.'

'You found it online?'

I really don't want to tell him I talked to Adriana. Especially because I was impersonating an FBI agent. So I let him think what he wants to think.

'How did you track it?'

'What, are you worried I'll be tracking you next?'

It's too dark for me to see his expression, but he's quiet for a second, and then: 'Tell me how you did it.'

'It's pretty basic. Anyone could do it.' I explain about the program that I used, how I remotely installed the app into Ian's phone without him knowing.

He gives me a sidelong glance. 'No, Tina. Not everyone can do that. Did you get the number from the cell phone company?'

Again, I let him believe that by not saying anything. I could have done it that way.

'Why is he staying at Tony's?' I ask.

'Because that's where he stays in Miami. You're sure it was the same car?'

Now that he's asked, I cannot be sure. It looked like the same one, but maybe it wasn't. Yet I'm not ready to concede. 'If it wasn't, then who was it?'

'Maybe it was another guest?'

'He was outside, watching me.'

'You saw him?'

'No.' Maybe I'm being as paranoid as he's suggesting. Maybe it was just a coincidence. If I believed in coincidences. I hate it that I'm doubting myself. That I am not trusting my own instincts. 'I may not have seen who was inside the car, but whoever it was, was watching me, my room. When I went outside, the car took off.'

'You went outside?' He is incredulous.

'Yes. Maybe it was stupid—'

'It was colossally stupid, Tina.'

Somebody's out to kill me. He doesn't have to say it. But I do have something I need to bring up. 'There's only one way Ian would know how to find me, if you're telling me the truth that you haven't told him I'm here.'

Zeke nods. 'Daniel.'

'Somehow he knows who I am. Maybe he's the one who put that other GPS in the laptop.'

He frowns, and we both speak at the same time. 'It's Ian.'

Even though I've been suspicious of Zeke, we are still in sync, like always. We both know that the reason Ian came to Block Island was for the money. He's still angry that he didn't get any after the bank job; he still thinks I have it or at least had it.

'Ian could be behind everything,' I say softly. 'He could have gotten Daniel to put that remote access Trojan into my laptop and shadow me.' I pause. 'How, exactly, did you end up working with him?'

He shakes his head. 'Let's get out of here first.' He starts up the car.

'I don't want to go back.'

'I don't blame you, but I think it's time to have a little chat with Daniel.'

TWENTY-SEVEN

He pulls out on to Crandon Boulevard, and I am wistful for the short time I have spent here, walking the beach, riding the bike as though nothing is wrong. When everything is wrong.

The bike. I need to return it. I point this out, and Zeke shrugs. 'I'll bring it back tomorrow.'

I sink back in my seat and watch the shadows of the trees as we speed back to the mainland.

'You went back to your house, didn't you?' Zeke asks after a few minutes.

'Yes.'

'How was it?'

Good question. I change the subject. 'I did something earlier.'

He glances at me and frowns. 'What?'

'I had one of those devices – you know, the ones that create their own wireless network?'

'You did? Where did you get it?'

'That's not worth discussing.' I don't want to go into the whole story. 'But I was able to get into a couple of computers.'

'Able how?'

'Like my shadow.'

He doesn't say anything, waiting for me.

'Someone was in the deep web.'

'Who?'

'I don't know. It kicked off because the battery died before I could find out. I didn't see much.'

'Where was this?'

'Near Tony DeMarco's house.' I don't wait for him to react. 'Ian wasn't home. I saw that by tracking his phone, and Daniel was at the apartment, right? So it couldn't have been either of them. But it could've been anyone in the area, not necessarily at Tony's. So it might be nothing. Just some hacker.'

'Where did you get it?' he asks again.

I sigh. 'I picked it up off some kid at a coffee shop. I took it, because he was clearly taking advantage of it.' I hesitate. 'I may have threatened him by saying I was FBI and could arrest him.'

Zeke chuckles. 'So you stole it off him, and then used his account to break into someone else's computer. You're FBI after my own heart. See, you belong with us.'

My silence tells him that I'm not so sure about that.

His silence tells me that he's deep in thought, and I have a feeling I know what he's thinking.

'This might be the way in,' I say before he does.

'Into Tony's deep web site, right.' He pauses. 'I don't know why I didn't think about this before.'

'Because you've been busy trying to hack in through the site, not directly through his computer. You know, you wouldn't need a team to do it that way.'

'All I needed was you,' he says. 'I knew that all along.'

'But now that you know how to do it, you don't need me, either.'

We have stopped at a light, and he gives me a sidelong glance. 'You haven't been listening to me, Tina.'

The car begins to move again, and I notice that we are not going toward the causeway. I don't have to ask where we're headed. 'It's out of juice,' I try.

He ignores me, and we ride in silence until we are passing my old house. The car slows enough for me to see that there are no lights on inside. The 'For Sale' sign feels ominous. In a way, I feel as though this is apropos. The house is best left to the ghosts.

As we approach Tony's house, however, it's clear that someone is awake here. The windows are brightly lit, although I see no one inside.

'It's just over there,' I say, indicating where I left the wireless router.

The car moves over to the side of the road, and I've got the door open even before we stop. In a swift move, I lean down, reaching down where I left it, my fingers finally finding it. I clutch it in my palm as I climb back into the car.

We are almost back to Crandon Boulevard when I see the headlights in the side-view mirror. They are coming up on us fast. Zeke glances in the rear-view mirror and then back at the road.

'Hold on,' he says softly.

I grip the armrest as the car speeds up, watching the headlights behind us. We have a rental, and the car behind us clearly has more power. It's dark, and I can't see what make and model it is, but I begin to suspect that this is not a random case of road rage.

Zeke jerks the steering wheel to the right, turning on to Crandon, the car fishtailing.

'The bike,' I say.

'It'll be OK.' His short, clipped tone doesn't do much to assuage my concern.

I'm not so sure when I feel the first tap. Zeke is trying to speed up more, but our car doesn't have the power and the one behind us is now pushing us up the road. I can't speak, even if I wanted to. My heart is pounding. Zeke's hands are tight around the wheel, struggling to keep the car under some kind of control, but I wonder how long he can keep it up. The speedometer reads ninety miles an hour now.

I spot brake lights ahead. Someone's turning; the blinker is on. I'm afraid my fingers will break, I'm gripping the sides of the seat so tightly. I glance over at Zeke and see his jaw is set; he's as tense as I am, which doesn't make me feel any better. I wish he had some FBI trick he could pull out of his pocket, get us out of this before we're killed or kill someone else.

Because the latter is looking likely as we are going even faster now, and the car ahead of us is waiting for cars to pass in the other lane before turning.

Just as we come up on it, the car turns, none the wiser, and suddenly the one that's been pushing us veers to the right, scraping the side of the rental and speeding past. Instead of slowing down, we speed up, Zeke's foot heavy on the accelerator as he tries to catch up to the other car, which keeps getting further away because the rental just doesn't have the same power.

A car turns from a side street into our lane; the yellow light turns red. Zeke slams on the brake. We jerk forward, the seat belt taut against my chest. I can hardly breathe and am afraid I'm bruised, although it's better than the alternative. We are merely inches from the car in front of us. I may never breathe normally again.

'Are you OK?'

I take a few deep breaths and nod, although I'm sure I'm really *not* OK.

'Did you see the type of car it was?' Zeke's asking. I can't tell if he's as shaken as I am, but maybe he's had more experience with things like this than I have, because he asks so matter-of-factly and his voice is calm.

'No. It's dark. I didn't see.' My voice sounds as though it's coming from somewhere else, almost like an out-of-body thing.

He doesn't speak for a few seconds, then says, 'I think it was a BMW.'

TWENTY-EIGHT

We are both thinking the same thing. It's Ian.

'He must have seen us when we got the device,' I state the obvious. 'But I didn't see anyone around. He came out of nowhere.' I pause. 'Besides him giving Daniel to you, how, exactly, are you and Ian working together? Or is that the extent of it?'

Instead of answering, Zeke pulls to the side of the road and starts to get out.

'What are you doing?' I ask.

'Your bike.'

I scramble out of the car, too, and meet him at the back. The bike is half out of the car and half in, but it doesn't look the worse for wear, considering. He picks it up and adjusts its angle in the trunk and tries to secure it, but is not very successful. 'We'll just go slow,' he says.

'Unless he comes back to finish the job,' I mutter.

'You're sure you're OK?'

'I'm fine. I just had someone try to run me off the road, but yeah, I'm OK.' I don't even try to keep the sarcasm out of my voice.

'Let's go.'

We climb back in, he starts the engine, and the car begins to move again, at a normal speed. The engine sounds a little bit louder than it was before, as though in protest that it has to continue working.

'So, to answer your question about Ian,' Zeke says, 'it started a few years after Paris. I knew Ian was working both sides, even though he really didn't give us too much information. Tony kept him at a distance; Ian had ripped him off once before and he wasn't going to let that happen again, but for some reason it seemed the old man liked him.'

Ian has that way about him, so this doesn't surprise me.

'I kept an eye on him. Even though he's been helping the FBI for years, our personal collaboration, so to speak, is relatively new. Within the last year, since you left Block Island.' He pauses a second, then adds, 'I know what happened between you two there.'

He's not talking about how Ian and I left it. He's talking about how we became lovers again – albeit for a short period. He's jealous.

'So let me get this straight. You found me to keep me away from Ian?'

'Initially, I guess. But he's the one who told me that Tony has some sort of site in the deep web. He didn't know any more than that, though. When I found you in Quebec, I knew you could help. You were the only one I could trust.' He studies me for a moment, then says, 'I'd like you to talk to Daniel. I think you might be able to get through to him.'

Because I know what it's like to be used by someone you trust.

Zeke continues. 'He's a kid. I'm pretty good at reading people, and Daniel's not bad, just a little misguided. His skills are good. He found a few things on the Waste Land site, but like everything else, it's not directly connected to DeMarco.'

'That could be on purpose. To throw you off it.'

'His father could be advising him,' he admits.

'You think Ian is sort of a double agent?'

'Wouldn't be the first time.'

'You're right. And Ian can be very persuasive when he wants to be.' I was so vulnerable. Maybe Daniel is, too. Maybe he's as anxious for his father's love as I'd been. 'I'm not very good with actual interaction,' I say.

Zeke chuckles. 'Understatement. But you have common ground.'

'If he's doing Ian's bidding, he's not going to tell me anything.'

'Maybe not directly.'

'If Ian is behind this, then why didn't he kill me when he was at the motel? I was there by myself. I came out of the room. No one would've ever known.'

Zeke takes a deep breath. 'He doesn't have the money yet. He still thinks you know where it is.'

'But that other Tracker told p4r4d0x that he did have the money.'

'Maybe he was lying.'

His words surprise me. 'So maybe he's setting up p4r4d0x?'

'Anything could be going on.'

I don't even want to speculate. There are too many things at play right now and too many questions.

'Tell me how you got Ian Cartwright's cell phone number,' he says when we are on the Rickenbacker Causeway, headed back to South Miami.

'What makes you think I didn't hack into the carrier?'

'You won't answer the question.'

Busted. 'I may have done a little social engineering.'

'You could get charged with impersonating an FBI agent.'

I stare at him. He knows what I did. 'Why did you even ask? Anyway, how did you find out?'

'Adriana DeMarco called the field office. She asked for Agent Nancy Lyon, and when she found out there wasn't anyone by that name, she threw a fit. She's a little bit of a princess, your sister.'

I ignore his comment. 'How do you know this?'

'I get a call if there's something to do with DeMarco. His daughter calling and saying that an agent called her warrants a red flag.'

'So she admitted that she gave me Ian's phone number?'

Zeke chuckles. 'No, she didn't admit that, but you just did. Hey, don't get me wrong. It was a good move. But why didn't you just get the number from the carrier?'

Good question.

'It's OK if you want to know more about her,' Zeke says. 'I understand.'

Although he understands a lot more than I wish he did, on this I don't know that he does. *I* don't even understand it. Why *did* I call her? I have no answer except that perhaps I wanted some sort of connection. It also told me something that she did have Ian's number.

I don't say any of this to Zeke, though. Instead, I ask, 'So how do you find your hackers?'

He gives me a sidelong glance, then says, 'Online in the chat rooms. How else?'

Except for Daniel. Daniel, who was handpicked by his father to join this team. Why? Why would Ian turn his son over to Zeke? There's no love lost between them; Ian only does things that will benefit him. I'm more convinced than ever that Ian is behind all of this. And then I have another thought.

'Daniel. The wireless router.' My head is spinning; I'm having a hard time getting the words out.

He knows what I'm thinking. 'You got into someone's computer with the router, but you think that computer was hacked. You were watching a shadow.'

I'd hacked the hacker.

TWENTY-NINE

'We need to get back in there,' Zeke is saying. 'The router's dead.'

'So we find a charger.'

'And how long will it take to power it up?'

'Then we get a new one.' He makes it sound so easy.

'And put it in the same place?'

Zeke nods. 'Someone's trying to hack into a computer in Tony's house. You set up the router so the network was automatic for anyone online?'

'Yeah. But I think you have to order those things by mail.'

Zeke gives me a lopsided grin. 'Tina, how many times do I have to tell you that I'm FBI? I can do anything.'

I make a face at him. 'What if Daniel's p4r4d0x?'

'We don't know that Daniel is p4r4d0x. Maybe he's Tracker.'

'But if we believe the conversation, then Tracker tried to kill Tony. Daniel's been here, right, the whole time? And I'm not sure I can see him as the one who tried to kill Tony DeMarco in New York.'

Zeke shrugs. 'What if the whole thing is made up? What if the conversations are fabricated?'

I hadn't even thought about that. Maybe I'm too quick to believe the worst rather than believe that maybe someone's messing with me. With us. 'What's the point of that?'

'To lure you out? Like the shadow did last summer? Whoever is doing this knew about the bike shop at the Cape. This is as much about you – about me – as it is about DeMarco.'

'It might only be about me.' He looks confused, so I continue. 'Tony's not dead, right?' He shakes his head, frowning, trying to see where I'm going with this. 'Whoever was hired to kill him—'

'Didn't succeed,' he finishes. 'Which means DeMarco might not be the target after all. It's you.'

'Or *us*. Look what just happened.'

He's quiet for a few seconds, then says, 'But he didn't finish us off. He could have slammed us into a tree. Why didn't he?'

I have no idea, but then I realize something, something Zeke had said earlier. 'Because he doesn't have the money yet.'

'Exactly.'

Although we've sorted this out, and I'm pretty sure we're on the right track, I begin to get that ominous feeling again. This place is not safe for me. 'I have to get out of town,' I say softly.

For the first time, Zeke doesn't disagree with me, which means he's drawing the same conclusions I am. 'You're right. You and I can work anywhere.'

'We've already figured out it's Ian.'

'But we need proof.'

I'm perfectly willing not to take this any further. I know how to disappear; there are plenty of places I can go where I won't be discovered. And bringing Zeke along is not part of any plan I've ever had.

I can see, however, that he's not going to let me go without a fight. He's got another card up his sleeve, too.

We've pulled into the parking lot behind the apartment building, but when he stops the car, he doesn't make a move to get out right away. Instead, he says, 'That hit was traced to you – and to me. You go into hiding now, you'll never be able to get out. We catch Ian, we prove to DeMarco that you weren't behind the hit, and you're free.'

I'd almost forgotten about that. 'OK, fine, sure. But I really don't want to go back in there.' I indicate the apartment.

'Talk to Daniel. See if you can get anything out of him. I'll get my stuff, you get whatever you left behind, and we'll head out.'

He's not going to let me off the hook, even though I really don't know what I'm going to say to Daniel. Resigned, I turn and head toward the apartment building, my backpack slapping against my side. Against my better judgment, I pause and turn around when I realize he's not right behind me. He's wheeling the bike toward me.

'Can't keep it in the car,' he says simply, and we go up the stairs and head to the apartment. I open the door and let him through with the bike. He leans it against the wall as I step inside. Jake and Charles are still hunched over their keyboards. It's quite possible that they have not even moved since I was here early this morning. Heather wears headphones as she stares at her screen. Empty cans of Red Bull are littered about; the scent of popcorn is in the air. No one looks up or acknowledges that we're here.

Zeke taps Jake on the shoulder. Jake looks up, lifts up one side of his headphones.

'Wassup?'

'Where's Daniel?'

He shrugs. 'Not my turn to watch him.'

Zeke doesn't even bother with Charles. He approaches Heather, who sees him and shoves her headphones up over her ears so she's wearing them like some sort of crown.

'Daniel?' Zeke asks.

She shakes her head, gives me a sidelong glance. 'He left.'

'For where?'

'I don't know. Said he had something to do.'

Zeke and I exchange a look. It's the middle of the night. Although it's perfectly normal to be here at this hour, it is not normal to have 'something to do.' Other than this, anyway.

'You sure he didn't just go to bed?' Zeke tries.

Her hands are on the headphones, ready to move them back down over her ears again. 'No. He left. Got a ride.'

Zeke's face grows dark. I can sense his exasperation with Heather's cryptic responses. 'With who?'

For the first time since we entered the room, she looks straight at me, and then back at him. 'He got a text and left. Said he'd be back.'

'When?'

'I don't know – couple hours ago?' Now she does lower her headphones and goes back to her screen, but she is still watching Zeke – and me. She's not that discreet about it. I'm doing the math in my head. Daniel left about the same time that car was idling outside my motel room. Zeke looks as if he's not finished with the interrogation, but I tug on his shirt-sleeve and indicate he should follow me. I can feel Heather's eyes on us as we let ourselves out.

'What's up?' Zeke asks when we're in the hallway, heading toward the other apartment.

'You can't do simple math in your head?' I roll my eyes at him.

When we get inside the apartment, the bicycle in tow, I take the laptop out of the backpack. The program that I used to track Ian's cell phone is still bookmarked. I hit a few keys, and there it is. The location of Ian's cell: at his house.

'That's not really a surprise,' Zeke says, but it's clear he's formulating some sort of plan.

I get tired of waiting for him, though, and say, 'If you can get your hands on one of those wireless routers, we can go set up another network. See what he's up to.'

He's already in his room, packing up his bag. I go into the bedroom and find the couple of T-shirts I'd left here earlier and stuff them into the backpack. Back in the living room, I scoop up the laptop and shove it inside, too. He's waiting by the door, his cell phone to his ear, murmuring something into it.

'We're all set,' he says, shoving the phone into his jeans pocket and closing the door behind us.

We move quickly down the stairs and past the fountain, the parking lot lights beacons in the night. But just as we are about to emerge from the courtyard into the lot, headlights flash. Zeke grabs me and pulls me back into the shadows. We peer around the wall and watch as the black car pulls to a stop. The door opens, and Daniel emerges. He's going to have to walk right by us to get upstairs, so I shrink back, ready to try to find another hiding place. But I stop when I hear his voice.

Ian's voice. Telling Daniel he'll walk him up.

THIRTY

The computer program showed that the cell phone was at the house. Not here. I'm confused. But I don't have time to think about it because another thought creeps into my head. Ian probably knows that I'm in town, but I'm not ready for that encounter yet, especially after what just happened. And even though Zeke wants me to have a heart-to-heart with Daniel, this clearly is not the time. It seems that Zeke is on the same page. He indicates I should follow him, and we hug the wall as we head around the courtyard. A door is just up ahead, and Zeke turns the knob, pushing me inside, his finger to his lips, indicating I need to stay mum.

He's got the door open a crack and is watching. I lean against the wall, my eyes adjusting to the dark. We're in the laundry room; a line of washers and dryers are in front of us in a row, like soldiers at the ready.

I barely have time to register it, though, when Zeke yanks my arm and we are running through the courtyard to the parking lot. The car's lights flash as Zeke hits the key fob to unlock the doors. We climb inside, and he peels out of the lot.

'Heather will tell them that we were giving her the third degree,' I say when we get to the South Dixie Highway. 'She'll tell them that we just left.'

'She doesn't know where we're going.' Zeke's eyes are trained on the road as he grips the steering wheel. The car weaves from lane to lane, around the other few cars, going through yellow lights, putting more distance between us and Ian. I twist around in my seat and look behind us, almost expecting to see Ian's car, but of course I don't. There are not many cars on the road, though, so I worry that Ian will catch up with us regardless.

It reminds me of something, however.

'The car that was behind us – the BMW?' I say. 'If it was Ian, then he had Daniel in the car with him.'

That sits between us for a few minutes. I'd like to think that if Ian's going to come after us, he wouldn't bring his teenage son along.

We're driving parallel to the monorail, and then suddenly we're veering left, underneath it. The seat belt is tight against my body; the back of the car feels as though it's hydroplaning.

'He must have left his phone at home,' I say to break the tension.

'No shit, Sherlock.'

'But who leaves his cell phone home?'

Zeke's head snaps around to look at me. 'Maybe it's powering up.'

'He could power it up in the car. You don't think he's on to us, do you? I mean, maybe he talked to Adriana. She could have told him that she gave his number out. I mean, she did call the FBI about the phone call she got, and she probably trusts him a lot more than the feds.'

His silence tells me that he thinks the same thing. I made a huge mistake getting the number from her rather than just hacking into the phone company records.

We're on Bird Road, then to the right, driving the grids. I peer into the side-view mirror and don't see anyone behind us now. The houses are dark. Only a couple of sets of head-lights pass, and the palms overhead cast shadows on the pavement. We're somewhere in Coral Gables, that's all I know, squat stucco houses with red clay roofs lining the street.

Zeke turns down another street, then pulls into a driveway of one of the small houses. He cuts the engine, and I open my door at the same time he opens his.

'No,' he says. 'Stay here.'

No one is around; shadows creep along the surface of the house. All the houses on the street have neat, tidy yards with palm trees and flowering bushes. This one is no different, except that there is something over the front windows; there's no glow from a TV and no light seeps through. 'I'm not staying in the car,' I say, starting to get out.

He leans over and opens the glove box, takes out a gun. I'm so startled that I don't speak for a moment. Who exactly lives in this house that he'd need a gun?

He slams the car door shut and sticks the gun in his back waistband.

'Isn't that dangerous?' I ask, finally finding my voice and cocking my head at him. 'I mean, what if it goes off? You could injure yourself.'

'Would you care?'

'Seriously, Zeke. Don't you have some sort of holster?'

He ignores me as he walks up the driveway, following a stone path around the back. I do a little jog to keep up. There's a door at the side of the house; the curtains in the windows are drawn. Zeke knocks; the knob turns and it opens. Zeke indicates I should follow. We slip inside.

It's a kitchen – very modern, with expensive-looking stainless-steel appliances, dark cabinets, and granite counters circling the room. An island sits in the middle with a couple of chairs on one side. The figure who let us in leads us into the living room, which spreads out the width of the house. But there are no sofas or chairs or fancy artwork on the walls. Four computer screens sit side by side on a long table, keyboards and wires cluttering the space in front of them. From the number of screens, I would have expected more than one person manning them, but I would have been wrong. He is a wiry fellow with a short ponytail fanned out on top of his head. His hands and feet seem too large for his body. He could be thirty or he could be fifty; it's anyone's guess.

'Tina, Spencer. Spencer, Tina.'

Spencer gives me a small salute, and I nod, a little taken aback that Zeke has used my real name in the introduction.

They huddle together, and I run my fingers across the keyboards. The screens are dark, but when I hit a key, one of them springs to life, and I scan the code. It's a jumble, until I see something familiar and lean forward to take a closer look. I glance over at them. They are facing away from me, whispering to each other. I take advantage of the moment and lean over the keyboard, my fingers moving swiftly, my eyes on the screen, watching the code as it scrolls. There. I hear Tracker's usual question in my head: *What do you see?*

I don't have time, though, to delve deeper, because Zeke clears his throat right behind me. I twirl around, like a child caught stealing a candy bar at the drugstore. Spencer has an amused expression on his face; his eyes meet mine and I catch the small smile at the corner of his mouth. He knows that I know. So does Zeke.

'Did you find it?' I ask Spencer.

He shakes his head. 'Not yet. But I will.'

He's been looking for the bank account, the one I put that two million dollars into after the job. The one no one could find. This is work that Zeke's team hasn't been commissioned to do, and I wonder how much Spencer is getting for it. Is he an outlier of the team, someone like me, who has a bigger purpose than searching for Tony DeMarco's deep web site and proof of his criminal activity?

'Come on, Tina,' Zeke says.

I want to stay here. I want to help Spencer, see if we can find that bank account together, see if the money really does still exist, like 'p4r4d0x' and 'Tracker' said in the chat room.

'How did you find this?' I ask Spencer, ignoring Zeke.

'It's all still there; it's just digging it out.' He is eyeing me curiously now. 'How did you do it?'

He's asking how I transferred the money, how I got it out of the bank accounts and put it into all those other accounts. I force myself not to look at Zeke. 'I had help.' Why isn't Zeke helping Spencer? He knows where that money went; he told me how to do it. Except that one account. The one no one found.

The one that Spencer is about to hack into.

THIRTY-ONE

He doesn't know what's there. He hasn't gotten inside. If what Zeke tells me is true, there isn't anything there. The account is a ghost, much like its creator. But what if it's not? What if it *does* still exist? My fingers itch for the keyboard; I have to know.

It dawns on me: Spencer *knows*. He knows about me, which is why Zeke introduced me as, well, *me*. I'm not the only one he knows about, either. It's pretty clear that he knows Zeke is Tracker, and he knows, too, about the bank job.

'Come on, Tina,' Zeke says softly, suddenly next to me, his breath tickling my ear.

'I want to stay. Don't you? He's almost in.'

Zeke and Spencer exchange a look.

'No, he's not.'

'Why not?'

Spencer shakes his head. 'It goes in circles.'

'What does?'

'Just when I think I'm in, I get kicked out. Whoever did this is a fuckin' genius.' He levels his gaze at me, and it strikes me: he thinks *I* did it.

'I don't know anything about this. I only transferred the money into the account. I sent the code to the back door to Tracker.' I don't even bother censoring myself.

'What back door?' Zeke asks.

He actually sounds as though he doesn't know. 'The back door that I set up in the code. Just in case.' Just in case someone locked the account. I wanted Tracker to have the money. I wanted him to pay everyone who helped. I narrow my gaze at Spencer. Did *he* help? Zeke says no, no one helped; it was only him.

'I never got any message about any back door,' Zeke says. He isn't even trying to pretend he isn't Tracker, confirming my suspicion that Spencer knows everything. He's still talking. 'Someone must have intercepted it. Maybe the same person who's sending us in circles now.' He pauses. 'Did you know the feds would freeze the account?' Zeke is staring at me so intently that it makes me uncomfortable, not to mention that *he* is 'the feds', so this is a loaded question.

I shift from one foot to the other and back again. 'No. But I was worried that someone else might get in there and the money wouldn't get to who it needed to get to. So I put in the back door and sent you the code so you'd know how to get in there without anyone knowing you were there. You could take the money out—'

'And leave the account empty.' He finishes my sentence for me, and I know he's right: someone else found the back door, intercepted the message I'd sent.

'You're not going to find the money,' I tell Spencer. 'You'll find the account, but it will be empty. That money's long gone.'

'I'm not so sure about that.'

Zeke and I both look at him at the same time. 'What do you mean?' Zeke asks.

But he doesn't answer. He's seated now, in front of the screens, his fingers on the keyboard. Zeke and I lean over Spencer's shoulder, watching the code scroll across the screen. He was right. I did do it. By creating the back door, I allowed whoever got in to write code that would send any hacker in circles. I wish I could take credit for that bit of magic, but it was completely inadvertent and unexpected.

'Who did this?' Zeke asks no one in particular.

'A fuckin' genius,' Spencer mutters. He hits a few more keys, and then: 'What the hell is that?'

We see it at the same time. In the middle of the beautiful code is a sloppy line, and it reminds me of something. It reminds Zeke of the same thing. We look at each other.

'The picture of Adriana,' we say at the same time.

'What picture?' Spencer has no idea.

'Move over.' Zeke gives him a nudge, and Spencer slips out of his seat as Zeke takes it. Spencer and I watch as Zeke – no, definitely Tracker now – works. I find myself concentrating on Zeke's face rather than the screen. If I had any doubts that he's truly Tracker, I don't have them anymore.

The screen changes suddenly, and a chill runs up my spine.

It's the ransom note that my shadow sent me last summer in Quebec.

Zeke stares at me. 'It's your shadow.'

My shadow is not just some hacker working for Tony DeMarco. He's the one who took the money out of the bank account sixteen years ago.

'That's how he knew,' I whisper. 'How he knew about the account that no one found. Because *he* found it.' My head is reeling. But then I have another thought. 'There is no way that network can be the same as it was sixteen years ago. They must have updated it.'

'Yeah, you're right,' Spencer says. 'But it's a piss-poor network to start with and they've got shitty security. Their IT guys must be middle school dropouts who are so cheap it's the only way they got their jobs.' He jabs his finger at the screen. 'Look at that fucked-up code.'

It's not the code for the picture of Adriana. That had been too easy to find, as though whoever put it there knew we'd come poking around eventually. This is something else, but I can't pinpoint it. Not exactly.

'What do you see, Tiny?' Zeke's voice sounds as if it's a million miles away. He slides off the seat, and I sit, scanning the source code on the screen. It's there, I know it's there, but why can't I see it? Where is it hiding?

I am vaguely aware of Zeke and Spencer talking behind

me, but I'm in a tunnel; I tune it all out. I make an empty promise to myself that if I find it, I'll never hack again, I'll earn that coin and do my steps and disappear again, forget about Tony DeMarco.

And then there it is. It's right out in the open, which is possibly why I didn't see it before. Hiding in plain sight, just like me.

Two million dollars.

THIRTY-TWO

I have the sudden thought that 'Tracker' is waiting for me to find the money, and once I do, he'll take it and then he'll kill me. I have not said anything yet; I haven't given any indication that I've found anything at all. It would take only a second for me to change the code and the money will disappear so no one can ever get it.

But if I do that, it will be lost to me, too, and I might never know who my shadow was, who did this. And I realize in this second that I have to know, that I need to know who has set me up. I need to know if it's Ian or not.

Zeke and Spencer are still talking behind me. That gun is still in Zeke's waistband, and I fixate on it for a second, remembering being in the car and almost getting run off the road. That could have ended so differently; why didn't it? I'm back to the fact that whoever is after me – us – still wants this money first.

I like to think that I make this decision carefully, but I would be lying to myself. It's rash, but without bringing any attention to myself, I change the code only slightly and the account disappears. I am pretty sure I'll be able to find it again.

Zeke's voice in my ear startles me.

'What did you do?'

I force myself to keep a neutral expression. 'I don't know how to get in,' I say, surprised that my voice is steady. I don't sound as if I'm lying. I get up out of the seat. 'Maybe Spencer needs to keep working on it. He's gotten farther than any of us.'

Zeke frowns, as though he knows I'm up to something, but he finally nods at Spencer. 'OK, man, we'll let you get back to it. Come on, Tina.'

I remember something now. He called me Tiny. Is that why Spencer's looking at me with that expression?

'Who are you?' I ask him. 'I mean, are you in the chat room? What's your screen name?'

Spencer looks at Zeke, who gives a short nod, then back at me. 'You might know me as Angel.'

Every muscle in my body tenses. *He* is Angel? Before this completely sinks in, Zeke says, 'Spencer's been trying to trace the other Tracker, find his IP address, but he hasn't been able to yet.'

'He's a slippery bastard,' Spencer says. 'But he trusts me.' He chuckles. 'Asshole. I'll get him. Don't worry.' He gives me a sympathetic smile, and I believe him. Zeke had been vague when I asked him about Angel; now I know it was because he's known who Angel is all along.

'Let's leave him to his work,' Zeke says, then waves something. It's a wireless router. That's right. That's why we came here in the first place. Zeke said he knew where he could get one, and I am not surprised that Spencer would have one just lying around the house. 'All set.' He starts for the door, but I hesitate, the screens drawing me back, and I am suddenly doubtful that I will ever find that account again.

'Come on,' Zeke says, his tone firm, and I follow him through the kitchen and to the back door where we came in. Spencer holds it open for us, gives Zeke a fist bump and nods at me. 'Nice to finally meet you.' There is a hint of respect in his voice, which surprises me. 'Come back sometime.'

'Sure,' I say, and follow Zeke out. When we are almost to the car, I finally speak. 'He's got a lot of equipment there. We've got one laptop. Maybe we should come back after we plant the router.'

'No.'

'He knows who you are.'

'Yes.' He gives me a look that tells me he may regret bringing me here.

'You told me no one knows.'

'He knows who both of us are. He knows everything.' He pauses. 'I'm sorry I lied to you about that, but we can trust him. Spencer and I go way back. Anyway, he's got a lot more to hide than we do. He's part of something. It's like Anonymous. They call themselves Incognito.'

I've heard of them. They're an offshoot of Anonymous. They've got access to things that I can't even imagine; they've hacked high-profile sites all over the world. If Spencer is part of Incognito, it's not surprising he got into the bank like he did. What is surprising is that he couldn't find the account. As I think about it, it suddenly seems too easy. I want to turn around and go back, confront him, but in case it wasn't a set-up, I can't risk it. Maybe later, when I'm by myself – granted, if Zeke leaves me alone – I can try to get back inside.

'You upset? I mean, about Spencer knowing?' Zeke asks after we get into the car. 'You don't have to worry. Really.'

'You said no one but me knew about you.'

'He's the only one.'

I raise my eyebrows. 'Sure about that?'

'Yes.' There's something behind that 'yes,' though, that tells me there's more to this. But it's pretty clear I'm not going to find out what it is – at least not now.

So I change the subject. 'Do you only have him working on finding the bank account, or is he looking for Tony's site, too?'

'He's not part of the team.' Zeke seems relieved that I'm not going to press the issue of Spencer knowing who I am – or who he is. 'If the agency finds out I've got any contact with him at all, I'll lose everything.'

I consider what he's telling me, and decide to leave it alone for now. Instead, I ask, 'So how come he can work alone and I can't?'

The corners of Zeke's mouth twitch, as if he wants to smile, but he doesn't say anything.

We're back in the car and heading toward Key Biscayne. Zeke is quiet, biting the corner of his lip. I find myself constantly looking in the side-view mirror, on the alert for that car.

'Don't worry,' Zeke says, noticing.

'Why not? Maybe we shouldn't have come back here.'

'We have to plant the router. It's a good way in.'

'But it's not like we're traveling under the radar. They already know our car.'

He doesn't say anything to that. Probably because he can't, because I'm right.

As we approach Tony DeMarco's house, every muscle in my body gets tighter. I'm not going to relax until we're far away from here. Zeke pulls over and hands me the router. I open the door and, without getting out of the car, hunch down, tucking it into the bushes where the other one had sat only hours ago. As soon as the door is closed, the car shoots off.

We travel in silence, my thoughts drifting back to Spencer. There was something oddly familiar about him, even though I'd never met him before tonight – and it's not the fact that I've seen him online. Maybe it's because I know that if I hadn't run, if I hadn't disappeared, I could have been him. I could have been the one who found myself holed up in a small house with a bank of computer screens as my only company. Right now, the idea of that is incredibly appealing.

'Where are we going?' I ask.

He shakes his head. 'Don't worry.'

But I do worry. That's my favorite pastime.

THIRTY-THREE

We leave Key Biscayne and go toward the city on the Rickenbacker Causeway. Although I doubt we'll end up at the South Miami apartment, I am still surprised when he pulls up to a high-rise hotel on Brickell Avenue. It's a little out of my price range, but he doesn't seem daunted by it.

'I'll get us a room,' he says casually, parking in front and getting out of the car.

I am uncomfortable here alone and find myself constantly looking in the rear-view mirror and out the driver's side window, just in case someone decides to come up from behind.

Zeke jogs back to the car and climbs in. We head into a covered garage and park. I grab my backpack as we get out and go to the hotel entrance. The hotel lobby is elegant, with a sleek white marble tile floor, a green wall of lush plants, and a bank of plush sofas. It's definitely a few steps above the Palm Court Resort. I give Zeke a sidelong glance, but he doesn't seem fazed by its luxury. I follow him into the elevator.

'You can afford this?' I ask when we reach our floor.

He grins and indicates I should go ahead of him.

The room is luxurious as well, with a large king-sized bed and dark mahogany furniture. Glass doors lead to a balcony overlooking the bay. The lights from the city bounce off the glass, and Zeke goes over to study the view.

I notice the handgun is back in his waistband.

'Isn't that dangerous? Don't you have a holster or something?' I ask. He hadn't answered me when I asked him that at Spencer's house.

'It's at the apartment. It bothers you?'

My gaze is fixated on the gun. He notices and pulls it out, the gun now hanging loosely from his fingertips. When I don't say anything, he holds it out to me, and I frown.

'Take it,' he says firmly.

I don't want it. I shake my head, but he isn't taking no for an answer. He grabs my hand with his free one and presses the gun into my palm, as he did with his FBI shield earlier. I have no choice. I look him in the eyes, and he's watching me, waiting for something, I'm not exactly sure. I don't know what I'm going to do; we stand there for a few minutes without speaking. Finally, he takes it from me, and I take a deep breath.

He chuckles. 'I think it's a testament to how much I trust you,' he says, clearly referring to the fact that I shot him in Paris.

I roll my eyes at him. He opens the sliding door and steps out on to the balcony.

'I'm going to take a shower,' I tell him, but I can't be sure that he's even heard me.

I head into the bathroom and strip off my shorts and T-shirt, stepping into the hot shower. I stand under the stream of water for a lot longer than I need to, washing away everything that's happened in the last few days. When I get out, putting on a clean oversized T-shirt from my backpack, Zeke is still on the balcony. But now he's seated at the small table, the laptop open in front of him. He doesn't even look up.

For the first time since this whole thing started, I have no curiosity about what he's doing online. I need a break from it; I need to clear my head. I towel-dry my hair and crawl into the bed, turning on the TV.

I fall asleep to the sounds of a night-time drama.

A sliver of sunshine splashes across the bed. It's morning; oddly, I am refreshed, despite having dreams where I'm inside source codes and I can't find my way out. I have no idea what time it is. The TV is off; I don't remember doing that, so Zeke must have. My stomach growls, reminding me that it's been hours since I ate anything.

He is still on the balcony. He's closed the door, and I slide it open, the heat clashing with the air conditioning. He glances up, dark circles under his eyes, but he doesn't look tired.

'Tina, check this out.' He indicates the laptop screen.

'Have you been out here all night?' I ask.

He reaches around and rummages around in the backpack, producing a power cord. 'It's almost out of juice.' He picks up the laptop and the cord and brushes past me, as though I'm barely there.

Although I'm curious about what he's been up to, I need some caffeine. 'I'm going out for coffee,' I say, following him in. He barely registers that I've picked up one of the room key cards off the desk and let myself out. I go down to the lobby and am told there is a coffee shop adjacent to the hotel. I go outside, the sun's glare making me squint, and around the corner to the shop. I order two coffees and a couple of bagels with cream cheese. I don't really know what Zeke likes for breakfast. Did we ever have breakfast together? Again it bothers me that I know next to nothing about him, about his life. Does he have an apartment somewhere – not one that he shares with a team of hackers, but one that he calls his own? Does he have a cat, a dog? A girlfriend? The last makes me pause.

I shrug the thought aside, balance the bag of bagels and coffee, and make my way back to the room, letting myself in with the card key.

Zeke is sitting cross-legged on the bed now, the laptop in front of him, completely engrossed.

I hand him one of the coffees and he takes it, sips, but it's not too hot so he chugs it down and sticks the empty cup on the bedside table. He looks up at me, his eyes bright with exhaustion, his five o'clock shadow pronounced, his hair tousled.

'You're a mess,' I say.

'And you, my dear, look refreshed.'

I make a face at him, but before I can ask him what he's doing, he volunteers. 'I've been watching the hacker all night through the router.'

'He's there?' I put my own cup down, forget about the bagels, and squeeze next to him, pulling the laptop toward me so I can see the screen better. 'Who is it?'

'I still don't know. The IP address jumps all over the place, so I can't pinpoint him, but he's definitely not at DeMarco's.'

The screen is dark, and I look up at him, frowning. 'Nothing's going on.'

Zeke nods. 'Yeah, he disappeared a little while ago. But he'll be back.'

'This is why we should have stayed at Spencer's. We could have used his set-up.'

'Spencer's got his own shit going on. You can't be involved in that.' The way he says it makes me hesitate.

'What else is he up to?'

Zeke turns his head to look at me. We are so close that our noses touch, and then he's kissing me, his arms around me; we're lying on the bed, the laptop has been shoved to the side. I think about stopping him, and for a second I try to pull away, but his lips are against my neck, his hand is on my breast, and he whispers, 'Tiny.' I close my eyes and he's Tracker, and I kiss him back.

Afterward, we lay naked on the bed, staring at the ceiling, his arm underneath my head. The only sound is the soft whir of the air-conditioning unit. I'm trying to decide if I regret what I've done and am only mildly surprised to find out that I don't.

'You OK?' he asks.

'Yeah. You?'

'I'm a little tired,' he admits.

'You were up all night.'

He doesn't respond, and after a few seconds, I hear his soft snores. I try not to jostle him as I climb out of bed, but from the look of it, I don't think a bomb would wake him. I stare at him for a few seconds. This is a man I thought just a day ago was going to try to kill me. As I watch him sleep, I realize that fear was unwarranted. His touch was so tender, and I shiver a little with the memory of it. I'm struck by the familiarity of him, but at the same time it's as though we've never been together before. It felt so *right*. Maybe because I've always been more than a little in love with Tracker.

The thought confuses me as I'm still trying to come to grips with Zeke being Tracker. Does this mean that I'm really in love with Zeke? Or am I just in love with the *idea* of Tracker?

I spot the bag of bagels on the dresser next to the TV. I grab his shirt and pull it over my head and reach for the bag, but I trip over the power cord for the laptop, which is on its side on the floor. I reach down and pick it up, and the screen lights up.

I see now what Zeke was waiting for.

THIRTY-FOUR

He is in the chat room. It must be the shadow. I wonder what he'd do if I showed myself, if I sent him a message saying that I know where the money is; that if I give it to him, will he leave me alone and let me get on with my life? Or maybe it's not about the money. Maybe it's about me, about revenge, getting back at me, and the money is an afterthought, something that would be nice, convenient, but not the ultimate goal.

I glance over at Zeke, who is still asleep. The sight of him distracts me again. I slept with Ian on Block Island, even when I knew he was no good for me, even though I knew he was using me. He awoke an old passion in me, a passion for him that I didn't think I had anymore. In retrospect, I knew he wasn't good for me even when I first met him, but there was a carnal need for him that I couldn't shake.

Am I merely chasing after the past, first with Ian and now with Zeke? Am I trying to reclaim all those lost years when I was living alone on Block Island, hiding from everyone, especially myself?

I shake off the thoughts as I turn back to the laptop.

The shadow is using a screen name I'm not familiar with: Betr@yD. *Betrayed*. A sudden affinity with the shadow rushes through me. I can relate. I want to have a conversation with Betr@yD, see if I can get any information out of him about himself. I go through the VPN and open the Tor software application. I find my way to the chat room site where I sign in as 4rt!sT, a screen name I've never used before. When I get inside, I see that Betr@yD has posed a question about back doors.

4rt!sT: What do you need to know?

Betr@yD: It might be a little too personal. Can you chat privately?

I'm not sure exactly why, and I'm uncertain about clicking on any link he'll give me, so I say: *Sure. I'll get a link.*

He doesn't seem to mind, and when I send him the link, he clicks through and we meet in the private room.

4rt!sT: What do you need to know about back doors?

Betr@yD: I already know about back doors. What do you know about the people in this chat room?

I am not here to gossip, but I admit I'm intrigued by the change of subject.

4rt!sT: Not very much. Are you talking about anyone in particular?

Betr@yD: p4r4d0x.

My heart begins to pound as I stare at the screen. I did not expect this. But I have to answer; I need to know what Betr@yD is looking for.

4rt!sT: I don't know who that is. I haven't been here that much to know everyone. What is your interest?

Betr@yD: What about Tracker? Everyone seems to know who he is.

My heart skips a beat. I am glad Betr@yD can't see me, to see my expression, because I'm certain that he would see right through me.

4rt!sT: I don't.

Betr@yD: He's FBI.

My fingers freeze above the keyboard. How does he know that?

4rt!sT: How do you know?

Betr@yD: I've been shadowing him.

I glance over at the bed and watch Zeke sleep. Does he know? I want to wake him, but I'm afraid if I wait too long to respond, Betr@yD will go away.

4rt!sT: How long?

Betr@yD: Long enough. And he's not the only one. Watch yourself.

And then he is gone.

I switch back into the public chat room, but Betr@yD is nowhere to be seen. I switch screens again so I can see into his computer, but it's dark now.

Who is Betr@yD? Is he really shadowing Tracker – Zeke? He's right that he's FBI, but how would he know that? The only ones who know Zeke's online identity are me – and Spencer. For a second, I consider him, but his Coral Gables home is too far away to be connecting to the router. If Betr@yD is in the vicinity of Tony DeMarco's house or even *in* Tony's house, he might actually be Ian. It's possible that Ian – through Daniel – may have discovered Zeke's online identity.

I am concentrating so much on how Betr@yD knows about Tracker that I almost forget his last words. How Tracker's not the only one he's shadowing. He told me to watch myself.

But there's no way he could know who I am; I've never been in the chat room with that screen name before. I've never been anywhere with that screen name. Is it just a general warning, that someone could shadow me, too?

I am trying to think logically about this when Zeke's cell phone begins to chirp, startling me. It's on the table next to the bed. I put the laptop down and start to go toward the phone when Zeke rolls over and snatches it up, answering it with a sharp 'What?'

It's as though I'm not even in the room as he listens intently, then says 'OK' before ending the call. He jumps up and pulls on his pants, then looks around for something. He finally notices me, and the all-business expression fades as he gives me a shy smile. 'I need my shirt.' He comes over and unbuttons the top two buttons, his fingertips tickling my skin. He doesn't seem to notice that I've tensed up, my head still online, in that chat room with Betr@yD. He leans in and kisses me. That's when he finally does notice, when I don't respond.

'What's going on?' he asks.

I gather up my clothes, pull on the bike shorts, and tug a T-shirt over my head, finger-combing my hair and adjusting my glasses on my nose. The laptop is still open on the bed, and I pick it up. 'I had a conversation with the shadow,' I say, telling him about Betr@yD.

Zeke's jaw tightens. 'He said Tracker's FBI?'

I nod. 'He left the chat room, and when I looked back at his screen, it was dark.' To show him what I'm talking about, I pull the laptop toward us.

But instead of a dark screen, Betr@yD is in the deep web, checking out the Waste Land site. Zeke pulls the laptop into his lap, settling on the corner of the bed, and I look over his shoulder as we watch Betr@yD click on a link to a site called Unicorn. I'm not sure what I expect, but what pops up is not it. It's a kiddie porn site, photographs of naked children filling the screen. 'This is new,' Zeke mumbles.

I lean in to see that whoever is looking at the site is taking screen shots and putting them in a folder on the desktop.

'I haven't seen this site before,' Zeke says. He peers at it a little more closely. I have to look away; the images are too disturbing.

Suddenly, the screen goes entirely black. I think I know what's happened. 'The router. It's out of juice.' I pause. 'He's connected to the router, so he's near Tony's house. Or *in* Tony's house.'

Zeke understands what I'm saying. 'It could be Ian.'

'He might know who Tracker is, who you are. Through Daniel.'

He doesn't want to believe that Daniel's been able to find out; I can see the denial in his eyes. 'See what you can find out,' he says again. 'I have to go.'

'What do you mean?'

'That call? I have to go.'

'What about me?'

'You stay here. I don't want you to go anywhere.'

He's reminding me of last night, of the BMW, of Ian.

If Betr@yD really *is* Ian and he's telling me to watch myself, I don't want to be alone.

Zeke knows what I'm thinking. He wraps his arms around me. 'He doesn't know who you are, even if he *thinks* he knows who Tracker is.'

'But he said to watch myself. It was like he knew exactly who I was.'

'There's no way he could have. I think he was messing around with you.'

I'm not so sure.

'You'll be fine here, safe here. Even if by some remote chance he knows who you are, he doesn't know *where* you are,' he says confidently, and he kisses me. When he finally pulls away, I feel dizzy and can't remember what I'd been thinking. He smiles, but then it fades. 'Don't let anyone in.' He pauses. 'See if you can find out anything about that kiddie porn site, too. It might be something.'

Or it might not, I think. But he's distracted, and I don't know what's going on.

'When will you be back?'

He shrugs and grabs the keys to the rental car off the bedside table. 'I'll call you,' he says, leaning over and brushing my cheek with his lips.

And then he's gone, the door closing behind him, and I'm alone.

For a moment, I consider following him, but there's no way he wouldn't see me. Absently, I pick up the TV remote and turn it on. I click through the hotel channels and find local morning news. I really just want it as white noise, but the scene on the screen catches my eye. It's familiar, the street that's filled with TV vans and reporters. I don't need to see the house to know exactly what's happening.

Tony DeMarco is coming home.

THIRTY-FIVE

I sit on the bed and stare at the TV. I find it more than a little fascinating that the local news has nothing else to feature, but Tony DeMarco has never been convicted of any crimes and has been a mover and shaker in the local political scene for years, so I suppose I shouldn't be surprised at the attention he's getting. Especially since someone tried to kill him, and that's no secret.

The camera is trained on the front of the house, and the door opens. Ian Cartwright, aka Roger Parker, saunters out as though this is the most natural thing in the world for him to be doing. I wonder exactly what his role is in Tony's world. Is it this? Is it warding off the media? Is it deflecting the bad and trying to point out the good?

I've missed the lead-in by the station's reporter, but the others are shouting questions. 'Have they arrested anyone yet?'

Ian turns at that and says loudly, 'No arrests. And you should ask the police why not.'

'Do you think they're holding back on the investigation?' The question comes from somewhere in the crowd; I can't see who asks it.

'There has been no word from the police about the investigation,' Ian says. 'You should go stand on *their* doorstep and ask what they're doing to find out who tried to kill Mr DeMarco.'

I mute the TV, wanting to concentrate on the scene, not the questions. Ian is a natural at this, and I watch him working the crowd. Again I wonder if he is Betr@yD and whether the real reason the screen went dark has more to do with this than the router running out of juice.

My attention goes back to the TV when the cameras swing suddenly, and I watch the arrival of a long, sleek black car that pulls up into the driveway. Ian is at the car's back door, opening it. A pair of long legs appears, and then Ian takes her hand and gently guides Adriana DeMarco out of the car. He leans down and gives her a quick kiss on her cheek, and she smiles up at him. I try to see if there's anything in that smile, but I am distracted by Tony DeMarco being brought out of the other side of the car. Adriana moves quickly around the back of the car so she is now at her father's side, taking his arm while a nurse has the other. Two bodyguards follow closely, their arms hanging stiffly, their heads swiveling to make sure no one is going to sneak up on Tony and try to kill him again. Ian waits at the door as Tony is helped up the steps.

Tony DeMarco is a far cry from the larger-than-life, boisterous man I remember from my youth. He has lost a lot of weight, which could be due to him being shot, or maybe he is sick, as I'd thought when I saw him last summer in New York. What had once been a full head of hair is now merely a few strands of white combed over his mostly bald pate. He is hunched over and has a visible tremor in one of his arms.

The camera is trained on the reporter now, whose mouth is moving, telling viewers what's going on. I don't need to hear her. Instead, I focus on what's happening behind her. Tony DeMarco disappears inside; Adriana pauses in the doorway, glances back, but then follows her father into the house. Ian is the last to go inside, leaving pandemonium behind.

I pick up the remote and hit the button, turning off the TV. I toss the remote on the bed, and it lands next to the laptop.

A nervous claustrophobia overcomes me. I jump off the bed and go to the sliding door, stepping out on to the balcony. The room is on a floor high enough that Biscayne Bay spreads out in front of me like a blanket, dotted with small islands. I remember a long time ago when the artist Christo surrounded them with floating pink fabric. My father hired a helicopter to fly us over the islands, giving us a bird's-eye view. It was the first and only time I've ever flown in a helicopter; the ear protectors were a little too large for my small head, and the vibration shook my entire body. But I wasn't afraid because my father put his arm around me as we leaned over to see the assault of colors: the dark green islands against the bright pink and cobalt water. I couldn't figure out how the artist did it, and in my head I imagined him a magician with a wand that cast out fabric like a spider produces a web.

I am struck by my childhood memory, and when I close my eyes, I can see it so clearly. I wish desperately that I had a canvas and my paints, because I could paint it, bring it back to life.

I'm not quite sure what to do now, except I have an overpowering need to escape this place. In my head, I know that Zeke left me here to keep me safe, but I am not comfortable being sequestered here any more than I was in the apartment in South Miami. My mind wanders as I go over my online conversation with Betr@yD.

The laptop is taunting me. I open it and hit a key, the screen springing to life.

But what I see is not what I expect.

It's a slideshow, with pictures popping up one after the other across the screen.

Pictures of kids. But these are not snapshots of children taken at the beach, on a swing set, in front of a Christmas tree. These are the photographs that the shadow – Betr@yD – was downloading from the kiddie porn site.

I force myself to concentrate on what's happened rather than the content of the pictures. We had managed to sneak inside a port to spy on him, but somehow he's turned it around on us. While I was having my conversation with him in the chat room, it's obvious he managed to find his way unseen back into this laptop and infect it with the kiddie porn.

I quickly power down the laptop, staring at it for a few seconds, my heart pounding, before I shove it into the backpack

that's on the floor next to the bed. Even though we've got a
VPN and the IP address has been rerouted, how do I know
that the hacker hasn't managed to compromise that, too?

Zeke was wrong. Betr@yD *could* know exactly where
I am.

I have to get out of here.

I sling the backpack over my shoulder and look around for
the room card key. There. I left it on the bedside table when
I went over to see what Zeke was looking at on the laptop.

But that's not the only thing there.

Zeke left his gun.

Did he leave it on purpose? Did he know I might need
something to protect myself? Not that I'm good with a gun,
but I don't have to actually shoot it. It could scare someone,
if necessary.

I tuck it inside the front pocket of the backpack, then realize
how noticeable it is. I don't want anyone to stop me because
I've got a gun. I put it into the next pocket, hoping that if I
need it quickly, I'll be able to get it easily. I'm not so sure.
All I know is that I am not going to put it in the waistband
of my bike shorts and risk shooting myself.

As I let myself out of the room, I am struck by the sense
that even though I have no idea what I'm doing or where I'm
going, it's as if a weight has been lifted off my chest.

I ride down the elevator, leaning against the back wall. There
is only one place to go.

Since I still don't have a phone that has an Uber app, I go
the old-fashioned way and have the concierge call me a cab.
He tells me to go outside and wait.

I'm standing in front of the hotel when I see her. Amelie.
She is coming out of the coffee shop next door. She's holding
a coffee in one hand, a briefcase in the other, a Louis Vuitton
bag over her shoulder. Suddenly, she turns and faces me.

I freeze. She gives me a small, tight smile, but I can't read
it. Is it a smile for a stranger who she's discovered is watching
her? Or does she recognize me?

I don't know if she knows about me. If she knows about
me and Ian, back in Miami, in Paris, on Block Island. Did Ian
ever tell her about me, or did he lead her on, telling her she

was the only one he would ever love? The way he used to talk to me.

I feel a little empathy toward her, since we were both duped by the same man for the same reason. He got her to provide those bank account numbers and gave them to me so I could steal for him. He ran away with me, but he ended up marrying her.

She is watching me so intently that she must know who I am. She studies my face, as though trying to see the woman whom her husband loved for a time. I shift uncomfortably, but I am unable to look away. I have the irrational thought that I have a gun in my backpack; that if I need to, I could defend myself. She has that sort of look in her eyes, one that tells me she will fight for what she believes is hers.

A cab pulls up in front of me. My ride. It distracts me and I look away for a second. When I look back, she is walking quickly in the opposite direction, her heels clacking against the sidewalk, looking cool in her white shift despite the heat.

Her presence makes me uneasy. No one else is on the sidewalk. This is a business district; it's morning. Everyone's at work. But as I look around, I see the logo for the bank where Amelie works. It's two doors down from the hotel. Relief rushes through me, and I find myself relaxing a little. Betr@yD has me too paranoid. I could also have imagined that she looked at me as though she knew me. My imagination is playing tricks on me.

I quickly climb into the cab, settling into the back seat, the backpack on my lap. I watch the meter as we make our way along the city streets. I'm going to have to take stock of my cash. I'm not making any money right now. I could take up Zeke's offer and get a bona fide job with his team, collect a regular paycheck, maybe even have healthcare benefits.

Those thoughts stifle me even more than being physically closed in a hotel room. I'm not cut out to tether myself to a job like that.

The palm trees hang over the road, and again I'm struck by how at home I feel. As the cab winds its way around to Coral Gables, I wonder if I could ever live here again. I dismiss the thought almost as soon as I have it. No, when I'm done here, I'm never coming back.

THIRTY-SIX

The house where Spencer lives looks a lot less appealing in the bright glare of the sun. The white paint on the stucco looks as though it was dipped in tea and is peeling. I take note, however, that the rest of the neighborhood is tidier, with its green lawns and landscaped plantings, smooth driveways, and pink and blue houses. Spencer's sticks out like the proverbial sore thumb, and I can't help but think that the neighbors talk among themselves about the mysterious guy who lives in the shabby home.

Zeke's rental car sits in the driveway. I'm not entirely surprised to see it here. I pay my cab fare and get out, leaving me vulnerable, out in the open. I have an unexpected sense of danger, but a quick glance tells me no one is around and I am being silly. Maybe.

I don't go to the front door, preferring to use the side entrance as we did last night. I walk swiftly around the house and note again that all the windows are covered. I can't see anything inside. When I get to the door, I don't bother knocking, just put my hand on the knob and turn.

It's not locked.

A faint smell of coffee permeates the kitchen, but there's no sign of a coffee pot or cups anywhere. Again, the strips of daylight that stream through the window are not kind to the house. The cabinets are worn, with gouges in the wood; the laminate floor is full of nicks; the countertop stained with rings that could be red wine or coffee or tea, or all of the above. It looked a lot nicer in the dark.

I move through the room and into the living room. Spencer has covered the windows with fabric, so it feels like night-time in here. He and Zeke are huddled next to each other, studying source code on a screen in front of them; they each have a keyboard in their laps.

'Come on in, Tina.' Zeke doesn't even look around. How did he know I was here? Did he hear the door open? But then, how would he know it was me?

I hesitate, and he turns. I expect him to ask me to explain my presence, but all he says is: 'Did you put a back door in the bank site last night?'

I shift a little, from one foot to the other. 'Maybe.'

He rolls his eyes and elbows Spencer, who's furiously working his keyboard, before saying, 'You'd better get over here and help, since you're the one who caused it.'

'Caused what?' I cross the room and Zeke pulls a chair on wheels over for me.

He jabs his finger at the screen. 'This.'

I scan the code and every muscle tenses. 'I didn't mean to do that.'

'So what, exactly, did you mean to do?'

I bite my lip and debate how much to tell him. The whole truth or just a portion?

'You can't bullshit me, Tina. The entire network went down. A botnet got in there. Through your back door. You made it easy for them.'

'Too fucking easy,' Spencer adds.

'The whole bank network is down?'

'The whole fucking thing.' Even though Spencer is trying to be angry, I can hear a hint of respect in his tone again. The back door was only supposed to be a place marker for me so I could find my way back in, but I have an unexpected sense of pride in what I did. The feeling subsides, however, when it's clear Zeke isn't thrilled.

'Tell us what you did.' Zeke isn't being patient, and he's definitely angry.

I sigh. 'OK.' I pause, uncertain how to say it, and decide I might as well just do it outright. 'I found the money.'

The shock is clear in their expressions. Before they can press further, I tell them. 'Last night, when you weren't looking, I found the money. But because I was here, I couldn't

do anything about it, so I may have created a little bit of a
back door so I could recognize it and get back in later.'

Zeke is frowning, trying to figure it out, but Spencer gets it.
'I knew it. Even though they updated their network, accounts
just don't disappear. How did you know it was yours?'

'The account number.'

'You remembered it after all these years?' Zeke is
dubious.

'I created it. It wasn't a legitimate account, but I tucked it
inside the code and made it look like it was. But it was sort
of a ghost; no one who was looking for it would be able to
find it.' I nod at Zeke. 'I really did send you the account
number and the code for the back door. I don't understand
what happened.'

'Someone got in there before me,' he says simply. 'That's
why there wasn't any money.'

I'm confused. 'But when I saw it last night, the two million
was in there. Like it had never been touched.'

'You're telling me that someone took the money out and
then put it back later?' Spencer said. 'That's fucked-up.'
Spencer might be a genius hacker, but he has a very limited
vocabulary.

I turn my attention back to the computer screens. 'A botnet?'
I ask. 'Who put that in motion?'

'Could have been anyone,' Zeke said. 'It might not have
anything to do with you or me or us at all. But your back
door let them in.'

So my little string of code allowed in an army of hacked
computers that apparently succeeded in waging a denial-of-
service attack against the bank where my secret account lives
– or lived – and took the whole network down.

I should feel guilty. Instead, a huge sense of relief rushes
through me. Although it was a thrill to have found the money,
I am better off without it, without the knowledge that it's still
out there.

I wonder, suddenly, why Zeke and Spencer are so interested
in this particular bank network. 'What's really going on here?
Why are you paying such close attention to this particular
bank? The one that . . .' My voice trails off.

'Tony DeMarco's got money in this bank. Legit money,' Zeke tells me. 'But we're keeping an eye on it, to see where it's coming from, where it goes. And this is not the only bank we're watching. He's got his money scattered all over the place.'

'So what have you found?'

'Nothing,' Spencer says. 'Guy's as clean as a whistle. At least on the surface.'

'What if he really is?' I ask. 'What if all this' – I wave my arm around to indicate all of Spencer's equipment – 'is a waste of time?'

Spencer grins. 'But it's not.'

'How do you know?'

'Zeke says you hacked into a computer at DeMarco's.'

'So?'

'And that whoever had hacked it was downloading kiddie porn.'

I am about to tell them about the laptop, but they exchange a look I can't read. Zeke nods, and before I can say anything, Spencer says, 'The botnet that took down the bank network? Flooded it with images of kiddie porn.'

THIRTY-SEVEN

'That's going around,' I say.

'What do you mean?' Zeke asks.

I tell them about the kiddie porn on the laptop. 'The hacker we were watching? Betr@yD? I'm pretty sure he's the one who did it.' I reach around, pull the laptop out of the backpack, and hand it to him.

We're all thinking the same thing. Whoever crashed the bank's network is the same person who hacked into that computer at Tony's.

'He must have known it was me on the other side of that conversation,' I say.

'If he's shadowing that laptop, compromising it, then he

knows what's on it. He knows that the data is yours.' Zeke confirms my suspicions.

'He played us for fools.' Saying it out loud makes me extremely anxious. Zeke's expression is dark. He's thinking what I am: that Betr@yD also knows who *he* is.

'He asked specifically about p4r4d0x, too,' I remind him. 'It's like he was telling me that he's behind everything: the shadow, Tony's hit.'

'And he feels betrayed.' Spencer's voice is low, but his words ring loud.

I think again about Ian. But he was busy with Tony DeMarco's homecoming right before Betr@yD showed up. If he were even capable of this, would he have had the time to do it?

'Who's keeping an eye on the kids while you're here?' I ask Zeke.

'I don't think it's Daniel.' He's not talking about keeping an eye on everyone. He's talking about who perpetrated the botnet, who compromised the laptop.

'Why not?'

'Because I've been monitoring his computer ever since he started.'

Spencer and I both roll our eyes at him.

'Yeah, I know,' he says, trying to defend himself. 'I've been shadowing him. I can see everything that everyone on my team is doing at all times.' As if to prove it, he puts the laptop down and hits a few keys on Spencer's keyboards. The screens in front of us change, and we're looking at the screens for each team member. At least that's what Zeke thinks.

'Any of them could be on to you, you know. We were watching the laptop and someone still downloaded kiddie porn into it right in front of us, without us knowing it was happening.' I can tell he's not thrilled that I've thrown this in his face, but I need to make the point so I don't feel as guilty about the back door.

'She's right, dude,' Spencer says. 'Any or all of them might have their own laptop stashed somewhere.' He gives me a sidelong glance. 'Sometimes I think he's been with the feds too long. He doesn't remember the shit he used to do, in case someone hacked *him*.'

'Someone did hack you – and me,' I say to Zeke, and I'm not talking about the laptop last night. 'Someone landed in that laptop at the bike shop, knowing where I was. Knowing that our names would be linked. How, exactly, did that person know where I was? You were the only one who knew, right? You didn't tell anyone?' I glance over at Spencer, then back to Zeke.

'He didn't know,' Zeke says. 'I really didn't tell anyone.'

'What did you do when you left me? When I gave you back the laptop?'

'You mean when you kicked me out?'

'Now this is getting interesting.' Spencer grins, leans back in his hair, and puts his hands behind his head. Zeke kicks the chair so he falls backward. 'What the fuck—'

I ignore him. 'Who knew you were coming to the Cape? Someone had to know I was there. Someone who knew what our relationship is.' I don't give him time to answer. 'You've been working with Ian, with his son. Did you make a flight reservation online? What about a car rental? Not when you came this time, but the first time.'

Zeke is uncomfortable now. He sees what I'm saying. That he wasn't careful.

But I'm not done. 'We may have hacked the hacker in DeMarco's house,' I say, 'but it's very possible that Daniel's been hacking *you* all along. And was still in that laptop even after you got your hands on it.' I have another thought. 'It's even possible that while we *thought* we were watching him through the router, he already knew we were there and set us up. He might not even be at Tony's house. He could be anywhere. He could be at the apartment.'

He pulls the keyboard toward him. As he tries to find out what Daniel's been up to, Tony DeMarco fills my head. Someone was 'hired' to kill him, but didn't succeed. The only thing he succeeded in was framing me – or my screen name – and Tracker. Someone's been impersonating Tracker and having conversations with my screen name. Whoever it is could have done it to pit me against Tracker. To make me fear him, to lose trust in him, to feel betrayed.

Betr@yD might be after revenge. Maybe he's getting it.

What sticks in my head is that the hit man did not kill Tony. Again, I wonder if this is because he wasn't supposed to. What if Tony DeMarco set this whole thing up himself, manipulating Ian – and, thus, Daniel? My father and Tony were master manipulators in their day. Even though he's now an old, sick man, Tony DeMarco's reach is as long as ever.

I'm not paying attention to the screens. I walk across the room, pull back the curtain over the front window, and peer outside. Spencer's car is still in the driveway; Zeke's rental is catty-corner to it, parked across the sidewalk. But something else catches my eye. A black car sits across the street, idling. It's a BMW.

I quickly let the curtain drop, hoping the driver of the BMW didn't see me.

'We've got company,' I say.

Zeke and Spencer look up at me, Zeke's fingers frozen over the keyboard. He jumps up from his seat and comes over. 'Where?'

'Across the street.'

He goes to the other side of the curtain and does exactly what I did, then lets the fabric fall back.

'It's Ian,' I say. 'It's the same car that was outside my room.'

'The same car that almost ran us off the road,' Zeke adds.

Spencer's eyebrows rise, but he doesn't say anything.

'Do you think he followed us? And he followed you here?' I ask.

'Possibly. Probably. How else would he know where we were?'

I shake my head. 'No, that can't be it. He was on TV. Right after you left.' I tell him that Tony DeMarco came home. I remember Amelie, though. 'She looked right at me. Like she knew me. I think she does.'

'So maybe she told Ian.'

'How would she know where I was going? I got in a cab.' I am confused. 'Maybe it's not him. Maybe it's one of Tony's other guys. Maybe he's been watching us ever since we got run off the road.' It would be like Ian to have someone do his dirty work for him.

'We can check the cell number, see where he is,' Zeke suggests.

I can't use the laptop with the cell phone locater program because it's been compromised. But that's not a problem for Spencer, who has a more sophisticated program at his fingertips. I look in the disposable phone, where I stored Ian's number, and rattle it off.

After a few seconds, a map appears on the screen, and a small dot begins to blink, but to my dismay, it's not here. It's back at Harbor Point. Back at Tony DeMarco's house. Then who is outside right now?

'Tina, where's my gun?'

I fish it out of the backpack and hand it to him, as though this is the most natural thing in the world. Spencer's gaze is fixed on the screen that shows where Ian's cell phone is.

'What do you see?' I'm mimicking Tracker by asking; the question came out of my mouth before I could stop it.

Spencer jabs at the screen, at the blinking dot. 'It's not really there,' he says, back to the keyboard, and suddenly he's in the source code of the site, searching for IP addresses. I'm trying to follow what he's doing, but my head is not in the game in front of me, but outside, across the street.

'Holy shit,' Zeke mutters, and I force myself to focus on the screen.

The map flashes back on the screen. Spencer leans back in his chair and threads his fingers together behind his head. 'Whoever's cell phone it is, they're clever,' he says. 'But not as clever as me.'

He's waiting for the pat on his back.

Because he's managed to trace the phone's signal – and it's not where it appears to be.

It's across the street.

'So it *is* Ian?' I'm still uncertain how he managed to pull this off.

'These programs have a lot of glitches,' Spencer says, downplaying his find. But then reality sets in. 'Maybe it's this guy you're talking about, maybe it's not. Either way, I don't know who's watching you, but I really don't need the attention.'

'It's not the agency,' Zeke assures him, although the alternative is not attractive, either.

'I don't really care who it is; I need to maintain my anonymity, and you two are threatening that right now.'

'So what, exactly, do you propose we do?' Zeke is asking Spencer. 'We can't just go out the front door and go about our business.'

'Why not?' I ask. Both heads swivel toward me. 'I mean, whoever is out there knows we're in here. But he doesn't know that we know about him.'

'Tina's right,' Spencer says. 'Maybe you could go out and get in the car and leave. Take your friend with you.' He really is squirrelly for some reason. I need to ask Zeke more about what he's up to.

'We could go back to the apartment,' I suggest. 'Daniel's there. I think you're right that we need to talk to him. Anyway, if Ian was going to do something, he has had the opportunity and he's not taking it.'

Zeke smirks. 'So you think that we're just fine and dandy?'

I shrug. 'We don't have any other choice.'

'OK.' Zeke pauses and picks up the laptop, setting it on the table next to Spencer. 'Maybe while you're looking for the money, you could also take a look at this.'

Spencer gives it a wary glance. He doesn't want to turn it on any more than I do.

Zeke ignores him and gives Spencer a fist bump. 'Whatever. Tina and I will call later and see how it's going.'

'Later, man,' Spencer says, but he's not even paying attention to us anymore. He's back to his computer screens. Again I envy him.

Zeke is still holding the gun, and he indicates that he's going to go first. I lay back a little, giving him some space. When we get outside and go around to the front of the house, however, the black BMW is gone.

THIRTY-EIGHT

The car is gone, but the threat remains. He's watching us, and there's nothing we can do about it. Even though he hasn't made a move beyond trying to run us off the road, the psychological toll is doing a number on both of us. He is in control, and we are on the defensive.

Zeke constantly checks the rear-view and side-view mirrors, but there's no sign of the BMW. I remind him about my theory about Tony DeMarco, about how, perhaps, he wasn't supposed to die.

'Yeah, I've been thinking about that.'

'It might be a set-up. To trap us.'

'The man did get shot.'

'He's Tony DeMarco. There are probably plenty of people who want him dead.'

'But he's sick.'

'Cancer?'

Zeke nods. 'He doesn't have long to live. It's possible he arranged that hit himself, but maybe not to get at us.'

'To sort of commit suicide?' I ask.

'Crossed my mind. I've been over so many scenarios, though, and none of them really sits well. Why does Tony DeMarco give a shit about either of us, especially if he's going to die anyway? Yeah, we stole from him, but it's not like he doesn't have money. He already got his revenge on your father.'

'Well, either way, if he thinks that I tried to have him killed, he's not going to let it go. He's not going to let me off, even if he *is* sick.'

'You're right about that,' he says thoughtfully.

We are right back where we started. We don't know any more than we did that morning in Falmouth when the FBI interrogated me. 'Do you think that whoever did this figured that you'd come get me?' I ask. 'Maybe he wanted us both in the same place? Betr@yD knows you're FBI. Knows who you are.'

'That would mean that somehow he found out about Tracker,' Zeke says.

'Maybe you haven't been covering your tracks as well as you thought.' The moment I say it, I see his face fall and I regret it. But I can't take it back now. I keep going. 'Let's say Ian planted Daniel on your team for a reason. And it wasn't to help his kid.' Again I feel sorry for Daniel. I've been in his shoes.

I've been in his shoes.

'I used to hack into my father's accounts,' I say, thinking out loud. 'I knew *everything*.' I was younger than Daniel when I started hacking; I'm not naïve enough to think that he's just started on this road, too. He had to have garnered quite a few skills in order to hack into his school's system and change grades.

It's almost frightening how parallel my life was with his at that age.

'So let's say Daniel's been hacking into Ian's accounts – not only Ian's, but DeMarco's, too,' Zeke says, caught up in my theory now. 'He knows DeMarco, but maybe he didn't know everything. And then he finds out a lot more than he was expecting. Maybe he went to Ian about it—'

'And the only way Ian can protect him is to turn him over to you,' I finish for him. It makes sense. 'But Ian also protects Tony by telling Daniel that he can't reveal what he's found.' I think another minute. 'It's possible that Daniel found out who you are online. You've been in close quarters with him; you've been working together. It's not beyond the realm of possibility. I think Daniel knows a lot more than you think.'

We mull that over a few seconds, then Zeke says, 'I'm going to drop you at the apartment. I want you to keep an eye on Daniel.'

We've been concentrating on how Daniel might know about Tracker, but if he does, then he might also know who p4r4d0x really is – not the imposter, but me. I'm not thrilled with this plan, especially since Zeke's going to 'drop me off.'

'Where are you going?'

'I have to talk to Ian.'

This is not a good idea, but I can see by the way his jaw is set that there is no way I'll be able to talk him out of it. 'I'd tread a little lightly on this. He can be pretty volatile. I mean, I really do think he's the one who tried to run us off the road. And I think he was the one in that car across the street from Spencer's. He's not stable.'

Zeke gives me a tight smile. 'I know. Don't worry.'

But I do.

We are at the apartment, and Zeke pulls into the parking lot. He gets out of the car, which is my cue to get out as well. He comes around to my side, and before I take a step toward the building, his arm circles my waist and he pulls me to him. He leans in and kisses me. When he stops, I reach for more, but he merely smiles, tracing my jaw with his finger and causing electric currents to run through my body. This is not how it ever was between us.

'I brought you here to keep you safe,' he whispers, his breath tickling my ear, his lips against my neck. 'I'm sorry.'

And then as quickly as he grabbed me, he lets me go and begins walking toward the apartment building. It takes me a few moments to grasp that I need to follow him, that I can't stand out here in the parking lot. I jog a little to catch up with him, and he slows down. His hand wraps around mine. I'm not sure what to make of this; it almost feels more intimate than the kiss. I try to remember if we held hands before, back when we were younger, but I can't. There were hours in bed, motorcycle rides to the beach, but all of it is eclipsed by the memory of how I shot him on that houseboat on the Seine.

I watch his profile as we climb the stairs and wonder what my life would have been like if I'd gone with him, if I'd left Ian right then and there. Zeke knew who I was, but would he ever have told me? I can't imagine that I would never have found out he was Tracker. Neither of us would have been able to stay away from a computer. Would Zeke and I – or Tracker and I – have ended up like a virtual Bonnie and Clyde? Him running from the FBI, me from my father and Tony DeMarco and Ian? It sounds so romantic, but the reality would not have been.

We reach the apartment, and he lets go of my hand. Despite the heat of the night, my fingers grow cold.

Zeke pushes the door open. They are lined up behind the computer screens: Jake, Charles, Heather – and Daniel. None of them looks up; they are all wearing headphones. It smells like popcorn and weed. Despite our misgivings about Daniel's loyalties, I can't help but think that he's one of us, regardless, and maybe we should give him a pass. That Ian is exploiting him is not his fault.

He is watching us over the top of his screen. Zeke cocks his head at him, indicating that he should follow us into the other room. Daniel gives me a curious look, then gets up. He's again wearing a white button-down shirt and chinos. He's the anti-Spencer.

When we get into the bedroom, Zeke closes the door behind us. Daniel slouches against the wall, his arms folded across his chest, a sullen expression settling into his face. I've had very little exposure to teenagers in the last few years, but I remember the attitude well.

I'm not quite sure what to say, how to start. Zeke senses my hesitation, and he tells Daniel, 'Talk to Susan. I'll be right back.' He slips back out, leaving me face to face with Ian's son. The resemblance is so striking, now that I know.

'What exactly are you working on for your father?'

His expression changes slightly. 'I don't know what you mean.'

I give him a small smile. 'My dad wanted me to do something a long time ago, and I did it. I didn't think I could say no. It didn't turn out so well for me, but I think Zeke could help if you talk to him.' I have no idea if that's true.

Daniel looks dubious, and I can tell I'm not getting through to him. I have no idea how to talk to him, so I just come right out and ask, 'Have you found out who Tracker is?'

Daniel bites his lip and shifts from one foot to the other. He really is so young, and I find myself getting angry with Ian for manipulating him like this. I am almost certain that Daniel does know about Zeke.

'Have you told your father what you've found?' I ask when he doesn't answer me.

Before he can respond, Zeke comes back in, an anxious expression on his face. 'Go back to the other apartment.' He presses a key in my hand. 'Ian's here.' He glances over at Daniel, whose eyes widen. I can tell that he's afraid we're going to tell Ian that we know. I feel bad for him, but not enough to stay.

I start to go, but it's too late.

THIRTY-NINE

I hear one knock and the doorknob turns. Daniel is right behind me, so I can't back up. I duck into the bathroom and shut the door. Maybe it's childish, maybe I should face him, but I don't want to do it here. Not in front of his son. Or Zeke.

Still, I put my ear to the door to try to hear what's being said. I'm unsuccessful, however, as the sound is muffled. I lean back against the wall and take some deep breaths. Zeke tells me I'm not a fugitive, but I certainly feel like one right now.

A knock on the bathroom door startles me, and I freeze as it opens. Heather's face appears around the corner.

'Susan? You OK?'

I brush down the front of my T-shirt and take a step forward. 'Yeah, sure.' I keep my voice down, straining to hear what's going on out in the living room, but I don't hear anything.

'They're gone.' She pauses. 'What's the problem, anyway? It's just Daniel's dad.'

'No problem.' I try to keep my tone light. 'I needed to use the bathroom.'

She doesn't believe me, but she doesn't push it.

I wash my hands to keep up the ruse, flush the toilet, and follow her out. For the first time, all eyes are on me, curious. I wonder again what Zeke and Ian said to each other. This was not played well.

Daniel is standing in the middle of the room. He looks at

me quizzically, as though trying to figure out exactly how much I know about what he's been doing for his father. I've handled this wrong. He's going to tell Ian that I questioned him about Tracker. I've probably played my hand. I don't want to get in any deeper. I still have the backpack over my shoulder, so I shift it a little and say, 'If Zeke's looking for me, I'm in my apartment.' I doubt that my departure is going to be considered as casual as I'd like it to be.

'Have you two found something?' Heather is bold. She stares me down.

I shake my head. 'No. Dead ends. Like all of you.'

I let myself out of the apartment and move into the hall that overlooks the courtyard with the fountain. I can hear them: Ian and Zeke. They're arguing. I shift the backpack higher on my shoulder, and instead of going directly to the apartment, I move along the hall to find a place where I can eavesdrop better.

They are directly below me now, and their voices carry on the still air.

'I don't know what you're talking about.' Ian's voice is clear. 'Where do you think I was? Some seedy motel?'

'It's not seedy, but it is a motel. Why were you there?'

'I wasn't. I don't know what you're talking about. I've been at DeMarco's since he came home. You do know he's home, right?'

'It was before. Before he came back.'

'Before what?'

'Before DeMarco came home, you were at the Palm Court Resort.' Zeke's voice is laced with exasperation, but he's not going to get anywhere. I've heard every lie out of Ian Cartwright's mouth, and he's not lying. There's no explanation for it, but he's telling the truth. I don't have to see him face to face to know that.

'I really don't know what you're talking about.'

'OK, fine. But if you're lying—'

'I'm not.'

'What do you have for me, then? Now that DeMarco is home, what's he doing about the hit?' To his credit, Zeke has switched gears, but he's being too confrontational. If this is the way he is with Ian, then there's no wonder he has to rely on his computer skills for information. If I try to intervene, though, he'll take it the wrong way. I tiptoe back to the apartment, careful to open and close the door without making any noise.

The air conditioning hits me in the face as I enter, and goosebumps rise on my arms. I hadn't realized how hot it is outside. I drop the backpack on the sofa and head to the glass doors. The small balcony overlooks the parking lot, and I slide the door open a little, letting in the heat. I peer over the railing, but from here I can't see Zeke or Ian. I can't even hear them anymore. I shut the door and take a deep breath.

The bicycle I rented and have yet to return leans against the wall. I run my hand along the handlebars, the cold steel comforting. I could use a ride right about now, but I'd have to go past Ian and Zeke. I couldn't go quietly.

It's late in the afternoon, and I rummage through the refrigerator for something to eat. I find a package of strawberries and pop one into my mouth. I don't expect it to be so sour and my lips pucker. A bottle of seltzer is in the door, so I pour a glass and take it into the living room. I put the glass on the coffee table. It's already begun to sweat, despite the air conditioning. I sit and wait.

He finds me here, in this spot. He stops in front of me.

'You want out?'

It rushes over me: the desperate need to escape. I can't speak, so I merely nod.

He watches me for a few seconds, then holds out his hand. 'Come on.'

I don't know what he's up to, what he's suggesting.

'It's time,' he says gruffly. 'You have to go.'

Does he really mean it? I grab the backpack as I reach for him. He takes my hand and pulls me behind him, out the door, and down the stairs. We're moving so fast that my feet can barely keep up.

We get to the car, and he takes the keys out of his pocket. 'Dump the car at the airport. You'll have to travel as Susan McQueen, but you can change your name as soon as you get wherever you're going. Find another island.' He shoves the key at me, and I take it, although I'm still uncertain whether he really means all this.

'Go,' he says. But he doesn't mean right this second, because he pulls me to him and kisses me, holding me so tight I'm afraid I might break in half. He finally breaks away, and I struggle to catch my breath, but he doesn't let go completely. 'You have to go now.'

I still don't completely understand.

'Ian knows you're here, and he's confirmed that DeMarco's got a hit out on you. Go as far away as you can and never come back.'

FORTY

I am vaguely aware that I have begun to shake. I put my hand on his arm to steady myself and look into his eyes. 'What about you?' I whisper.

'I'm fine. Get to the airport. Get on the first flight you can.'

'But won't he know where I'm going?' Daniel's upstairs. Ian's probably got him checking on flight lists as we speak.

'You just need to get out of the city right now.'

Tony DeMarco's empire stretches far and wide. Miami is not the only place he can find me.

'He's after you, too,' I remind him.

'He's after Tracker.'

'Daniel knows who you are, which means Ian does, too.' I am as sure of this as I am of anything.

'I'll be OK,' he says.

'You have to be careful.' I hear the fear in my voice – fear for him as much as for me.

He reaches up and touches my cheek. 'I will be, but you have to go,' he says. He reaches into his pocket and pulls out a cell phone. He hands it to me. 'Take this. You'll need something.'

I remember the disposable. 'I've got one in my bag.' All

I have to do is fill it up with more minutes. I take it out and put his number into it. 'How's that?'

'OK.'

'I can't go to the airport,' I tell him. 'That's the first place they'll look.' I have another thought. I shove the keys back at him. 'I'll be right back.'

I take the stairs two steps at a time. When I reach the apartment, I push open the door and see the bike. I wheel it out and down the stairs, where Zeke is waiting for me. I tug on the helmet. He reaches over and fastens it under my chin.

'I don't know how far you'll get—'

I put my finger to his lips. 'I've been here before.' I give him a small smile. 'I know how to disappear.' Already a plan is formulating in my head, but I can't let him know. Not yet. In case someone comes too soon. He needs to be unaware of where I am.

I straddle the bike, and he kisses me again.

'Go,' he whispers, and I mount the bike and begin to pedal. I don't look back, even though I desperately want to. He is in as much danger as I am. He says Tony's got a hit out on me, but I'm willing to bet that he's also got one out on him.

I see the car as I cross the South Dixie Highway. A black BMW, tinted windows. It might be Ian. It might not be. My heart pounds; I can't take any chances.

I don't think the driver has seen me. If he has, then he may not be registering that I'd be on a bicycle. Nevertheless, I pump the pedals hard as I go up one side street and down another, zigzagging my way around the neighborhood and into the next.

Despite what Zeke thinks, I have no illusions that I can get far enough on the bicycle. It feels wonderful to ride, but it's not practical.

I pedal down Bird Road, finding my destination with little trouble. The windows are still covered. I hop off the bike and wheel it around to the side of the house, tucking it next to the palm trees that line up against the fence that separates the property from the neighboring one. It's as hidden as it can be.

I rap on the door three times before I hear movement inside.

The curtain over the door's window moves slightly; I can see his eyes, then the knob turns. He opens the door only a sliver, searching behind me for the person who's not here.

I don't have time for this. Because he's not expecting it, I easily shove the door open and push my way inside. 'I need your help,' I tell Spencer.

His hair is no longer pulled back into a ponytail and is longer than I thought, falling down just past his shoulders. He's got a five o'clock shadow that is patchy. His green eyes are glassy and his mouth twitches as though he wants to smile. He's stoned. His T-shirt wants me to stay calm and carry on. Maybe the carry on part, but the staying calm is a challenge.

'You shouldn't be here,' he says, but indicates I should follow him into the other room.

'I need your help,' I try again.

'You need more than my help, Tiny. What, you've got a bicycle? Seriously? How far do you think you'll go on that?'

I roll my eyes. 'That's why I'm here.' I don't bother explaining further, just grab a chair and park myself in front of a keyboard. He hovers over me as I check out Craigslist for a used car. It's probably the least hacker thing I could be doing right now, and it clearly disturbs him. He pulls the keyboard away from me.

'What do you think you're doing?'

'I have to ditch the bike. I'm not going to get too far on it.'

'What happened?'

'Gig is up.' I don't have to explain further.

'What about Tracker?'

I shrug. 'He says he's OK.'

'For now, maybe. Maybe not.' He hesitates. 'You need wheels, you take mine.' He digs keys out of his pocket and drops them in my lap.

'What'll you do?'

'Bike. Fair trade.'

'The bike is stolen property.'

He grins. 'I wouldn't expect otherwise. Where are you going?'

'I don't know.' And I don't. I considered Key West, but it's isolated with little means of escape if I need to get away. A boat to Havana isn't out of the question, especially now that we can go there legally, but it's not an ideal solution. I'm going to get in the car and just drive.

I give Spencer a nod and start to go, but he says, 'Don't you want to know what I found?'

I don't. I really don't. Yet I turn back. It's almost as though the source code on the screen has magical powers. Maybe it does. 'What did you find?' This is my downfall, my addiction at its worst. I have an out, a way to escape, and still I can't leave.

'I found the money.'

My heart skips a beat. 'The money that disappeared?'

'After it reappeared.'

'I thought you said it went in circles.' I'm closer now, peering at the screen in front of him.

'Whatever.' He waves his hand like a game show model. 'It still went in circles. I mean, whoever it is has a VPN. I managed to trace it, though. The money went into a bitcoin wallet.'

It is all I can do not to shove him out of the way and take over the keyboard myself. He senses my impatience. He points to the code on the screen. I scan it, but I can't make sense of it. 'What's going on?' I ask.

'This money went through a site on the deep web. A kiddie porn site. Doesn't that sound familiar?' He pauses, letting this sink in. 'Whoever's working on it is smart. But not smarter than me.'

He hits a few keys and it's clear.

Spencer is a genius. He's managed to track the bitcoins through a tumbler. Right back into a bank account owned by Roger Parker, aka Ian Cartwright.

FORTY-ONE

Daniel must have done this. And if he did, he is as much a genius as Spencer. Ian is taking a huge risk, though. If Tony finds out what he's done, he'll target Ian just as he's targeting me. Perhaps because Daniel is his son, Ian feels safe, confident that no one will find out.

Zeke needs to know what's going on. He needs to know what Spencer has found. I shift the backpack around and take the disposable phone out of the front pocket. Spencer gets up and goes into the kitchen. While the phone rings, I hear him opening and closing cabinets.

'Staying for dinner?' he calls out.

It's getting dark outside, and my stomach growls, reminding me about the sour strawberry, the only thing I've had to eat for hours. I should be going, though, after I talk to Zeke. I don't have time to answer Spencer, because Zeke finally picks up the phone.

'We've got something,' I say. 'Well, Spencer does.'

'You're with Spencer? You need to get out of there.'

'But we've found something. Daniel—'

'Get out of town. Now.' He hangs up as the fear rushes through me. I head to the kitchen. 'Something's wrong,' I tell Spencer. 'Something's not right.'

'He wants to keep you safe.'

'Tony's after him, too. He's implicated in all this. What if—'

'He can take care of himself. He's been doing it for years.'

The way he says it makes me wonder. 'How long have you known him? I mean, in person, not online?'

Spencer pulls a plate out of the microwave. Spaghetti and meatballs. He raises his eyebrows, and my stomach growls again. I can't hide it. He puts half the portion on another plate and hands it to me, along with a fork, then leads me back into the room in front of the screens.

'We met in juvie,' he says when we're settled.

'Prison? What did you do?'

He laughs. 'Not nearly what I'm doing these days, but I'm better at it now. Better at not getting caught.' When he realizes I'm waiting for an answer, he says, 'I took down a major website. Denial of service. Like this guy' – he cocks his head toward the screen – 'did with the bank.' I want to ask which site, but he's already moved on. 'I did three years. Tracker did a year, but he had better connections than me.'

'Did he take down a site, too?' I'm curious about Spencer, but I'm more curious about Zeke.

Spencer nods. 'Took down the feds. The FBI. Showed them where they had a hole in the system, how he could get around the firewall. Really showed them up.'

'Wouldn't they give him more time, then?' I can't see the FBI being magnanimous toward a kid who hacked their system.

'Not if your father is a fed.'

Again I'm reminded about how little I know about Zeke's background, about his life. I've always felt that the criminal in me was genetic. Zeke's criminal past probably came more from rebellion. Either way, I'm lucky that I only got expelled from university after my hack into its system. And then I have another thought. They could have put me away, too, but my father pulled strings, just like Zeke's.

'Why does he still do it, then?' I don't realize I've asked it out loud until Spencer answers.

'He can't stay away. But he's trying to do it for good instead of evil.'

'He's riding a fine line.'

'That he is. He's obsessed with taking down DeMarco.'

'What happened when he was undercover? Do you know?'

Spencer's expression goes still and he shakes his head. 'No.' He gives a short snort. 'It's your fault.'

'What?'

'He went after DeMarco because DeMarco was after you because of the bank job. You disappeared, but he was always afraid your body would show up somewhere. He wanted to make sure you were safe, wherever you were.'

I put my plate on the desk next to the keyboard and stand. 'I don't need a guilt trip.'

'No guilt, Tina. Just fact. Guy's had a hard-on for you ever since he was a kid.'

'But he got married.'

'And he left her after he found you. You think that was an accident? Him showing up at your house like that? You left a trail of bread crumbs. He followed you there.'

I always told myself I didn't know how Zeke had found me, but maybe I'd done it subconsciously. I'd left that trail for Tracker, not Zeke, but I didn't know they were one and the same. I can't stay here any longer. I don't want to hear any more. I can't be held responsible for what's happened to Zeke, and I can't be responsible for what will happen when Tony DeMarco finds out who Zeke is.

'I have to go back.'

He's not as stoned as I thought he was, because he moves fast, jumping up and grabbing me around the waist. 'No. You're going to do like he said. Get in the car and leave Miami.'

He lets me go abruptly, and I stumble, struggling to balance myself.

'I'll tell him. Let him know what your ride is. He'll find you.'

'What do you know?'

'No more than you, but if he's telling you that you have to go, then listen to him. He's got ears everywhere.' Spencer's eyes flicker toward the screens. I doubt I'll get any more out of him. What I need is to get online.

I no longer have a laptop, since it's been compromised.

'Can I at least check out a few places to stay?' I indicate the computers. 'Just tonight.'

Spencer's a little edgy right now; his eyes are darting all over the room. Maybe the paranoia that comes with being stoned has set in. I can only hope.

'Why don't you finish your dinner and I'll just take a minute,' I tell him.

'I'm not sure that's a good idea.'

I'm already seated. Before he can stop me, I'm inside the

code, checking out his history. Spencer's been busy – not that I don't already know that from what he's told me, but busier than I thought.

He pulls the keyboard out from underneath my fingers and holds it in front of him.

'Too late,' I say. And it is. I've already seen enough, and I'm already plotting my escape. I should have left but I had to know. I hate it when I'm right.

He's p4r4d0x.

FORTY-TWO

The good news is that I don't think he has a weapon nearby. He could try to hit me with the keyboard, but that's not going to do anything.

The bad news is, he's been plotting my death.

I take a couple of steps backward, clutching the car keys. Zeke told me he was Angel, but so many of us have more than one screen name. 'Does Zeke know?' I ask.

'Of course he does. It was his plan.' His tone is so matter-of-fact that it takes me aback.

'And what is that?'

'I've been chatting with Tracker as p4r4d0x.' He lets that hang between us a few seconds. 'Not Zeke – the other guy,' he feels compelled to explain when he sees my confusion. 'Every time I get him online, I try to get his IP address. I've even gotten into his computer with a RAT, but it's never him. He's got some serious security. I also can't find the real p4r4d0x.'

I don't want to point out that there is no 'real' p4r4d0x.

He's still talking. 'p4r4d0x hasn't been online, except for me, since the hit was ordered. Fortunately, Tracker doesn't seem to realize this. I think I've been pretty convincing.' He takes a moment to pat himself on the back. 'Anyway, I think Tracker's working alone now, even though he thinks he's still working with p4r4d0x.'

'So what happened to p4r4d0x?' Against my better judgment, he's got me intrigued.

'Your guess is as good as mine.'

We let that sit between us for a few seconds. I don't like the implications. I remind him about my conversation with Betr@yD. 'He knows Tracker is FBI.'

'But does he know there are two of them?'

'Does it really matter? Someone out there knows Zeke is Tracker.'

'No, someone out there knows that Tracker is FBI, but we don't know for sure that he knows he's Zeke.'

I hadn't thought about it like that. It's an interesting premise and might explain why Ian hasn't yet gone after Zeke. But it doesn't make sense. Zeke's been really careful as Tracker not to drop any clues about himself. No, if Betr@yD knows Tracker is FBI, he must also know Tracker is Zeke.

I turn my attention back to the computers. 'Can you find Tracker? Right now?'

'OK, but then you have to do what Zeke says and leave.' Spencer swivels around in the chair. I feel a tickle at the base of my neck. I reach for the keyboard, then pull my hand back. Spencer hits a few keys and suddenly we're in the chat room.

'Go ahead,' he says, 'check it out.' He nods, reaches over around the screen, and pulls out a joint. He holds it up, offering me some.

I shake my head. 'I have to drive.'

He shrugs and lights up, one hand on the keyboard. I slide into the chair next to him. And suddenly there's Tracker, joining the chat. I lean forward and glance over at Spencer, who raises one eyebrow as if to say, *See, you can believe me.*

'So p4r4d0x is you?'

'Right.'

'And this Tracker, it's not Zeke?'

'No. Just watch.' He asks Tracker to go into a private chat. He gives him a URL link, and I can see he embedded a remote access Trojan. If we're lucky, we'll get inside his computer. 'Don't get your hopes up,' he warns. 'This guy is slippery.'

Tracker shows up in the chat room, and says, *I've got the money.*

Spencer and I look at each other. 'Shit,' he says softly, then begins to type.

p4r4d0x: Where is it?

Tracker: In a safe place.

p4r4d0x: That network crash was pretty impressive.

Tracker: Some of my best work.

p4r4d0x: So what about her?

I assume that the 'her' he's talking about is me, and I take a deep breath, not sure I want to see where this goes but unable to look away.

Tracker: I'll take care of her.

p4r4d0x: Where is she?

Tracker: Don't worry about it. I've got it taken care of. By morning, it will all be over. She'll be gone, and we've got the cash.

p4r4d0x: What about him?

Tracker: I've got a plan for him, too, don't worry. Later.

And then he's gone. p4r4d0x lingers for a few seconds, then he disappears, too, when Spencer puts the keyboard back on the desk. He leans back, blowing smoke rings.

'You didn't exactly catch him at anything,' I say.

'But we know he's got the money, and he definitely set off the botnet.'

'Betr@yD is the one who dumped the kiddie porn in the laptop, so—'

'He's Tracker. *This* Tracker,' Spencer finishes.

We also know Ian Cartwright has the money because of the deposit in the bitcoin wallet. But he couldn't set off a botnet – that I'm sure of. He probably got Daniel to trigger the denial-of-service attack on the bank to try to circumvent the money when the network was down.

I still doubt Ian would put out a hit on Tony DeMarco, but I have no doubt that he would put one out on me – and Zeke.

As long as I'm in Miami, I'm vulnerable. Zeke is right. I have to leave the city as soon as possible. Still, I feel so helpless. There has to be something I can do. And then I know what it is. I reach for the keyboard. Spencer watches me, intently, but I don't know if he's truly curious or if he's just really stoned. Probably a little bit of both.

'So, did you get it?' I ask.

'Yeah.' Remote access Trojans are too easy, and although I've thought that 'Tracker' is so smart, he has just let us inside his computer. But Spencer is shaking his head.

'What's wrong?'

'It's like it always is.'

But maybe it's not, because I recognize the computer we've hacked into.

It's Betr@yD's.

FORTY-THREE

'This is the computer we got into through the router.' I tell Spencer about how I put the router near Tony DeMarco's house.

'That's why you wanted it,' he muses. 'So this guy is remote accessing someone else? And using that computer to get into the chat room?'

He's a little slow, and I attribute it to the fact that he's stoned. Admittedly, it's a little complicated and I'm about to add to the complication.

'Yes, and also dumping kiddie porn into our laptop and the bank network.'

'Our friend has been a busy bee,' Spencer says, spinning in his chair and setting the keyboard on the table in front of the screen. He's checking out Betr@yD's computer.

'Check the history,' I tell him.

He scowls at me because that's exactly what he's doing and he doesn't need me to micromanage. I lean over his shoulder and scan the websites in the history file. It's been wiped clean except for the chat room, but Spencer knows what I do: deleting something on a computer doesn't really get rid of it. Before he can do anything, though, we watch a browser pop up on the screen and a map appears. My heart beats a little faster when whoever is navigating the site types in an address.

It's not until the location is pinned by a small icon that it registers. Spencer sees it at the same time I do.

It's this address.

It feels as though a huge weight has landed on my chest, and I can't breathe for a second, then I ask, 'How did he trace us?'

'No fucking clue,' Spencer mutters. 'There's no way he could have gotten through my VPN, the firewalls.'

But somehow he did. He's better than we thought. So much better. This can't be Ian. Can it be Daniel? Is he *that* good?

We don't have time to figure it out, though. 'Whoever it is knows where we are,' I say softly.

Spencer's eyes grow wide, taking in all his equipment. It's probably taken him years to build up this operation. He's stunned that someone has managed to hack him – and seemingly so easily.

'We have to leave,' I say. Zeke's warnings resonate in my head. But now they include Spencer. Whoever it is can't find him here either – can't find all of *this*.

Spencer is one step ahead of me. He's already clearing hard drives. 'I'm on Tor,' he says, more to himself than to me. 'What the fuck.'

He's got a lot more to lose than I do, since he's part of Incognito.

He gets up and starts unplugging everything. I don't say anything, but I begin to help him, shutting off the monitors. 'Do we leave it all here?' I ask.

'We don't know what kind of time we've got,' he says. It could take a while to wipe everything clean. He leaves the room and comes back with a couple of screwdrivers. He hands me one. I have already started pulling out all the wires. I know what we need to do. Without saying anything to each other, we move quickly, until we have a pile of hard drives on the floor. Spencer finds a plastic bag, scoops them up, and puts them into the bag.

'It's road trip time.' Spencer pulls on a sweatshirt, yanking the hood over his head.

'It's a hundred and fifty degrees out there,' I say.

'I live in Miami. This is, like, fucking winter.' He is walking toward the door, the bag of hard drives slapping against his thigh, a laptop under his armpit. He takes one last look back at his monitors, and then he's got his keys in his hand, and we go outside. I've got the backpack over my shoulder.

'When was the last time you were outside? You're probably allergic to the sun, like a vampire or something.' I don't think I'm too far from the truth. I recognize the signs: empty pizza boxes from a place in Coconut Grove that delivers and bags from the local supermarket's delivery service.

He ignores me.

Once in the car, he turns to me before starting it up.

'Where are we going?' I ask.

'Trust me,' he says, and we're on the move.

For the first time in a long time, I actually do find myself trusting someone. Spencer was as surprised as I was to see that he'd been hacked, that someone was probably on his way to his house. I wonder again about who could have had the skills to get through his security so easily.

'Use your cell and call Zeke. Tell him what's going on,' Spencer says.

I pull it out and find the number.

He answers quickly. 'Where are you? I hope you're long gone.'

'Working on it.' I am about to tell him about the hack.

'I told you to get out of town.' Something in his tone makes pause.

'What's going down, Zeke? Have you found out something?'

'No.' His answer's too quick, too final.

'What's up?' I press.

'I can't say. Not right now. But trust me, it's not good and we're all in danger. Where are you?'

I glance over at Spencer, whose eyes are shaded by a surprisingly classic pair of Ray-Bans. I would have expected something more John Lennon-like.

'We were at Spencer's,' I say, 'but Betr@yD found us there.

We broke down the hard drives and are on our way . . .' I stop, not sure.

'Tell him Hollywood,' Spencer says. 'He'll know where to meet us.'

'He's not taking you to Hollywood, is he?' Zeke is asking.

'That's right,' I say.

I hear a heavy sigh. 'I'll see you there.'

'You can't tell me *anything*?' I don't want to hang up until I get an answer. I don't like being in the dark, and Zeke is a little bit too much about keeping everyone in the dark. I know it has to do with the fact that he's FBI, but we're all involved and we all need as much information as possible.

'You're not going to like it,' he warns.

'I haven't liked anything about any of this, so what makes this different?'

'I've been with Adriana.'

It takes a few seconds for this to register. 'DeMarco?' I ask, the name curdling on my lips as soon as I say it.

'She needed my help.'

A hundred questions pepper my brain, and the one that comes out is 'And are you helping?' It is not the question I really want an answer to, but it's out there and I have to live with it. For now.

'It's not what you think.'

I don't know what I think. I only know that there is a pit in my stomach that's getting bigger with each moment. I tell myself there is a logical explanation for this. That I am a reasonable woman who, especially after this morning, should not feel threatened.

Yet still I do.

'I'll meet you in Hollywood and explain,' he says. And then the call ends.

I take the phone away from my ear and hold it limply in my hand, the landscape whishing by in a blur as we head north.

FORTY-FOUR

By the time Spencer parks the car, I am overwhelmed with claustrophobia. This has more to do with the fact that I don't have the whole story, that, despite my best efforts, my imagination has run away with me. Why would Zeke be with Adriana? And why couldn't he have just told me on the phone?

The sky has grown darker as the day winds down. When the car finally stops, I stumble out and make my way to the beach. I am only vaguely aware of Spencer following me as I pull off my sneakers and dig my toes into the sand. The salt water rushes over my feet, and I feel the pressure as it tries to pull me back with it. I want to go.

Spencer is standing next to me now, his sandals in one hand. He's smoking a joint with the other, offers it to me. I stare at it for a second, then take it. It's been a long time, and I choke on the smoke that's invaded my lungs. I give the joint back to him, doubled over until it passes.

He chuckles. 'You are going to get *so* high.'

I stand back up, and I get a head rush. I'm not used to this; I'd make do with a glass of brandy, a beer. Grown-up highs.

'How long has it been going on?' I ask him.

'What?'

'Adriana DeMarco.'

Spencer nods. 'Oh.'

'How long?'

He hesitates only a second before answering. 'He hasn't been with her since he found you.'

Even though I asked him outright, I didn't really expect this and it hits me in the gut.

He's still talking. 'It was his undercover thing. I don't know what it's all about.'

'But he told you about her.'

Spencer takes another hit and offers it to me again, but I shake my head. He shrugs. 'I've known him a long time,' he adds. 'He doesn't just screw around.'

That really doesn't make me feel better. I try to empty my head, breathe in the salt air, willing it to calm me, as it has so many times before.

'Let's go.' Spencer grabs my hand, but it's not what I think. Instead of leading me back to the car, he's guiding me further into the water.

I stop short, yank my hand away. 'What are you doing?' I'm trying to sound angry, but I'm too high. This was definitely not a smart move.

'Let's go for a swim.' He pulls his T-shirt over his head, revealing a pasty white torso with a little bit of a gut. He is so white that he almost glows in the dark.

I can't help myself. I start laughing. 'You live in Miami. How can you not be tanned?'

He gives me a grin and runs into the surf. I move a little closer, and while I don't plan to go in, I soon feel the water rushing around my calves. It feels so good. I watch Spencer splashing several feet away, his head under and then back up, tossing his long locks around his head. I think about the backpack in the car – and the disposable phone. If Zeke is trying to call, then no one will answer.

My head is spinning with the weed, and I am so relaxed. Far more relaxed than I've been for days. Without realizing what I'm doing, I drop down. The water is warm, womb-like, and I sit as it rushes over me. All I can think is, when I can get up again, I'm going to make Spencer take me to a hotel, sleep it off, and leave in the morning.

I don't know how long I've been sitting here when a long shadow crosses in front of me. I stiffen, uncertain.

'Water nice?'

Zeke wades in next to me, his chinos yanked up around his knees, his shoes in his hand. Spencer is suddenly there, too, in front of us, and he shakes himself off like a dog.

'Dude,' he says to Zeke.

'How did you find us here?' I ask.

Zeke and Spencer share a look that tells me they've been

here before, that this place holds memories that maybe I'll never know about. 'OK, fine, so keep your secret,' I mumble.

I hear a quick intake of breath. 'Jesus. You're stoned.'

'I am not.' But even I can hear the singsong tone that indicates I just might be.

'Uh-oh. I'm in trouble, aren't I?' Spencer asks.

Zeke rolls his eyes. 'I can't leave you alone.'

'Dude, your shadow found us. He was coming after us.'

'So you thought it was a good idea to come to Hollywood?'

Spencer shrugs. 'Thought we should get out of the city.' He gives me a glance, then says, 'You two need to have a conversation.' And with that, he wades past us and goes up on the beach. I twist around a little to see that he doesn't stop, but heads for the boardwalk.

Zeke leans over and holds out his hand. 'Come on, Tina. Let's take a walk.'

I don't like to think that I need his hand to steady me as I get up, but I do. Spencer was right. I am really high.

Zeke continues to hold my hand as we walk along the water's edge. 'There's nothing going on. There's a reason I saw her.'

'I bet there is.'

'I'm not that big an asshole.'

For some reason – probably the weed – this strikes me as hilarious and I begin to laugh.

'Someone hacked into her laptop.'

That stops me short. 'What?'

Zeke pulls his hand out of mine and folds his arms across his chest. 'OK, here's the deal. Adriana thinks I'm with tech support.'

'Tech support? Where?'

'I may have been wearing a polo shirt with a logo on it when she was bringing her laptop in for servicing.'

I narrow my eyes at him. 'You *may* have been? Or you were? I can't believe you're poaching business.'

'She thought I had just gotten to work. We were still in the parking lot. I offered to fix her laptop at a discount.'

'You didn't take her money?'

'It would've looked suspicious if I hadn't.' His lips twitch, as though he wants to smile.

'And it wasn't suspicious that you were lying in wait in the parking lot and just happened to be able to fix her computer? How did you know? That she needed tech support?'

'It was over a year ago. I had the brilliant idea that maybe I could get to her father through her, and maybe her laptop might help me get inside. But she's clean. Really clean. But since then, if she's got a computer issue, she calls me.' He hasn't answered my question, but by saying this, he's addressed another one.

I shake my head. 'I can't believe you're keeping it up.'

'Maybe I still hold out a little hope I'll find out something about her father.'

'Fair enough. But you could have told me.' I pause. 'So she called you today?'

Zeke nods. 'She has a shadow, and whoever got in there is asking for ransom.'

A little chill runs up my spine. 'Let me guess. He wants a million in bitcoins.' Exactly what my shadow asked for last year.

'That's right.'

My head is spinning. I had assumed that my shadow was asking for the money in response to the bank job and what I'd stolen. Adriana DeMarco didn't steal from anyone, especially not her father. 'What does this mean?'

'It means someone is playing all the angles.'

FORTY-FIVE

'Is it hers, the computer that we saw through the router?' I ask.

'No, I don't think so.'

I hear someone coming up from behind, and I turn to see Spencer jogging toward us, his breath loud and ragged. 'Come on, dudes. Taco Beach Shack.' He looks directly at me. 'You've got to be hungry.'

The moment he says it, I realize I'm starving. The

spaghetti at Spencer's wasn't nearly enough, and tacos suddenly seem like a wonderful idea. Zeke rolls his eyes, but he follows us.

The Taco Beach Shack is more of an upscale beach shack, with couches and pillows under a huge canopy. The small wooden building looks more like its moniker, a row of barstools surrounding it, 'Happy Hour' in neon on one of the open windows. We find an empty table and sit, reading the menu on surfboards. When the waitress finally arrives, Spencer takes over and orders shrimp tacos, nachos, and beers. I am salivating with the thought of the food, and Zeke watches us both with an amused smile on his face.

'I had no idea you'd be so susceptible to his charms,' he says to me, but then his expression darkens. 'I don't know what you two were thinking, whether you even thought about what would happen. A RAT? Seriously?'

'It was a good idea,' I say. 'We didn't know he'd be able to hack us.'

The waitress shows up with the beer, and when she leaves, Zeke leans in toward us and says, 'So tell me exactly what happened.'

Spencer and I take turns relating how we'd tricked 'Tracker' and put the remote access Trojan into the link.

'He used it against you.'

'We were inside his computer. Tina says it's the same one you saw through the router,' Spencer says.

'It was Betr@yD,' I add. 'I think he's Tracker, too.'

'So how did he get through your firewalls and VPN?' Zeke asks.

'Beats me.' Spencer sighs. 'Years I've been at this, and no one has ever caught me. Not since . . .' His voice trails off and I know what he's thinking. Not since he got caught and thrown in prison all those years ago.

'You had to have let him in somehow.'

'I know. But I can't figure it out.'

'You wiped everything clean, right?'

Spencer gives him a look that says *I'm not stupid*. 'Bag of hard drives in the car.'

'What I don't understand,' I say, 'is the connection between my shadow and the one inside Adriana's laptop. Who is targeting both of us? Tony wouldn't do that. Would Ian?'

Zeke leans back and takes a drink from his bottle. 'Maybe he's covering all his bases. Maybe he's trying to get as much money as possible so he can get away. Make his own life.'

'But he's got kids. It's easier alone.'

We all look at each other. That's it. What if he's not planning on taking anyone with him? What if his plan is to leave them behind? Make a new life somewhere, like I did? He already has a name that's not his own. I know how easy it is to take on another identity.

'What's awful,' I say, 'is that he's using his son for his own purposes, even if that's not what he plans on doing.'

'I've got access to Daniel's computer in the apartment, but I also managed to get into his laptop,' Zeke said. 'That wasn't easy; he's got a lot of security. A lot more than I expected. But I can shadow him, see what he's up to. I've got a laptop, and you've got yours, right?' He's asking Spencer. 'After we eat, I've got a place we can go.'

My hands begin to sweat with the thought of it. For someone who just days ago had sworn off hacking, I'm in it so deep right now and I still feel that thrill. I tell myself again that I will still walk away after all this. I will cut myself off. But is it an empty promise?

Our food comes, and conversation ceases, although I can tell from the thoughtful expressions that we are all trying to work out how we're going to go about catching the shadow at his own game.

After we've paid our bill, we head back to the parking lot. When we reach the cars, Zeke tells Spencer, 'I'll take Tina and you follow.'

As I'm strapping on my seat belt, Zeke leans over and brushes my lips with his.

'Hey,' he whispers.

I give him a small smile. 'Hey, back.' I hesitate.

'What?'

'Spencer seemed to think that something was going on. I mean, with you and Adriana. He said you hadn't seen her since you found me.' I wait for him to contradict this, but he's silent a little too long. 'He's not right, is he?'

'No, no, he's not right,' Zeke says. 'I don't know why I let him think that.'

'But he did know about her?'

'He helped me a couple times. I mean, helped me hack her. That's when I found out there wasn't anything there. To do with her father, anyway.' The way he says it, I know he found something else.

'What is it?' I prod.

Zeke shifts in his seat and looks at me. 'She knows about you, Tina. She knows she has a sister and that it's you. She had all those news stories about your father on her computer. She had the stories about the bank job.'

For a second, I wonder if I can meet her. If I can come out of hiding long enough to let her know that I know about her, too. Zeke senses what I'm thinking and says, 'You can't do it. She said a couple of things to me, things I'm not going to tell you, but I can say that it wouldn't be a good idea to meet her.'

She doesn't want anything to do with me. I let that sit a few seconds before I give him a shrug. 'OK. I've lived my whole life without a sister, so it's not a big deal.' But as I say it, I know I'm lying to myself. He knows, too.

To his credit, though, he doesn't press it. Instead, he straightens back around and starts the car. He presses the accelerator, we shoot forward.

The side-view mirror tells me that Spencer, who's been waiting on us, is close on our heels, but something else catches my eye.

A dark BMW is coming up behind Spencer, gaining ground on us.

FORTY-SIX

'Um, Zeke,' I say, indicating the car.

He's already seen it. 'Hold on,' he says, and we are going faster.

Suddenly, I hear a popping noise. I sit up straight in my seat. 'What's that?'

I can barely get the words out as the car skids to the side of the road. Zeke is struggling with the wheel. More pops.

'Get down,' he orders, his hand on the back of my neck, shoving my head to my knees. He's hunched over, too. I thought we were going to stop, but the car is still moving. I can feel the blown tire in the back, hear the scrape of metal against the pavement.

This is different than the last time we were chased. They're shooting this time. It's Tony's hit on us. Someone's actually trying to kill us.

I wonder where Spencer is, if he's witnessing this from behind. I desperately want him to call the police, but somehow I think the last call Spencer would make is to the police.

I peer up over the dashboard and then into the side-view mirror. We are zigzagging along the road, but I see Spencer's car coming up fast next to the BMW, which has gained ground. Spencer passes it, and I hear a screech of brakes. The BMW spins and lurches into the median. It doesn't matter that we're driving on metal; Zeke speeds up. Blue and red flashing lights come up behind the BMW, and we leave it behind us.

'You OK, Tina?' Zeke's voice is tinged with concern.

I take a couple of deep breaths. 'Yeah, I think so. What just happened?'

Zeke chuckles. 'If I'm not mistaken, that BMW just ran over a couple of Spencer's hard drives.'

'That's one way to destroy them, I guess,' I say. 'Do you think that was Ian?'

'I don't know. Could have been Tony's guys.' He pulls into the parking lot of a small strip mall. Spencer comes in behind us. 'Time to go.'

We get out and climb into Spencer's car, although Zeke makes him get in the passenger seat so Zeke can drive. I'm in the back, looking out the window, making sure that the BMW isn't going to spring another surprise on us.

'I guess the rental company isn't going to rent me any cars for a while,' Zeke says.

'That's what happens when there's a hit out on you,' Spencer reminds him. 'It's just not good for business.'

Zeke sighs. 'I can't believe you went rogue on me, then went to the beach and got stoned. I told you to go somewhere safe.'

'How was I supposed to know Hollywood Beach wasn't safe? It's always been safe before. Someone must have followed you.'

'No one followed me.'

'Well, we didn't have any trouble until you showed up.'

'You were too stoned to notice.'

'I would have noticed.'

They are like a bickering old married couple. I am more than curious about how Hollywood Beach plays into their history, but although my heart has finally stopped pounding, I can't keep the anxiety at bay, worried that whoever is after us will find us. Wherever we're going.

Which seems to be somewhere in North Miami. And not a great neighborhood.

Zeke pulls into a parking garage and gets out, sliding the seat up so I can climb out. He takes the backpack so it's easier for me and slings it over his shoulder. I feel naked without it. I want to take it from him, but it would be a childish move.

The three of us head up a stairwell. It's an apartment building, white stucco that's clearly seen better days. On the third floor, we go down a hallway. Zeke stops in front of a door and puts a key in the lock.

I find myself wishing for the apartment in South Miami, because this one is dark and smells like old socks and cigarettes. Zeke turns on a small light and it basks the room in a golden glow that under other circumstances and in another environment might be romantic. Here, however, it only accentuates the worn, sagging sofa and stained coffee table. I don't even want to know what the beds look like.

'Can't the FBI swing for a nice hotel?' I ask.

Zeke grins. 'It's a safe house.'

'For Palmetto bugs, maybe.'

'Beggars can't be choosers.'

'I choose to go to a hotel.'

But he's not paying attention. He and Spencer have pulled laptops out and are setting them up on the coffee table. Zeke looks up at me. 'Can we find that cell phone locator?'

Instantly, my exhaustion disappears. I squeeze on the sofa next to him, trying not to think about what might be living inside the cushion. I download the program and again put Ian's cell number into it.

The phone is on the move down the South Dixie Highway. I'm a little surprised, considering where we'd left him just south of Hollywood. If, in fact, he was driving that BMW. Perhaps Zeke was right, though, and it was Tony's guys.

'Maybe he's going to the apartment,' I say. 'Do you think he's going to see Daniel?'

'Maybe. Maybe he thinks we went back there.'

'He thinks we're stupid, then.'

Zeke chuckles.

But then the little dot changes direction, heading now to another familiar location.

Spencer's house.

'Damn,' Spencer says.

We all share a glance.

'Did you actually see a car there, or were you just tracking online?' Zeke asks us.

'Tracking,' Spencer and I say in unison.

'We did see a BMW there before,' Zeke muses softly, thinking out loud.

Spencer is very quiet. I reach over and put my hand on his arm. 'I'm sorry,' I say. I can't even imagine what he's going through. To his credit, he gives me a wan smile and reaches in his front pocket. He produces another joint, his eyebrows rising with the question. Zeke shrugs and grins. 'What do you say?' he asks me.

'What the hell.' I feel like I'm in my teens again, rather than over forty. 'There's nothing we can do tonight anyway.'

Spencer takes a drag and hands the joint to Zeke. 'That's what you think,' he says. I forgot that he probably does his best work like this. Me, I curl up at the end of the sofa and rest my head on the cushion.

'Wake me if you find something,' I say and immediately fall asleep.

Someone's nudging me. 'Tina, wake up.' I open my eyes and squint, trying to focus. Zeke is leaning over me.

'What's going on?'

'You have to see this.'

I unfold myself so I'm sitting next to him. Spencer is on the other side of Zeke, engrossed in something on his laptop screen.

'Remember how I said that the money went into a bitcoin tumbler and from there it went into Roger Parker's account?' Spencer asks.

'Sure.'

'Well, it didn't stop there.'

I frown. 'What do you mean?'

'We only traced the money to its first stop. Which was Parker's account. It hadn't gone anywhere beyond that at that point.'

I don't say anything, just wait for him to finish.

'Since then, the money's moved again.' Spencer looks at Zeke, who takes over.

'Tina, the money went into an account with *your* name on it.'

FORTY-SEVEN

I set up the original bank account, but my name had never been attached to it, for obvious reasons. It was an offshore account in the Channel Islands that I created online. I haven't had an actual bank account in my own name in over sixteen years. 'Whoever's doing this is setting me up. It's easy to create an account online through a back door using anyone's name.'

'You didn't let me finish,' Zeke says. 'It's a local bank. A bank here in Miami.'

I'm not sure what he's trying to say.

'The account was opened in person.'

In person? I still don't get it. 'What do you mean?'

'It was opened this morning. The person who opened it went to the bank. In person.'

Spencer takes over. 'The money was transferred into it at noon. The transfer was done online, but the account was opened legitimately, with a deposit of a hundred dollars.'

'How is that? They need documentation, right?' I struggle to remember how to open a bank account. It's been so long.

'Driver's license and social security number,' Spencer says. 'And you had both of them.'

I get a sick feeling in my stomach. 'What do you mean, *you*?'

'The account was opened in your name. Tina Adler. The documentation matches. I already got into the Social Security Administration website and the number they used is a match.' Spencer pauses.

Someone really is impersonating me. It's gone from impersonating me online in the chat rooms to physically impersonating me. Which begs a question.

'The photo ID, the driver's license, whose picture is it?' I ask.

And then it's on the screen, the image I expect: Adriana

DeMarco. It's the picture that Zeke and I found in the code when we were hacking the hacker. Someone made up documents using my actual information and Adriana's picture. I turn to Zeke.

'You were with her today. You *saw* her.'

'She didn't say anything about opening a bank account in your name. That never came up.' He is trying to sound angry that I've asked this, but he is clearly flustered.

'But she told you someone hacked her laptop and was holding it for ransom. I wonder if this was before or after she opened the account in my name.' I pause. 'I guess you never thought that she might be using you. If she knows enough about me to open an account with my name, then she might know about my shadow; she might have already known what happened with *my* laptop.' I realize I am very quick to judge her, but it seems that she's guilty of something. Possibly everything. 'Does she know anything about hacking? Maybe she's a hacker, too.' It would be rather convenient for Ian to have two hackers at his fingertips. Right. Ian. I remember now how she rattled off his cell phone number so quickly without having to look it up. He is such a master manipulator that it's very possible he's got everyone working a different angle for him.

'She knows about me,' I say. 'That might explain how we both got implicated in the hit on Tony. Maybe she knows you're not just some random IT guy.'

'I've been really careful,' Zeke says. 'She doesn't know who I am.'

'But she does know who Tina is,' Spencer tells him.

I remember something else. 'Patricia Hale,' I remind Zeke.

'Who's that?' Spencer asks.

'Adriana went to Block Island to get information about me from my friends there. She told them that her name was Patricia Hale. That was my mother's name.' I pause. 'If she knows so much, we can't assume she doesn't know about you, too. How well does she know Daniel? What if she saw you and Daniel together and then asked Daniel about you?'

I remember how she called Tony DeMarco 'Daddy.' If she thinks I had anything to do with ordering the hit, then that could be motive. The only thing it doesn't explain is who put the hit out on Tony. She wouldn't do that. Not even to get back at me. But then I have a thought. What if she did? That could explain why he's still alive.

Zeke is busy with something. I'm trying to follow what he's doing, and when I finally think I've got it, he's found it.

It's video of Adriana DeMarco at the bank.

'How did you get that?' I ask.

He grins. 'I'm FBI, Tina, don't you remember? I've got access to systems.' I make a face at him. 'OK, this is the camera that's on the ATM machine inside the foyer when someone goes into the bank. All I had to do is check for the time that the account was first opened and that's the time I looked for on the video.'

I open my mouth to ask just how he's able to access this when Spencer shakes his head. 'Don't bother. If I was able to get inside as easily as he can, I'd be a lot richer.'

'So we know it's Adriana,' I say slowly. 'What do we do about it?'

Zeke gets up and climbs over me. He disappears into the small galley kitchen and comes back with three beers. He hands one to me and another to Spencer.

'You're going to have to see her,' Spencer tells him.

Zeke looks at me. 'It's Ian. He's pulling the strings.' He isn't willing to admit that it could be Adriana, for some reason.

'She's not entirely blameless,' I say, not wanting to let her off the hook. 'She did do this.'

'You of all people must know how he can be.'

The implication is that Ian has seduced Adriana, just as he seduced me all those years ago. Did Adriana go along with it, like I did? Is she in love with him? Is she willingly betraying her father?

Or does he know about it, too?

I voice my thoughts. '*Tony* might be the one who's pulling the strings, at least on this,' I say. 'If he thinks that I put out the hit, this could be his way to get back at me.'

'But the money—'

'The money might not be the same money. Spencer said it went in circles. All Ian had to do is have his son manipulate the code to throw off anyone who might have noticed it. He could have set it up so you and I *thought* that the money was back, when it really wasn't.'

'So it's all a trick to get back at you?' Spencer speaks up.

'And get Tony DeMarco to order repercussions.' Zeke swallows the last of his beer. He leans over and puts the bottle down on the coffee table next to my laptop. That's when I notice the gun has reappeared, although now it's neatly in a holster at his waist. It's too bad he couldn't have used it while we were being shot at, but it would have been hard, since he was driving. 'If I'm going over there, then I have to have it,' he says, explaining even though I haven't asked.

'Over where?'

'He has to see Adriana.' But Spencer is distracted. He's trying to figure out how Zeke has gotten into the bank's video system.

I get up and face Zeke. 'Why? We can access her bank account.'

'*Your* bank account. And yes, we can, but I have a feeling that's what they're expecting. The moment we get in there, they'll capture the IP address and that'll be the end of us.'

'I never thought Tracker would be so pessimistic about his own skills.' I turn to go back to the sofa, but he grabs me around the waist and pulls me down the dark hallway. The scent of old socks is worse here, but I don't have time to focus on that, because Zeke is kissing me, pushing me up against the wall, his hands underneath my T-shirt. I struggle against him and manage to move my head so he's no longer kissing my lips.

'Adriana,' I whisper. 'She probably knows who you are. You have to be careful.' I don't have to say that she's Tony DeMarco's daughter. That violence is part of their world.

He leans his forehead against mine. 'I'll be OK.' And he kisses me again.

'Spencer's out there,' I whisper as his lips find my neck. He stops, and despite the darkness, I can see the intensity in his eyes.

'If I don't get back in an hour, you and Spencer have to leave. Somewhere far away.' He kisses me one more time, then lets me go, leaving me trying to catch my breath, worry seeping into my head.

I hear him say something to Spencer, but by the time I'm back in the living room, the door is closing and he's gone.

FORTY-EIGHT

'You let him go?' I demand.

Spencer is still fiddling with the laptop. He doesn't acknowledge me.

'You let him go?' I ask, louder this time.

'I'm not his keeper. Neither are you. He's a big boy. He's a fucking FBI agent.' He still hasn't looked up.

'But he's got a gun.'

Spencer does look up then, an amused smile on his lips. 'What do you think he does for a living? He chases down the bad guys. He knows how to use that gun. They trained him. That's what happens when you sign up.'

'But he's a hacker.'

'They don't know that. Well, they do a little, because he's got that team. But they don't know what he can really do. What he's done.'

He's alluding to the bank job. 'When did he tell you about that?'

'I knew something was up. That he was helping you with something. I had a feeling it was something illegal, but he wouldn't tell me and wouldn't listen to me. If they find out, he'll be cut loose, probably sent back to prison, and no one can help him this time.'

'Don't lay a guilt trip on me,' I say. 'He didn't have to help me.'

'Yes, Tina. He did.' Spencer's stare is unnerving, and I have to look away.

'So what do we do for an hour?'

He chuckles, and I roll my eyes. I find two more beers in the fridge and bring him one, sitting down next to him. We clink bottles and drink, and I notice what he's been doing online.

'What's that?' I ask.

'That kiddie porn site – you know, Unicorn. I'm trying to trace the IP address, but it's cagey since we're in Tor.'

'It's not impossible,' I say, reaching for the keyboard. We've got an hour, after all.

We are no closer to finding the IP address after the hour has passed. We've each had two beers and finished off a bag of chips we found in the cupboard. Spencer lit up a joint, but I don't want any. I don't have the tolerance to it that Spencer has. It dulls my senses too much, and I want to be on alert for when Zeke gets back.

I remember something Spencer said about getting rich. 'How do you make a living?' I ask him. 'You can't just have that house and a bunch of computers. Or are you breaking into banks and stealing?'

'Only you do that.'

'I've supported myself as an artist for the last sixteen years. I also gave bike tours.'

His eyebrows reach up into his forehead. 'Really?'

'He didn't tell you?'

'He just said he'd found you last summer. He didn't say where or what you were doing.'

'I lived on Block Island for fifteen years. Off the coast of Rhode Island,' I add automatically because I'm not sure he knows where it is. 'I didn't have a computer. I didn't go online at all.'

'No shit?'

'No shit. Found out that there's life after hacking.'

'So why are you back at it?'

Good question. And Spencer seems to really want to know. So I tell him about how Ian found me, how he gave me a laptop, how I can't seem to stop, that the addiction is back, maybe even worse than ever.

He's quiet for a few seconds, then says, 'I built a company. I decided, like Zeke, to use my skills for good rather than evil. After I got out of prison, I started doing computer security work, finding back doors and getting rid of them so hackers couldn't get in. It was huge. *I* was huge.'

Now I know why he seems so familiar. I had figured it was because of the way he was living, with the bank of computers in his house, but that's not it.

'You're Spencer Cross.'

He takes a hit off his joint. 'I *was* Spencer Cross. Now I'm just a stoned, middle-aged hacker working with Incognito, staying under the radar and hoping that homeland security doesn't find me.' The way he says it, he's concerned about those cars at his house. That they have nothing to do with me and Zeke and everything to do with him.

Spencer Cross publicly released documents that showed the government was covering up the fact that it wasn't vetting refugees like it said it was. He discovered this when a mass shooting victim's family hired him to investigate how two terrorists were able to get into the country disguised as refugees.

I might not be a fugitive, but Spencer Cross is. 'Zeke—'

'Would lose his job, probably get arrested for obstruction, if they ever find out he knows where I am.' He grins. 'He seems to have a thing for criminals like us.'

I don't point out that by helping me, Zeke is as much a criminal as the two of us. That he also spent time in prison so he's not exactly free and clear, either.

'It's been an hour,' Spencer says softly.

'Should we give him a few more minutes?' I don't want to think about leaving without him, without telling him where we're going. We don't even have a plan. And then I have an idea. 'Didn't Zeke say he had access to Daniel's computer?'

Spencer doesn't hesitate. He grabs Zeke's laptop. We need a password to get in. Spencer gives me a grin and within minutes is inside. 'He's too predictable,' he says, although I know he's downplaying it. Zeke wouldn't have a password that's the name of a pet or a birthday. I don't have time to speculate, though, because Spencer's already found Daniel's desktop. I am in complete awe of his skills, forgetting that I am vowing to forego it all when this is over.

'It doesn't look like he's been doing much except poking

around in the deep web. He hasn't found much.' Spencer checks out Daniel's history, which shows a few sites via the Waste Land.

'If he's Ian Cartwright's puppet, then he's not doing a great job,' Spencer says.

This doesn't make sense. Daniel is Ian's plant on Zeke's team. Or is he? I think again about Adriana.

'It's just like the money,' I say. 'Everything goes in circles.'

Spencer frowns. 'Zeke says this kid is talented. I don't see it. But maybe it's not on the surface.'

'Maybe there's something . . .' I lean over and take the laptop. Spencer doesn't stop me. I try to think like Daniel, like I used to think back when I was a teenager – with a cocky confidence. I learned how to hide in plain sight. What if Daniel is doing the same thing?

It's easier to find because I'm looking for it. I turn the laptop toward Spencer so he can see, too. He gives a low whistle. 'Holy shit,' he whispers.

We weren't the only ones who got into the cameras outside the bank. Daniel did, too. But he took it a step further. I am sorry now that I blamed Adriana for anything. Because what Daniel did was genius.

He was able to put Adriana's image inside the footage, like someone creating a game would create an avatar.

She wasn't at the bank. It was a mirage.

FORTY-NINE

D aniel has set up Adriana, like Tracker and I were set up, and this could be a trap. He probably knows Zeke has access to his computer. I think again how Betr@yD knows Tracker is FBI, which makes me think he's made the connection to Zeke. An ominous feeling has settled in my gut.

'Zeke's in trouble,' I say softly. 'That's why he's not back yet.'

Spencer pulls a cell phone out of his back pocket. He tosses it in my lap. 'Call him.' When I don't respond, he adds, 'His number's in there.'

He's listed under 'Chap,' which is really not original at all. 'What, you think because you use part of his last name—'

Spencer holds up his hand. 'That was his nickname.'

Again, something I don't know about Zeke. I find myself wanting to know more about him beyond Tracker. I hit the phone icon and hear it ring, but it doesn't even go to voicemail. My worry increases.

'Track it,' Spencer says. 'Cell phones are just little computers. You can hack into them as easily as a laptop. Remember how the feds wanted to get into that phone that the terrorists in San Bernardino had? I could've gotten in there so fast it would've made their heads spin. Zeke even offered, but they said it wasn't his job.' He snorts. 'They have no idea.'

By the time he's finished lecturing me, I've already installed the same application on Zeke's phone that I put on Ian's. The phone's location pops up on the map on the laptop screen.

Spencer gives me a funny look. 'OK, so you know how to do that.'

'You doubted me?'

'I forget sometimes.'

'That you're not always the smartest person in the room?'

He rolls his eyes at me.

'Looks like he's in South Beach,' I say, pointing at the icon on the screen.

'I don't want to go to South Beach.' The way he says it, you'd think it was the third circle of hell.

'What's wrong with South Beach?'

He magnifies the map so we can see the exact location. 'Shit. It's a club. He's at a club.' Spencer sighs. 'I don't like those kinds of places. Too open, too many people. Too many people who might recognize me.'

I give him a sidelong glance. He doesn't look like the Spencer Cross in the newspapers and magazines. That Spencer Cross was bigger than life. That man was dressed in slacks and polo shirts, with a hip, short hairstyle, clean-shaven. It's hard to see that Spencer in this one with the five o'clock shadow, long ponytail, tattered jeans, and grungy T-shirt.

'I don't think you have anything to worry about,' I say.

'You're one to talk. You've been hiding for years.'

I have another thought. 'Why would Zeke be at a nightclub? I figured he went to see Adriana.'

'Unless that's where he found her.'

Spencer's got a point. But her father is still recovering. Would she leave him to go party?

I don't know Adriana at all to know what her lifestyle is. It's possible that Tony is doing a lot better – it's not as if we've been keeping tabs – and he encouraged her to go out on the town for a little fun.

Or it's possible that Zeke contacted her and arranged to meet there.

The latter is probably closer to what's happened, since I'm sure Zeke wouldn't go to Tony's house. He would definitely have Adriana meet him somewhere.

Spencer is still dubious about going.

'We probably won't even get in,' I say, indicating our salt-water-crusted clothes. 'We're not exactly red carpet candidates.' But then I have an idea. 'Maybe, though, it might not be a bad idea if we were.'

'What does that mean?' He's suspicious.

'I think it would be better if we fit in. Because like this, we'll stand out a lot more.'

He reluctantly agrees. 'I am going to seriously regret this, aren't I?'

'Possibly. Probably.'

I scoop up the laptop, grab Zeke's, and put them in the backpack. Spencer shoves his laptop under his armpit, grabs the bag of hard drives that are left, and we head for the parking garage.

Spencer's car is still there, which means Zeke must have arranged other transportation. Was it in anticipation that we'd need the car? I shake the thought aside as I settle into the passenger seat. Spencer leans over and opens the glove box. The light inside illuminates a small handgun.

'Take it,' he instructs.

'No.'

'You're not going to shoot anyone. We just need to scare people. Make them *think* that we'll shoot them.'

'Why?'

'We don't know what's going on with Zeke. This might be the only language they'll speak.'

'*They*? Who is *they*?'

'The bad guys. The ones who are after you.'

I don't want to get into it further. 'Have you ever shot a gun?' I ask.

'Well, not exactly. I got it for protection, but I never needed it before.'

'So you haven't even gone to a shooting range or anything?'

'No.'

This does not instill any confidence in me. The two times I've shot a gun, I've shot people accidentally. I don't know the first thing about shooting. 'We're not cops,' I say. 'We're hackers.' I shut the door of the glove box. 'We're not carrying a gun.'

Spencer shrugs. 'Suit yourself,' he says, starting the car.

Lincoln Road Mall on South Beach is like nothing I've seen in a very long time: an outdoor mall with spectacular fountains and palm trees and restaurants, bars, and shops. Although this is my idea, I share Spencer's feeling of panic. We are recluses suddenly thrust into the middle of a bustling throng of people. I crave peace and quiet, and this is anything but.

We go into the first store we see and are overwhelmed. The backpack on my shoulder looks shabby, but at least I have some cash inside. I only hope it's enough. From the look of things, it may not be.

Spencer monitors Zeke's phone on his own cell. 'We have to hurry,' he says. 'We don't know how long he's going to stay there.'

I pull a pair of black slacks off the rack and find a plain black T-shirt, shoving them at Spencer. 'Try those,' I say.

He holds them as though I've given him poison, but he finds his way to the fitting room.

A saleswoman approaches me. 'Can I help you?'

I push my glasses up further on my nose and wonder if I can really be helped at all. 'I'm looking for something that would be appropriate for a club or restaurant,' I say, overwhelmed by the bright lights and mirrors that reflect a middle-aged woman who has no business doing what she's doing right now.

The saleswoman, to her credit, does not discriminate. She smiles kindly and takes me over to the women's section, pulling a few dresses. 'These would look lovely on you. Why don't you try them on and I'll find you a pair of shoes.' She really is good.

When I put the first dress on, I am transformed back into the girl I used to be – who I was before I became Nicole. Miami is full of my ghosts, and this one stuns me more than I expect. The sleeveless dress is black, short, and tight. It is something I would have worn to go dancing. I look at myself from all angles in the three-way mirror in the dressing room. The biking has made me leaner, more muscular, than I used to be, and the dress is flattering. The girlishness is gone, but I've settled into myself more, and my years of tranquility on Block Island show in my face. There is only a trace of anxiety about my current predicament in my eyes.

When the saleswoman comes back with a pair of wedge heels, the outfit is complete.

'You look incredible, dear,' she says.

She gets paid to say that, to sell clothes, but I look a lot better than I did when I came in, so it's not really a lie. I fluff up my hair, wishing again that I had contact lenses.

'Who are you, and what did you do with Tiny?' I hear behind me.

I turn to see Spencer Cross, the one I remember from the papers, from the magazine covers. His transformation is as stunning as my own. Besides the slacks and shirt, he's managed to slick his hair back and knot it at the nape of his neck. His five o'clock shadow actually works with this look. Someone's found him proper shoes, too. He would hate it if I told him that he's exuding a confidence he didn't have just a few minutes ago, standing up straighter, his hands casually in his slacks pockets. He could be on the cover of *GQ*. We've both been transformed into our previous selves.

He comes over to me in front of the mirror and slings an arm over my shoulder.

'Look at us,' I say with a shy smile.

'We have to go,' he says, then lowers his voice. 'Do you have money for this?'

I rummage through the backpack and produce the cash. We stuff our regular clothes inside the backpack, and while I'm sorry the pack isn't fancier, I'm not going to let go of it, even though the saleswoman tries to get me to relinquish it for a classier, smaller black bag.

We go back out into the night, Spencer still checking his phone. 'It's walking distance,' he says. 'You OK in those shoes?'

Surprisingly, I am, so I nod. I just hope that all of this is worth it and we find Zeke.

We approach the entrance to the club, where there's a red velvet rope and a large, burly man looking at IDs. It's early yet, and there are only a few people ahead of us. The bouncer gives us the once-over and waves us in after we hand over our cover charge. I'm going to have to sell a few more paintings to recoup the expenses from tonight's excursion.

The interior is dark, with black walls and a neon strobe light flashing alternate colors across the room. It's not nearly as crowded as it will be a few hours from now, and its patrons aren't nearly as drunk. Spencer had a few hits off a joint for courage before we came in. I order a Scotch at the bar. My dress is not nearly as tight or as short as others in this place, but we do fit in. When I get my drink, we take a walk around the dance floor, scanning the room.

'He's not here,' I say. The music is too loud for Spencer to hear me.

But someone does hear me.

'Who are you looking for?'

I spin around at the sound of his voice and come face to face with Ian Cartwright.

FIFTY

'Tina?' He is as surprised to see me as I am to see him. He's not faking it. His eyes run down my body, and I hate myself for the familiar thrill it gives me.

Spencer suddenly appears at my side and his arm snakes around my shoulders. 'Can I help you?' he asks.

Ian frowns at him. 'Who's this?' He doesn't bother to wait until I answer before he leans over and says in my ear, 'You really shouldn't be here.' He takes me by the elbow and steers me away from the dance floor, away from Spencer, who grabs his other arm. Ian shakes him off. 'You have to get out of here.'

I trip over my shoes, stumbling a little, and Ian lifts me back up. We are now in the long hallway that leads to the restrooms, but I see a sign for an exit door up ahead. Spencer is on our heels. Ian ignores him, though, as he practically drags me now to the door and opens it. The sticky air slams into us, and we're outside, the door closing behind us. He finally lets go of me.

'What was that all about?' I demand.

He steps closer. 'Be quiet,' he says in a hushed tone. 'Do you have a car?'

I glance at Spencer, and Ian finally acknowledges him. 'If you brought her here, you have to get her out.' He speaks to me again. 'Go far away. You're good at that. At disappearing. It's time for you to do that again.'

'This is about the hit, isn't it?'

He takes a deep breath. 'You shouldn't have done it.'

'I didn't do it. I don't have any reason.'

'It doesn't matter. It all leads back to you.' He pauses. 'And me. But he knows I don't shit where I eat.'

Exactly what I told Zeke.

'You don't have any idea who did this?' My accusatory tone causes him to hesitate.

'You *do* think I did it.'

'And you framed me for it.' There. It's out in the open.

'You know I don't know anything about computers.'

'But your son does.'

His face grows dark with anger, but voices nearby make Ian glance furtively around. 'We can't stay here. *You* can't stay here. I'm helping you. Take my advice and get out.'

'That's not a bad idea.' I'd forgotten about Spencer.

Ian gives Spencer a puzzled look. 'And who the hell are you?'

For a second, I think Spencer is actually going to tell him, but then he says, 'Just call me Angel.'

'I'm not going to call you anything. Get her out of here.'

A long shadow at the corner of the building catches my eye. Ian's fear is contagious, because that's what it is: fear. He's afraid for himself – and for me.

'What's going on?' I can't help but ask.

'You know this is one of Tony's clubs, right?'

I should have known, but I didn't. This explains why Ian's here.

'Why are you helping me?' I ask.

He gives me a tight smile. 'Maybe someday you can pay me back for this.'

It's always payback with him, but I'm not going to argue. 'Just tell me one thing. Where's Zeke Chapman?'

Confusion crosses his face.

'He was meeting Adriana DeMarco here,' I say.

'Adriana was here,' he admits. 'But she left.'

'Where did she go?'

He shrugs. 'Back home, I guess. She left with Amelie.'

Amelie was here? I skip past that and ask, 'So you didn't see Zeke?'

'I saw him earlier. In South Miami. But you already know that.' Daniel must have told him that I'd been there. 'I haven't seen him since.'

Spencer and I exchange a glance. Where is Zeke?

'You need to go,' Ian says again. 'If you find Zeke, tell him to take care of Daniel.' For the first time I hear vulnerability in his tone. Something's going on beyond me, beyond

Daniel. I begin to wonder how much of his fear is not for me but for himself. Before I can speculate any further, he leans over and brushes my cheek with his lips, whispering, 'I'm sorry.'

And then he disappears back through the door we just came out of.

I have never thought that Ian Cartwright would be sorry for anything, but it does make me pause. What does he think he would have to apologize for?

'Come on, Tina,' Spencer says, taking my arm.

We walk a few feet, but I'm at a distinct disadvantage in these shoes. We are well to the side of the building now. There are so many people milling around – the night-time clubbers – that I can't help but think there is safety in numbers.

'Hold on,' I say to Spencer as I reach in the backpack and pull out the sneakers. I spot a place to sit, a small brick wall surrounding a patch of greenery and some palm trees, set back a little from the main walkways. I take off the heels and tug on the sneakers, welcoming the way my feet are now allowed to spread out. Spencer sits next to me, his elbows on his knees as he watches the pedestrians and cars pass. South Beach is hopping tonight; we can hear the bass from music in three different clubs nearby.

I am about to turn to Spencer, tell him we should get going, that we should check the app to see where Zeke's phone is now, when I see it. A long black car slows down next to the curb in front of the club we were just in. It's not a BMW – not *the* BMW – but it sends chills down my spine just the same. Am I going to have this reaction every time I see a black car from now on?

And then I know that I should always trust my gut instincts.

Two big men get out of the car. They could be twins: barrel-chested with bald heads, dressed in black suits. They head to the club entrance, chat for a second with the bouncer, then look around.

I am staring right at the one who sees me. He points, and the two men begin to walk toward us.

I don't need to tell Spencer that we have to get out of here.

He is up, and we are already running, weaving through the people on the sidewalk. I have the irrational thought that no one would try to shoot us with so many witnesses, with so many possibilities of killing someone else. Is this what Ian apologized for? Did he set them on us in order to save himself? I wouldn't put it past him.

I don't look around, afraid that if I do, I'll fall. Spencer is keeping up next to me, although I can hear his labored breathing. We're going to have to stop at some point or he'll pass out. I'm grateful for all the time on the bike, although running is a different sort of animal, and I can feel it in my lungs, a stitch in my side. My only hope is that the two large men are more out of shape than we are, and it's possible they didn't expect us to be so swift.

We have run at least four blocks, and I can't help myself. I look around.

As I feared, I tumble to the ground, rolling on the sidewalk after landing on my knees. I end up on my back, staring up into the faces of a crowd that's surrounded me.

'Are you OK?' I hear from at least three of them.

A hand reaches down and grasps mine, helping me up. I am about to thank my good Samaritan when I see who it is.

Zeke.

FIFTY-ONE

'Where have you been?' is the first thing out of my mouth.

He shakes his head. 'No time.' Spencer is standing behind him, and the two of them usher me to the curb and into a waiting car. Zeke gets into the driver's seat and the car shoots off. It has a lot more power than the rental car. Probably because it's a Porsche.

'Nice ride,' Spencer says from the back seat. He's crammed in the back, but he's not complaining.

'What happened back there?' Zeke is asking. I'm looking

out the side-view mirror, trying to see if anyone's after us. 'We're OK,' Zeke tells me when he notices what I'm doing.

'But it's not exactly as though we're in a car that's not noticeable.' It's cherry red. 'How did you find us?'

'I was passing by and saw the commotion.' He pauses a second, glances in the rear-view at Spencer. 'You look different. Different, but the same. Are we going back to our roots?'

'Not for long,' Spencer says. 'Now that you found us, we can change back.'

'It's a good look for you,' Zeke says. Then his gaze settles on my sneakers. 'That – well, that's not a great look.'

'I couldn't run in the heels.'

'You didn't do a great job in the sneakers, either.'

I study my knees, which are scraped and bloodied. My hands are scuffed as well, from where I landed. 'It was Tony's guys,' I say. 'We saw Ian. He told us to leave, but I think he told them we were there anyway.' That would be typical of him, always playing both sides.

'They were looking for him, too,' Zeke says softly. The implication of that hits me.

'Tony figured out what he's been up to?' I hate it that, after everything, I'm still concerned about Ian. But I am. 'Will he be OK?'

Zeke's grip tightens on the wheel. 'We went in after him. Right after you made your run for it.'

'What's going to happen to Daniel?'

'We're going to get him now.'

'In this?' Spencer indicates the tiny back.

But then I see where we are. The parking garage where Spencer and I parked his car. We took the long way around, but ended up where we were originally headed. Zeke parks the Porsche, gives it a little pat on the roof as we go over to Spencer's car, a fifteen-year-old Honda that is not nearly as conspicuous.

'So where are your people taking Ian?' I ask just as we're about to get into the car.

'Do you really want to know?' Zeke's expression grows dark, but I can't take it back now, even though I wish I could. He takes out his cell phone. 'Let's see just where he is.'

That's right. The locator app we downloaded on to Ian's phone, which Zeke has conveniently put on his own phone. Zeke looks at it, then frowns. 'That's not right. Have either of you messed with this?'

He wants to know if we've hacked it. 'No,' Spencer and I both say at the same time.

'What's wrong?'

'This shows Ian at Tony DeMarco's house.' He holds it up for us to see. He's right. The dot is blinking on Harbor Point. 'This isn't right.' He steps away from the car, away from both of us and makes a call.

'What's going on?' Spencer asks.

I shake my head. 'No clue.'

After a few moments, Zeke comes back, shoving the phone in his pocket. 'Get in.' He climbs into the car without saying anything else. We follow suit, although I can see Spencer is bursting with as much curiosity as I am.

'I'm going to bring you to the safe house,' he explains. 'You have to stay there.'

'I really wish people would stop telling me what I have to do,' I say. 'Maybe you should just tell us what's going on.'

Zeke hasn't started the car yet. He leans back, twisting around so he can look at me head-on. 'I'm going to drop you off, and then when I get back, I'm going to take you to the airport. Spencer can get documents for you. We can have them in a matter of hours. Go to California. Go to Europe. Go somewhere and disappear for a while.'

I've got a nervous feeling in the pit of my belly.

'I'll give you a cell phone, and we can be in touch. No computers. You have to stay offline.'

I've done it before; I can do it again. But I still don't say anything. I don't know if I can.

'If they find you, you're dead. You're not going to be able to escape this. DeMarco is convinced that you and Ian did this together. He thinks Ian is Tracker.'

Ian. I finally find my voice, but it sounds as though I'm speaking in a tunnel. 'What happened, Zeke?'

He takes a deep breath and chews on the corner of his lip,

looking from me to Spencer and back to me again. 'You're really lucky. Ian, not so much.'

Dread fills me. 'What happened to Ian?'

'Those guys? They ran after you, but not too far. You weren't their primary target right then.' He pauses. 'Our guys went in for Ian, but they were too late.'

I hear his words but I can't seem to understand what he's trying to tell me.

He sighs, puts his hand to my cheek. 'He's dead, Tina. Ian's dead.'

FIFTY-TWO

Even though I knew what he was going to say before he said it, it is still a complete shock. Ian can't be dead. I just saw him. I close my eyes and can still feel his breath on my cheek as he said he was sorry. My entire body begins to shake, and I put my hands up over my face. Even though Ian did me so wrong, I loved him once, and I am grieving for the young man I met so long ago, the man who made me feel normal when everything in my life wasn't normal at all.

'What happened?' I manage to ask.

'We thought we'd be able to get him out of there.'

'What happened?' The urgency laces my words. I need to know.

'Those guys went in, but we were too late. Ian was in the back, near the restrooms.'

Where he'd brought Spencer and me and told us to leave.

'He was shot once. In the head.'

I can barely breathe. I fold my hands tightly together to keep them from shaking, but it's futile. 'But the guys got caught, right? The ones who shot him?'

Zeke doesn't meet my eyes. 'No. They were already gone.'

How can that be? They were big; they couldn't just disappear. But the words won't come out.

'It's not your fault,' Zeke says.

I give a short snort. I know it's not my fault. It's all Ian's fault for everything he's ever got himself into. If Tony DeMarco hadn't killed him, someone else would have, eventually. That charm couldn't have lasted forever. It didn't. You can't play both sides of the fence without someone finding out.

While I am struggling to sort this all out, Spencer has no such distraction. 'How is his cell phone in Harbor Point, then?' he asks.

'Good question,' Zeke says, his eyes still on me.

Spencer has taken out one of the laptops and is powering it up. I want to tell him that it's not going to work here, that we have no Wifi network, but then I remember who he is and what he can do. It's easier to think about something other than Ian, but then it sucks me back in again, what's happened.

While Spencer concentrates on the laptop, Zeke gets out of the car and comes over to my side, opening the door. 'Get out, Tina,' he says, but not unkindly.

I do as I'm told, and he wraps his arms around me. 'I shouldn't have told you like that,' he whispers.

'Does Daniel know?' I manage to ask.

'No. Not yet.'

'He's just a kid. If they found out about Ian, maybe they found out about him, too, and what he knows.' I shiver. 'You have to go get him now, Zeke. And your team. They might not be safe, either.' I hear the panic rising in my voice.

'I made a call. I've got people going over there,' he says. 'Everyone's getting cleared out; everyone will be safe. Don't worry. I've got it covered.'

I'm not used to someone else making decisions. I've been on my own for so long and making my own way, and I don't like the lack of control.

'This is interesting.' Spencer gets out of the car, holding the laptop. I move away from Zeke, but he keeps a hand on my waist, as though to ground me. We both look at what Spencer is showing us.

It's the cell phone locator, and it's still showing Ian's phone at Harbor Point.

'I don't understand,' I say. 'Is this right?'

Spencer nods. 'Yeah, it's right. But we've been following the wrong phone.'

'What?' Zeke leans down to look at the laptop more closely.

'It's not here, dude,' Spencer says, then hits a key and an alternate screen pops up. 'It's here.'

All he did was a simple reverse number search. Rather than put a name in the search to find the phone number, you do the opposite: a phone number for a name.

Spencer's right. We've been following the wrong number all along.

The phone number is Amelie's.

'Who is she?' Spencer's asking, but I'm one step ahead.

'Adriana gave me the number. She said it was Ian's. At least that's the number I asked for. I never mentioned Amelie.' Reality hits me. 'Amelie is the one we've been tracking all along. The one who was outside my hotel room, at the apartment.' My head is spinning with a million thoughts that I struggle to sort through. 'She's the one who ran us off the road.' Finally, I take a deep breath and it's clear as day.

The shadow in my laptop knew about the bank job. Knew about the accounts. Knew everything. I kept wondering who would go after both me and Zeke – *and* Tony DeMarco. I kept coming back to Ian, but as he so aptly put it, he doesn't shit where he eats. But it's more than possible that Amelie does. That she knew about me all along, even though I didn't know about her. She gave Ian those bank account numbers; she knew about the bank job. It's possible she did know what happened between Ian and me on Block Island, and everything that happened since was revenge for that. She may have been the one he married, but she's threatened by me. Enough so that she'd set me up – with the FBI, with Tony. Ian has a hacker son, but so does she. All along, it felt personal. And it is.

She is Betr@yD.

I recall how I saw her outside the hotel on Brickell Avenue. I figured she was just stopping for a coffee before work, but what if it wasn't that innocent? What if she's been on our trail the entire time?

Zeke's eyes grow wide as I hash it out, and he holds his

hand up to stop me. 'It *is* her, isn't it? Why didn't we see it before?'

'Because we weren't supposed to. Because she has kept a low profile. But we know about her role with the bank job, which *was* pretty big, when you think back on it. All these years I assumed that she didn't really know what she was doing. But she must have worked it out, maybe after Ian found me on Block Island. Maybe she found out all about that.'

'That would explain the shadow. That was after you left Block Island.' Zeke is thinking out loud, too.

I remember something. 'I got into Amelie's computer with the wireless router. Everything looked pretty benign. But what if it's not? I wasn't looking for anything there. I saw some pictures, some work stuff. But then I got into that other computer, too, and that seemed a lot more suspicious, so I concentrated on that one. Maybe I should have looked closer at Amelie's.'

'What happened with the router?' Spencer asks.

'Ran out of juice, I think.'

We all exchange a look. But what if it didn't? What if Amelie found it? What if that was how she got into our laptop as Betr@yD and downloaded the kiddie porn? She turned the tables on us.

'We should assume that Amelie knows someone's spying,' Zeke says. 'But we need to get back into her computer. We have to prove it.'

'I know where we can get another router,' Spencer says, 'but it's better if I go alone.'

Zeke looks uncomfortable with that, but he finally nods. 'OK. How long do you think it'll take?'

'An hour?'

'All right. I'll take Tina back to the safe house. Meet us back there?'

I don't like the idea of that apartment. 'Why don't we go back to Key Biscayne? We'll be closer to where we need to drop the router.'

'Not a good idea. It's too close to DeMarco. Regardless of what Amelie has done, DeMarco is still after you. We can't make it easy for him.'

I think about Ian again. Did he have any clue that Tony

would go after him there, at that time? He couldn't have, otherwise he wouldn't have been there. Ian was all about saving his own skin. I know the worst about him, but still a sadness rushes through me again. He did not deserve to die.

And then it strikes me: Amelie did it. She set him up. She might as well have pulled that trigger herself.

'We need to keep an eye on Amelie. What if she tries to leave? We have to make sure we know where she is.'

'We've got the cell phone tracker,' Zeke says.

'But what if she's figured that out, too? We've underestimated her, and she's come back and caught us every time.'

'I'll go. Alone. After I drop you at the safe house.'

I shake my head. 'No. I have to see this through.'

Spencer holds up his phone. 'You kids hash it out. I'll go get the router. Call me when you know where you're going to be,' he says as he heads out of the garage on foot. He's been under the radar, too, and I'm not worried about his survival skills. Especially since he's not with me or Zeke.

'Do you think he misses his other life?' I ask, genuinely curious. I don't really miss my life here, but I do miss Nicole Jones's life. Sometimes so much it hurts.

'No.' He says it so definitively that it's clear they've talked about it. 'You're not going to give in on this, are you?' he asks. I shake my head, and he takes a deep breath. 'OK, I have a place we can go where no one should find us. You might not like it, but we'll be close by, and I don't think anyone will think to look there.'

'I promise not to complain,' I say.

'I'll hold you to that.'

FIFTY-THREE

Zeke doesn't pay any mind to the 'For Sale' sign. He takes out a key and opens the lockbox on the gate of my old house. I watch him from inside the car, where I have been stooped down so no one can see me. He opens the gate, then comes back and we drive through. Besides my quick intake of breath when we first drove up, I have not said a word. He keeps looking at me out of the corner of his eye, expecting some reaction. Between knowing that Ian is dead and this, it's as though a weight has landed on my chest, and I can't breathe normally. I take small breaths, trying to keep a panic attack at bay.

I want to ask him how he got the lockbox key. How we are able to come inside. Because now we are out of the car and going up the front steps. I am having the strongest sense of déjà vu, but of course that's not it.

I reach the door, and Zeke is holding it open. The backpack feels as though it weighs triple what it really does, and I drop it next to me. I am unable to take another step.

'How?' I ask, my voice barely a whisper.

'Don't worry about that,' he says. 'You OK?'

I shake my head.

I see the other car then, the one that is parked outside the gate. I can make out two people inside. He sees me noticing.

'Security,' he says simply as he leans down and picks up the backpack, slinging it over his shoulder. 'Come on in, Tina.' He walks through the door and a light goes on at the end of the foyer. I can see through to the great room – and the ocean beyond. The mirror I remember is gone; so is the side table. The emptiness lures me in.

He's got the sliding doors open, and he's staring out over the pool to the water. I drink in the view. Although there is no furniture, no signs of life, this sight gives me strength and I begin to breathe a little easier.

'I remember this,' he says, and I know what he's referring to. The first day he came here, the day I was sitting on the chaise longue by the pool. I didn't know then that we already knew each other, that he was my best friend.

I don't know that I can handle all the ghosts that have begun to swirl around us: my father, my mother, Ian. Tracker.

'That car out there – those agents. Won't it make anyone suspicious?'

'We've always got someone looking in on DeMarco,' Zeke

says casually, and in a swift movement he's got his laptop out and he's sitting cross-legged on the ground.

I remember that. How the FBI always sent agents here to check up on my father. That's what I thought Zeke was doing, the first time he showed up.

'We're close enough to Tony's house that we might be able to get into his network,' Zeke is saying, interrupting my memories.

He's right. I drop down next to him. I've got Spencer's laptop, so I open it. There are several networks in the area, though. 'Even if we can get into the right one,' I say, 'how do we know Amelie has left her computer on so we can access it?'

'It was on before, right? A lot of people just let their computers or laptops sleep and never turn them off.'

'So we might not need the router after all,' I muse. 'Spencer's not going to be happy that he went on a fool's errand.'

'It would be easier with it than without it,' Zeke says, 'but I think we can get in. Spence'll understand.'

If anyone would, it would be Spencer. As I concentrate, my surroundings disappear and my focus is solely on the work. I want to get in before Zeke does. I know I can be too competitive, but I still want to prove myself, show that I can do it without help.

It doesn't take too long, either. I grin at Zeke. 'I'm in.'

He scoots over next to me to see my screen. I've already managed to get back into Amelie's computer. I recognize the desktop, the photographs, from the last time I was here.

'This is her?' Zeke asks.

'Yeah.' I'm not done, though. I have to get inside further, see what she's been doing online. The history shows the usual suspects: social media pages, searches for local restaurant menus, directions to a vintage clothing shop. There has to be something here.

'Check her email,' Zeke urges.

She's got one account bookmarked, so we go there first. Nothing of any interest: notices from department stores about online sales, links to news stories from the local paper, emails from women in a book group about the next meeting, reminders about hair appointments.

'This is a waste of time,' I mutter. But then I go into the computer's programs and find the VPN – and Tor. 'Bingo.' I am kicking myself for not looking further when I was here before, otherwise we might have been able to figure out she was behind everything a lot sooner. Ian might still be alive. I shake off the thought and force myself to concentrate.

As we delve deeper, it's clear that Amelie is much more well versed with computers than Ian – and possibly Daniel. 'You don't think any of this is Daniel's work, do you?' I ask Zeke.

'Some might be,' he admits, 'but let's assume this is all Amelie.'

'Daniel did play a role in this,' I say. 'We found the image of Adriana in his computer.' I try to give him the benefit of the doubt, though. He's just a kid. It would have been difficult for him to say no to his mother. I turn back to the laptop.

Amelie has been busy. She's been in the chat room, and it's not so difficult to discover that she's been using my screen names. I ignore the shiver that shimmies up my spine when I see this.

'We're wasting time,' Zeke says, turning the laptop toward him. 'Look here,' he says, pointing. 'She's been to this hidden service.'

'What is it?'

He doesn't answer, his fingers tapping the keyboard, revealing that Amelie has downloaded a Tor descriptor. Zeke follows it to find the public key and the circuit that Amelie created, revealing a rendezvous point. It's here that we see it. The communication between Amelie and an unknown user about how the hit on Tony is going to go down.

Betr@yD: He's going to his daughter's apartment in the morning about eleven. It's quiet in that neighborhood then.
XXit: Doorman?
Betr@yD: Don't worry about him. I've got it covered. Make sure it's the leg. Not too high up or you'll hit the artery. Low enough to do some damage. So he'll be in the hospital a while. Make it look good.
XXit: How do I know it won't come back to me?

Betr@yD: I've set it all up. Conversations online that will point everyone in the wrong direction. No one will ever know.

XXit: When do I get paid?

Betr@yD: I've already transferred money into your account. You'll get the rest afterward.

It's as we suspected: Tony wasn't supposed to die, and Amelie set it up so it would look as though I was responsible – me and Tracker. Amelie somehow knew where I was, because the IP address of the laptop at the bike shop is on the screen.

'Who is XXit?' I ask as Zeke takes screen shots of everything we've found.

'I've never seen that screen name before,' Zeke says. 'It could be anyone, someone she found online just for the hit. I bet he doesn't know who she is. He could be the original p4r4d0x, too, and even though he disappeared after the hit, she didn't realize that because Spencer was communicating with her as p4r4d0x.'

I think about the Waste Land – how you can find anything on there, possibly even find someone who will kill for you for the right price.

'Maybe we can find the money she paid him.'

'Maybe.' From the way he says it, I can tell he's already thinking about how to go about it.

'So how did she find out where I was so she could set up the laptop at the bike shop? Who did you tell?'

Zeke shakes his head. 'No one, Tina. I was the only one who knew where you were.'

But then it hits me. 'You have been working with Ian.'

'What about it?'

'She knew Ian found me, and she probably knew about you and me, too.'

I can see from his expression that he knows where I'm going with this.

'She tracked you,' I say. 'Maybe she hacked into your phone or something, like we did.'

'What do you mean, *like we did*?'

I sigh. I probably shouldn't have mentioned it, but it's too late now. 'Spencer and I downloaded the phone locator app on your phone. You know, the one that we downloaded into Ian's phone, or, rather, Amelie's. That's how we knew you were at Tony's club when you were meeting with Adriana.'

'You hacked me?' Zeke shakes his head. 'I don't believe it.'

'That's beside the point now,' I say, eager to move back to Amelie. 'I bet she put two and two together, and if she was the shadow, she was able to find out that you were Tracker through the laptop.'

I feel so stupid that we hadn't thought about Amelie from the start, but why would we have? How long has she been planning all this? Has she been consumed by it for years? Eager to get her revenge on me, on Ian? An unbearable sadness overwhelms me. Again, I remind myself that I'm not grieving for the Ian I've known the last couple of years, or even the one who used me for the bank job, but the one I met at the university, the young man who was so eager to please, who loved me. I know he loved me once, despite all his lies.

Zeke is watching me, and he sees the emotions that I'm wearing on my sleeve. I want to tell him I need this time, just a little bit of time, and somehow he knows. He always knows.

Zeke's phone rings. He puts it to his ear. 'Hey, Spence.'

He's quiet as Spencer talks. I can hear Spencer's voice, but I can't make out what he's saying. I turn my attention back to the screen, and I can hardly believe it.

'What do you see?' Zeke's voice sounds as if he's a million miles away.

The code doesn't lie.

'Tony DeMarco's site. It's definitely Unicorn. That kiddie porn site.'

FIFTY-FOUR

I vaguely hear Zeke telling Spencer to meet us here as I peruse the code. All I did was trace the invitation to the hidden site backward and it ended up in a link to the site. I still don't have an IP address, though.

My thoughts stray back to Amelie. I don't like having a target on my back, and I don't like that it's her. She's got a lot to hold a grudge about, and I don't blame her. But Ian was with *her*, not me. He chose *her*. Why did she have him killed?

'You're right. I need to disappear again. This isn't going away. I can't throw some code in there to change things. I can't put money in Tony's account to make it all better. She did a good job.' I give him a small smile. 'At least now you've got Tony's site. You can take him down. I doubt she thought that would happen.'

'Or maybe she did. I think she's had this all planned for a very long time,' Zeke says thoughtfully.

'What can you do about her?'

'I can use all this' – he indicates the laptop and what's on the screen – 'to show that you didn't have anything to do with it.'

I think again about Daniel. He had to have been involved, considering how he'd inserted Adriana's image into that video footage. But maybe he didn't know what his mother was up to. Maybe she asked him to do it, and he was happy to and didn't ask any questions. And now he has to deal with his father's death. He'll find out his mother was responsible for that, too. He'll grow up with a parent in prison. I know what that's like.

As I think about my father, my thoughts stray to Adriana. She was set up, too. She had a shadow in her laptop, the ransom note, the bank account with my name but her picture. 'Do you think Amelie is after Adriana, too?' I ask.

Zeke's expression tells me this is something he hasn't thought about. He jumps up. 'Stay here,' he orders.

I can't stay here. Not with all of the memories, the ghosts. Especially since I know where he's going, especially since I see he's got his gun out.

He's already out the door. He leans into the car that's idling out in front, talking to the agents inside. When he stands back up, he gives me a glare, holds his hand up as though he's a traffic cop telling me to stop. I do, watching him disappear around the corner. The two agents are on his heels, and that's when I start moving again. I stay back when we get to Tony DeMarco's house, which is quiet, dark. A black car sits out front. I suddenly regret my rash move. I shouldn't be here; Tony's inside, recovering. He's got a hit out on me. He's had Ian killed. I've talked my way out of things before, but I doubt I could do it this time. I turn to go back, to slip into the darkness, but it's too late. The house door opens, and Amelie steps out.

'You got here sooner than I thought, but then you were only a few houses down, right?' she says.

Zeke has not raised his gun; I don't see she has a weapon, but we are all on alert. She must have been watching us from inside her computer. Against my better judgment, I am impressed with her skills.

'Where's Adriana?' Zeke demands.

She smiles. 'You would like to know, wouldn't you?' Her voice is playful, teasing.

I glance up at the dark windows. I have an unexpected thought that she's killed them all: Tony, Adriana, anyone else who she feels betrayed her.

'If you come quietly,' Zeke says, 'and tell us everything, maybe we can make it easier on Daniel.'

'I don't know what you think I've done.'

'We've got it all,' Zeke says.

'I don't know what you think you have.' She takes a few steps forward, leaving the door open. She must feel very confident that this is as far as it will go.

I hear the sirens somewhere in the distance. They're coming. I can't be here when they arrive. I may not be a fugitive anymore, but my instincts are still to flee. As I turn to go back, I hear another voice.

'What's going on?' It's Adriana. She's come out of the house behind Amelie.

'This nice FBI agent is just asking some questions,' Amelie says as though nothing is wrong.

Adriana focuses on Zeke. 'FBI?' And then she spots me. She takes a few steps forward. Zeke turns to see what's got her attention, and he frowns. It's clear that I am no stranger to Adriana, as Zeke has told me. I wonder if Tony told her – or if Amelie did. Either way, the secret's out, and I take a step back as if that will make everything OK.

'Maybe you should go tell your father he's got visitors,' Amelie says to Adriana. 'I'm sure he'll be very interested in them.'

'We're not here for him,' Zeke says. 'We're here to make sure Miss DeMarco is OK.' He pauses. 'And we're here for you.'

Amelie smiles. Her beauty strikes me again, and there's a calmness in her expression, even now as she faces FBI agents who are ready to arrest her. 'I have no idea what you're talking about,' she says.

'We have screen shots.'

Her expression doesn't change, but then her gaze finally falls on me. Her jaw hardens, and I can see it in her eyes: hate. I force myself not to react, but it's difficult not to look away, to face the woman who has always only been an after-thought to me, but who clearly considers me an enemy and has tried to destroy me.

The sirens are getting even closer. I have a small window of time. I break the connection with Amelie as I spin around and race back. Zeke has left the door unlocked, and I stumble to the back patio, the laptops still open, proof of Amelie's guilt.

I close the laptop covers to put them to sleep and stare out at the water. Somehow it seems as though it's come full circle. It started here and it's ending here. As long as it truly ends.

*   *   *

I wake in the morning to the sun streaming across the bed. I look at Zeke next to me. He came back for me after a couple of hours, gave me the car keys, and told me where to go. He stumbled in just before dawn, Amelie still declaring her innocence, Tony DeMarco alive but dying in his house, his daughter by his side. Daniel, upon finding out about his father's death, did the right thing and told them everything he knew, what he'd been asked to do. He's in FBI protection now, and although he'll survive this, the scars will remain. I know.

Tony DeMarco has not lifted the hit on me. I am still a target, and it has nothing to do with what's happened recently. He wants his revenge on me, on my father, even all these years later. Amelie didn't need to set me up, but she made it more convenient for him. No amount of money will make it right, because it's as I thought in the beginning. It's not about the money. It's personal.

Turns out Zeke has his own place in Miami, away from the South Miami apartment and his team. It's a small house not unlike Spencer's, in Coconut Grove. He says no one knows about it, but as recent history is showing, he may not be keeping all his secrets as well as he thinks he is.

I pack up my backpack and leave the laptop on the top of the dresser. I won't need it where I'm going, even though it probably would be best if I took it. I don't think I'll really be able to stay away. I have to stop lying to myself.

I also have to stop lying to myself about Zeke. We have a connection that I can't ignore.

Zeke rolls over, and I hold my breath until I see that he's just settling in. I don't want a long goodbye, and I'm afraid if I wake him, I'll never leave. It's hard enough to walk out like this now.

I hear the car pull up outside, and I let myself out quietly. Spencer is waiting for me. He's back to his usual attire of jeans and T-shirt, his hair in a messy ponytail. His eyes are glazed over, and I'm a little worried about him driving.

'You all set?' he asks. I nod. He hands me a cell phone. 'You need this. I've got your boarding pass in the app, so you just need to show it at the airport.'

I glance back at the house.

'We'll make it right for you to come back,' Spencer promises as he starts the car. I never thought I'd pray for an old man's death, but it could be the only way I'll ever be free. But I don't mention this. Spencer doesn't know everything, even though he thinks he does.

As we drive off, I glance in the side-view mirror and see Zeke standing in the doorway, watching. He lifts his hand in a short wave, and then he goes back inside, shutting the door behind him.

EPILOGUE

I stand on the deck of the ferry, ignoring how cold it is, my hands shoved in my pockets. I don't have gloves. I've layered with a sweater and a fleece jacket, but I'm underdressed; I should have gotten a parka. I lived here long enough that the weather shouldn't be a surprise. It's November, after all, and New England.

There are only a handful of other people on the ferry. They're inside, where it's warm. But I want to be out here. I want to watch the island getting bigger the closer we get. I breathe in the salty air; the boat bounces against the waves, the whitecaps surfing the surface of the water that's so dark it looks almost black. The sky is full of gray clouds, and I wonder if it's going to rain – or maybe snow. It's very different from the last time I came this way; it was summer then, hot and sticky, and the sun shone bright against the crisp blue water.

I want my paints. I want to capture the island, the water, from this vantage point, an angle I never had when I lived here because I was always looking out toward the water, not the other way around.

Despite the churning sea, a sense of peace rushes through me as we approach. The National Hotel towers majestically over Old Harbor, and the line of shops where Veronica's gallery sits grows larger as we get closer. I have nothing for Veronica now, unless I can get hold of my watercolors from Woods Hole.

I spot the little house. The one where I spent fifteen years of my life. It looks exactly as when I left it, unchanged. How can that be? I am so different.

The boat's engines are cut and we slow down, bouncing slightly against the dock. I stumble a little, unsteady. I never spent any time on the ferry; I just watched it come and go, the tourists filing off its decks and on to the island for their holidays. I waited for them at the bike shop, ready to take

anyone who wanted to go on a tour. And then I'd meet
Steve for dinner at Club Soda, for hamburgers and beer and
laughter.

He's not waiting when we dock. I am momentarily
disappointed, even though there is no way he could have known
I was coming. I haven't called ahead. I don't want to risk
anyone knowing I'm here.

Instinctively, when I get off the ferry, I look around to make
sure I'm not being followed.

There are two taxis waiting for the ferry, but I don't need
a ride. I want to walk, even though my toes are frozen inside
my sneakers. I wiggle them a little to try to warm them up,
but it's futile. I zip up my fleece jacket so it's tighter around
my neck. There's nothing I can do for my ears; my hands are
still in my pockets. I walk briskly, faster and faster up the hill.
I'm not quite as cold as I was when I got off the ferry by the
time I reach the door at Club Soda.

He won't be here; I know that. It's lunchtime and a Thursday,
and he's always here for dinner on Friday nights. At least he
used to be. Could be he changed it up after I left, set up a
new schedule. He and Jeanine.

I should have stopped at the spa to see her. But I'm hungry,
and I want to get used to the place again, just for a little while
by myself. I want to feel comfortable, relaxed first. I am a
little concerned that Abby will be working; I'm not ready to
see anyone I know. I don't recognize the waitress or the
bartender, which surprises me a little, but I've been gone a
while. I can't expect that things wouldn't change even a little.

I sit at a table near the bar and order a hamburger, onion
rings, and a beer. It feels so natural; I was afraid I wouldn't
be able to come back.

One thing I've learned: Miami is only where I grew up;
here on Block Island, I'm home.

It's too far to walk to Steve's, so I have the bartender call me
a cab. It's habit, really; I have a cell phone in my pocket but
I don't like using it and I don't need one here.

Again I feel a little pull of disappointment when the cab
that drives up is not Steve's, but I climb in and give his address.

The cabbie glances at me in the rear-view mirror but says nothing.

Butterflies are fluttering in my belly by the time we pull up to the little gray Cape Cod house. The red and blue and white buoys that hang from a rope along his small white picket fence almost make me cry. I pay the cabbie and tumble out of the car, dragging my backpack with me.

I take a deep breath, push my way through the little gate. I don't go to the front door; Steve hasn't used it since Dotty died. Instead, I go around the side to the door to the porch that leads into the kitchen. I know this house as well as I've known any of my own.

I peer through the window. It's dark, but that's not a surprise. Steve is the quintessential New Englander: save electricity, and thus money. I take a deep breath, raise my hand, but before I can knock, I hear a familiar buzzing. I consider ignoring it, but reach around and unzip the front pocket of the backpack. The number on the phone is 'unknown.'

I answer it. 'Yes?'

'Tina?'

The voice is familiar. 'Spencer?'

'You have to come back.'

'No. It's too soon.'

'It's important.'

Before he can explain, the door swings open and Steve is suddenly there, standing in front of me, his eyes wide, a smile spreading across his face. 'Nicole?'

I am unprepared for the emotion that rushes through me. Tears spring to my eyes, and I nod, but I'm still holding the phone next to my ear, and what Spencer says next makes me freeze.

'Zeke's gone.'